RICHARD NEER

Photo credit: Michal Bednarek©123rf.com

Other Books by Richard Neer

FM: The Rise and Fall of Rock Radio

Something of the Night

The Master Builders

Indian Summer

The Last Resort

The Punch List

An American Storm

Wrecking Ball

(Coming) Heart of the Matter

For Vicky

PROLOGUE

1972

He lay in their small bed, shivering.

It wasn't cold, in fact, it had been an exceptionally warm and humid late spring day. He was shaking because he knew that one way or another, his life would change dramatically in the next hour.

The drone of her hairdryer serenaded him from down the hall as he waited for his girl to join him in bed. She would be like she always was on these Saturday nights after an antiwar rally. Full of adrenalized zeal and eager to join her glorious body to his.

But tonight was different.

They were listening.

He asked himself for the hundredth time how he had agreed to this, how he had agreed to betray the love of his young life.

Wendy Walton was everything he'd ever dreamed of.

God, she was smart. The smartest person he'd ever known, more so than his professors. She understood the inner game of politics like no one he had ever met. Her insights into human psychology were those of a much more mature woman. And she was older than he was, maybe as much as a decade. As if that mattered.

And she was beautiful. Classic features. Deep blue eyes. Cheekbones to die for. Lean athletic body. But what put her over the top for him was her long blonde hair. Like his idol Joni Mitchell. Or the goddesses of his youth. Marianne Faithfull. Mary Travers. Dusty Springfield.

She was so clean. Always smelled great. The hippie chicks he ran into these days were raw. Hairy legs, underarms. Yuch. Going back to nature, they called it. He found it off-putting.

Wendy was different. She even shaved *down there*. A huge turn on when he first saw it, something he'd never encountered before.

She was the first real love he'd experienced in his twenty years. Everything he'd fantasized as a boy growing up in Ozzie and Harrietville, Long Island. The perfect, All American girl.

Except she wasn't. Or so they said.

The scent of Shalimar announced her presence, as her naked body silhouetted against the dim hallway light. The sight and smell had never failed to arouse him. But tonight was different.

They were listening.

She climbed into bed, under the sheets and immediately noted his lack of interest. "Are you okay, baby? Something on your mind? That record company guy upset you?"

"No, that's not it. We need to talk."

She laughed, her dusky alto attempting to lighten his dark mood. "Oooh, this sounds serious. Hey, I heard what he said. Don't listen to him. He's part of the establishment. He wants you to write stupid love songs and your music is so much deeper than that."

"I know. He just thinks that protest songs aren't what people will want to hear when the war is over and I need to expand my range. That's all."

"Well, speaking of expanding, let me see what I can do about that."

She started to work her way down from his chest, her soft lips caressing his body in all the right spots. But nothing was responding and he stopped her.

"Wendy. This is serious. We need to talk."

"It must be. What's wrong, babe, I don't turn you on anymore? Is there someone else?"

"No way. You could make a dead man hard." He'd have to use that line in a song sometime. But music was the furthest thing from his mind now. "Look, I'll come right out with it. You know my dad is a cop."

He felt her stiffen. "Yeah, I know that."

"And you have a problem getting your head into that."

"I know where it's at. You were raised in the 'burbs, typical middle class education. It makes me love you that much more, because I know how hard it was for you the go against your dad. I never call the police *pigs* like our friends do. Out of respect for you and your father."

"My dad's never approved of what we're doing. He fought in the Pacific against the Japanese. He thinks we're unpatriotic. He trusts Nixon's doing what's best for America."

"Babe, that's one of the terrible things about this war. It's divided fathers and sons. Your dad's generation will never accept that the government is lying to them."

His stomach was in knots. He was blaming his father for something he had no part in. But it was the only way he could make his case without telling her the truth about his own duplicity.

He said, "That's not the problem. He called me today and said everything you've told me about your past is bullshit."

"That's insane. Jason, your dad is dying of cancer. Those treatments are affecting his head, the way he thinks. He's paranoid."

"He called a cop friend upstate. He checked birth records in the town where you said you were born. Asked around at your high school. Researched your family. There was no Wendy Walton matching your description in Oswego, New York. No Walton family in the neighborhood you say you grew up in. You were never there. Dad thinks you're a fraud, a spy. He went to the FBI with what he found. He says they're going arrest you --- charge you with espionage."

The truth was the other way around. An FBI agent named Richard Gilmore had developed the evidence against Wendy and had contacted his father, hoping to recruit Jason to work undercover against his lover. The only way Jason could hide his own role in the deception was to lay this at the feet of his father, who had no knowledge of the tactic. But he would have approved if it meant busting a Commie who was using his son.

Wendy was naturally fair skinned, but this turned her face even whiter. “I was born in Oswego. Grew up there. Records get destroyed or misplaced all the time in a small town. Did you know everyone in your high school class? Damn it, Jason. This fucking Nixon is out of control. He’s going against anyone who disagrees with him, using Gestapo tactics.”

“Wendy, much as I hate the man, Tricky Dick had nothing to do with it.”

“It’s how he divides us. Pits us against each other.”

“All that’s not important. It doesn’t matter to me. You matter. I love you.”

“And I love you.”

“But I need you to be honest. You tell me you’re a spy, I’ll help you do whatever you need to do. I’ve already gone against my dad again by tipping you off. He made me swear not to. He only told me because he wanted me to break up with you before it all goes down so I won’t get caught up in it. Just tell me the truth.”

“How can I prove a negative? This evidence is bogus.”

“I don’t know how they know, but they do. The bottom line is --- I’ll stand by you to the end. I’ll run away with you if it comes to that. Wherever you need to go. Canada. Cuba. Wherever.”

He took both of her hands in his and squeezed hard. “But if it’s true, I need to know.”

Wendy could see that Jason desperately *wanted* to believe her. Her handlers had told her what could happen to her in an American prison if she was caught. They said suicide would be a better option.

If what he told her about an imminent arrest was true, she had to get away. Now. Maybe she could make use of Jason one last time to make her escape.

She made her voice small, as if he had broken her resolve. “I can’t lie to you anymore, my love. I was born in the Soviet Union. I was sent here with an assignment. It’s one I really believe in. Do everything in my power to stop this illegal war.”

So they were right.

He couldn’t believe that she had deceived him all these months. All he could do was stammer, “You really think you have the power to do that?”

“Aren’t you doing everything you can to stop it? Jason, you and I see things the same way. Your government’s betrayed its people. This war is immoral. Your country would be better off if it just accepted the inevitable defeat and walked away.”

“So I was just a stupid kid who had some pull in the movement because I could sing and write songs. You played me for a sucker all along, didn’t you?”

“I fell in love with you. That wasn’t the plan, it just happened.”

The feds had given him the clinching line and he recited it as instructed. “So you admit, you came here as a Soviet agent?”

“Yes. But what we have is real. I love you so much. You have to believe that.”

"I can't think straight now. If you really love me, you could defect."

"I can't do that. I can't betray my country. I'd rather die. I have to leave."

"Let me come with you."

"Jason, that's not possible. Maybe someday things will be different and we can find a way to be together, but I have to go by myself."

"They'll be watching the trains and airports. Wendy, they could kill you trying to get away."

"Give me the keys to the car. I'll let you know where I leave it when I'm safe."

What happened next destroyed him. Six FBI agents burst into the tiny house. They wrestled Wendy from the bed. She was naked. They didn't care.

Jason fought them off.

It wasn't supposed to be like this. He was thrown to the ground and handcuffed. Richard Gilmore had promised him that her arrest would be done with as much dignity as possible.

It was the last time he laid eyes on his lover, as she was dragged from their bed. Wendy was tough and it took three large men to subdue her. Finally, a needle full of something got her under control. Her limp, naked body was dragged from the house and spirited away in a white panel van.

Gilmore appeared after the remaining agents left the house. He was calm, smoking a cigarette. He didn't apologize for the degrading arrest. He merely said that Jason had done a good job, served his country well.

Jason Black was furious. He called them Storm Troopers, Nazis, Fascists. He said Gilmore had deliberately lied when he promised that she'd be treated with respect. The FBI man shrugged and said that things had gotten out of hand. She shouldn't have struggled.

Wendy Walton had sworn her love for him right until the end and he had given her ashes in return.

I

2017

The interview was at the campus radio station, a few blocks from the ancient hotel room they had booked for him. He'd slept in worse places, even at the height of his stardom. The accouterments didn't matter much.

Back in the day, his record label dispatched a promotion person or two to limo him back and forth to major radio stations. The rep would arrive in a comfortable town car, bearing coffee and a hearty breakfast. They delivered and so did he.

The appearances were booked in advance and he knew most of the interviewers. They asked polite questions based on his latest work. They affected an easy rapport as if they were old drinking buddies, although few of them were. The questions weren't even questions, just agreeable statements he was invited to comment upon. There was nothing challenging or embarrassing. Usually, they just gave him space to advance whatever product he was promoting at the time.

The campus radio station was merely the setting for this interview, which would be exclusive to social media, never penetrating traditional airwaves. If Jason was lucky, a few hundred might hear it, and luckier still if it moved a dozen followers to download his latest album. He might clear a hundred bucks from the effort.

He had never met the kid doing the interview. He wasn't interested enough to explore his background or how many regular followers his podcast boasted. Jason Black was an old pro --- he just showed up on time and played the game.

It was an unusually cold morning for Savannah, hovering around freezing. The studio had yet to reach a comfortable temperature and probably wouldn't, given that it was a weekend and the rest of the building was vacant. It was probably the only time the young podcaster could book. After some hasty greetings, Jason donned the tinny headphones and gave a level check. The kid nodded and began:

Todd: Hey, music lovers, Todd the Shark here with the latest entry in my series of podcasts with people who make music, big and small. I'm with Jason Black today. I know most of you have no idea who Mr. Black is, but I bet your parents do. He was a big deal in the seventies. Had some songs that the older generation considers classic. Toured with Joni Mitchell, Bob Dylan, James Taylor and some other biggies. I believe you even opened once for the late Tom Petty.

Jason: Back when his band was called Mudcrutch, he opened for *me*.

Todd: Wow. I bet that didn't last long. You're playing the student union tonight. I can't make it, but I hear there are a couple hundred tickets sold. Big crowd for you these days, I'd imagine.

Jason: Size isn't everything. I don't count numbers, just happy to be able to provide an evening's entertainment

Todd: Still, it's gotta be a comedown, half full auditorium considering you played places like Madison Square Garden in New York in your heyday. See, I did my research.

Jason: Uh-huh.

Todd: And what happened to your band, the Americans? That song *Only in America* was pretty big.

Jason: You're thinking of Jay Black. Jay and the Americans. They were great, but that's not me. No relation

Todd: Hmmn. I thought you just started saying Jason instead of Jay, like that whole singer songwriter thing in your day. So, why no new material? Kinda dried up?

Jason: Actually, I released a new album six months ago.

Todd: Must have missed that and I'm pretty media savvy. Sounds like you need a new marketing plan or maybe more interesting product. Anybody download it?

Jason: Again, I'm not about numbers. Hey Todd, It's been a pleasure talking with you. Good luck with your podcast.

Jason had a temper, a weakness he detested but had given up trying to tame. He had tried all kinds of therapy and mental exercises, but he finally accepted that it was an unfortunate part of who he was. It came and went quickly, but it was intense when he succumbed to it. He shed the headphones, stood up and walked out of the studio. He'd never done that in the past, but this punk had gotten under his skin.

Jay and the Americans, indeed.

Todd the Shark sputtered a few apologies to his audience, knowing that it was likely the brief chat would never see the light of day, unless he wanted to edit Black's comments and make a mockery of him. But if he did that, who would care? Jason Black was yesterday's news. Last century's actually.

2

He gazed at the body in the bed beside him. Was her name Diane? No, it was Dina. Or something more exotic, he couldn't really remember.

Jason Black had had many such encounters over the years, although their frequency had diminished to a slow drip. The pattern was the same. Right after the concert, they'd tentatively approach him, asking for an autograph and telling him how much they loved his music. Lately, more of them tossed out the unintended insult, "My mom was a big fan and she turned me on to you."

He'd long since stopped taking offense at the slight and was thankful that his music was able to cross generations. He'd slept with a few of those mothers, but he still gravitated to the younger bodies.

And Dina or Diana was certainly one of those. She was a bit older than the norm for him, maybe thirty five. As a paid employee of the school, she had arranged his concert in the student center of The College of Savannah. He'd accepted the gig via email before meeting her, not expecting the bonus she provided after the show.

She was old enough to understand the rules. He'd be off in the morning to the next stop, and it was unlikely that their paths would cross again. She was a tick short of pretty; her body was the main attraction. She worked out five days a week and it showed.

The fact that she was available to him, no strings attached, on a Saturday night, although fortunate for him, was sad for her. Did she have a lover, a husband? Children? In the rush to consummate their evening, he hadn't asked and she hadn't volunteered.

He wondered if she had similar misgivings about him. He rarely gave in to the idea that he was lonely, but he had no female partner with which to share his good fortunes or his sorrows.

The few concerts he gave these days were the closest he came to fulfillment. Although the raw number of attendees was laughable given his early fame, their appreciation for him seemed just as passionate. Hearing him perform his old chestnuts made them feel young again and on occasion, it worked that way for him too.

When he was writing about lost love, the road, and anti-war politics, he believed that he had an original message, or at the very least, a fresh way of expressing it. With older eyes and ears, he realized that his best work was a product of the times and didn't hold up. Besides, he was uninterested in repeating the same worn out saws of yesteryear. Maybe Todd the Shark was right about him.

The problem was that his new themes failed to strike a resonant chord with modern audiences. Even though a dwindling number of boomers appreciated his latest dive into their concerns, they weren't much inclined to attend concerts or download albums. Mortality was slowly taking its toll and his few devotees weren't being replenished. As an artist, he felt spent --- his most relevant work was decades old.

He got out of the bed, trying not to arouse his partner. She stirred for a moment, then turned over and went back to sleep.

Good, he thought. No awkward goodbyes. No polite kisses on the cheek. False promises to stay in touch. As many times as he'd been in this situation, he still hadn't mastered a clean getaway. He left a note on hotel stationery, thanking her for, well, everything.

~~~~~

Jason was set to move on to the next stop on the tour, except that there was no tour. He only did ten shows a year now. He lined up appearances at colleges, small clubs and private parties, mostly in the Southeast. His old manager had died years ago and he couldn't stir up interest amongst the newer crop of reps. He had an oft-neglected website that encouraged those interested to contact him directly.

His five year old Ford pickup was parked at the hotel. He'd already checked out of the hotel, so nothing was keeping him from heading home. Maybe he'd stop at a Cracker Barrel on the way and grab breakfast before making the two hour trek back to his place near Charleston.
~~~~~

As he left the hotel, he noticed a large black SUV parked at the curb. A black suited man he assumed to be a chauffeur was standing by the driver's side door. Jason flashed back to the days when there would be a promoter inside, waiting to ferry him to his next appointment, where he would be treated like music royalty. Not like today.

The man spoke. "Excuse me, Mr. Black. My employer would like a word. Would you kindly step into the car?"

Jason hesitated. Could this be Dina's rich husband, angry that he had violated his wife? A brother or boyfriend? He could think of no other nefarious purpose.

He said, "My mommy warned me about getting into cars with strange men, and you haven't even offered me candy. Who's this employer of yours?"

"Mr. Gilmore says you know him well. I can assure you, you're in no danger."

Jason stole a quick look at the license plate. A rental. The driver held the door open and Black got into the car. The surge of heat was a welcome relief from the cold although the smell of stale cigarettes almost choked him. He sat, not looking at the man seated across from him.

The man said, "Thanks for joining me without making a fuss, Jason. Good to see you after all these years. I apologize for showing up unannounced but you know how these things work."

"What things work?"

"Why the attitude? Your last assignment came out rather well for all concerned, I thought. For us, it was mission accomplished. For you, the satisfaction of knowing you served your country. I'm here to offer you the opportunity to do it again and this time, the stakes are even higher."

Jason looked up at the man. His hair had turned white, still clipped short like back in the seventies. It fit his deeply lined face better now. He was geeky in his earlier incarnation, now he looked distinguished. The intense brown eyes had softened, but still projected intelligence. He was wearing a gray worsted suit, white shirt and silver tie. In the middle of the bench seat lay a Brooks Brothers greatcoat, trimmed with a fur collar. Black was grateful for the distance it provided from his former handler.

He said, "I thought you understood that I'd never do that again. My days helping the FBI are over, Gilmore."

The man raised an eyebrow and nodded. "So you said years ago. I hoped you'd had time to reconsider. The thing is, you have a pretty special résumé. Your music career makes you perfect for this assignment. Trust me, I wouldn't ask if I had an alternative."

"I'm not interested. Look, I'm at a point now where I'm happy to do a few shows a year and work at my day job: Renovating historic houses in Charleston."

"A regular Daryl Hall, you are. I can guarantee you that Hall and Oates aren't playing student union centers to sparse crowds. What a career he's had. Too bad you couldn't parlay your past into a TV show like he did."

"That'd be nice but it's not in the cards. Look, I need to get home now."

"Maybe it could be in the cards with a little encouragement. Like back in the day, when we encouraged that record label to sign you. Maybe you would have made it without our help, maybe not. I must say, you weren't in such a hurry last night when you screwed that college administrator."

Jason chuckled. "You guys don't miss a trick, do you? Was she one of yours?"

"I'm shocked that you'd suggest we'd do such a thing. Corrupt a distinguished educator? Perish the thought. I was hoping to catch you after the show but I decided to let you enjoy whatever pleasures she might bring and talk to you in the morning. Thought it might put you in a good mood. Nor did I wish to intrude on your interview. How did that go, by the way?"

"You mean there's something you don't know about my life? Let's just say I've had better."

"How about this? Let me buy you a nice breakfast. There's a place along the river called Huey's. The best beignets this side of New Orleans. I'll lay it all out for you and if you still feel the way you do now, tell me to go to hell. What say?"

Despite what he'd told the man earlier, he was in no rush to get home that Sunday morning. A friend was feeding and caring for his dog. He never worked on Sunday with houses he was rehabbing unless they were under a tight deadline. Jason had been to Huey's before and the man wasn't lying about the beignets. They were excellent.

The lure of fried dough doused in powdered sugar held some appeal despite his qualms that he'd be conscribed into one of Gilmore's schemes. He'd trusted the man once and it had devastated his young life. Could there possibly be an upside for him now? A boost to his music career? Unlikely, but it couldn't hurt to hear the pitch, could it?

Jason said, "Okay Gilmore, I'll listen. But that's it. My days helping the FBI are over."

Richard Gilmore's smile was as cold as the morning. "I think in a short time, you'll be eating those words along with the beignets."

3

From River Street in the dead of winter, Huey's appears to be no more than a hole in the wall with a fancy awning. In the summer, the outdoor tables give it the flair of a Paris bistro, but in January the exterior is cold and gray, like the rugged cobblestone street it fronted. Even the river across the street is unappealing in the winter. Steamed up windows afforded no glimpse of Huey's interior, and unknowledgeable tourists don't give it a second glance.

Inside is a different story. The stone floors, walls of exposed brick and timber beams give it a rustic charm. Thick, white paper toppers grace the small tables. They are crammed in so tightly that you could barely navigate around them, even when the place is empty.

Upon entering, Jason was greeted by the heady smell of their enticing omelets. The aroma of onions, peppers, cheese and bacon sent him back to his childhood, when his mom would awaken him weekend mornings, eager to have him sample her latest experiment.

The room tinkled with the sound of silverware against the sparkling white china. The place had yet to fill up, as it would a couple of hours later, when the street would be lined with affluent Savannah residents.

They'd arrive fresh from Sunday services, ready to devour their reward for waking up on a cold winter's morning to hear their holy man of choice's interpretation of God's will.

The driver had dropped them off and disappeared to park the SUV. Apparently, whatever Richard Gilmore had to say was not for his ears. The hostess at the front of the restaurant ushered the pair to a secluded table, away from the kitchen and the few other early patrons.

Typical of Gilmore's arrogance, Jason thought. He'd arranged everything with the absolute certainty that he would go along with the plan. He wouldn't be shocked to find that Gilmore had somehow instructed Todd the Shark to belittle him, to make him more vulnerable. Gilmore couldn't be that thorough, could he?

After they were seated, coffee and a half dozen beignets ordered, Gilmore said, "Don't think we have to eat them all, Jason. I've put on a few since last we met, but you've stayed in shape. I guess that manual labor restoring those old shacks suits you."

"I'm not a member of any fancy health spas if that's your point. It's honest work, and I do a lot of it myself. Hands-on."

The coffee came. Rich, dark with a slightly nutty taste. Real cream was served with it, not half and half or the chemical stuff. Cost a little more in dollars and calories, but the bureau was paying and Black's labors made the calories irrelevant.

Jason said, "So, what's your angle? You've turned into a talent agent and you're trying to recruit me? I'd think a deputy manager to the assistant director of the FBI or whatever the hell you are these days would have better things to do."

"Okay, I deserve that. Look, we haven't been in touch for years. It's not like your music is going great guns now. I did a little research. Looks like your career could use a boost."

"So you arranged the concert last night?"

"No, that wasn't me but I did buy a block of tickets and pass them out for free. A small donation to help pay the freight."

These small favors always demanded something in return. The last time, the price was far too high. Jason was rethinking his decision to listen to Gilmore's plan. His rehab business was his main focus now. As much as he still loved music, it had become a hobby and he couldn't see any amount of federal intervention changing that.

He said, "Don't want your help, don't need it. The fewer ties I have with you guys the better."

The beignets arrived and lived up to their reputation. They were hot, fresh from the oven and smelled heavenly, a blend of powdered sugar, nutmeg and cinnamon. Black's negativity softened as he took the first bite.

"Haven't been to New Orleans in years, but they can't make them better than these," Jason said.

"Enjoy, my friend."

"Let's get one thing straight, Gilmore. I'm not your friend. You screwed me years ago and I went along with you like the idiot that I was in those days. But I'm done and that's that."

"I didn't plan on revisiting the past, but since your perception of it is distorted, let's. You rebelled, typical of that generation."

"Blah, blah, blah."

"Hear me out. When those protests against the war were going on, we had strong intelligence that the Commies were supporting it. I was a young agent, just making my bones. We needed somebody on the inside back then to confirm what we believed. With your dad being a cop and all, we figured you were that person."

No amount of powdered sugar could remove the sour taste from Jason's mouth. "You turned me into the worst kind of snitch."

"Sorry that's the way you remember it. The way I remember it was that we broke up a Soviet cell that had infiltrated your group. Their influence was spreading throughout your movement. Once they were busted, your protests were clean. Naïve perhaps, but pure."

"Bullshit. Face it, Hoover and his cronies wanted to shut us down, and if they proved that the Russians were funding us, it would turn public opinion against us."

"See, your memory fails you. Hoover died in 1972 and Pat Gray took over. Mark Felt, aka Deep Throat was an associate director. The Red influence never came out publicly until years after the war ended when that Soviet defector wrote a book about it. Not saying that had Hoover lived, things might have been different, but we kept it under wraps. And your participation was never revealed."

"*I* know what I did. That's what matters."

"Admit it Jason, you still carry this around with you for one reason. The girl. The girl you thought you were in love with was a Russian spy. And she was arrested for that, due to your efforts."

"Arrested and thrown into a dark hole, God knows where. Interrogated by you guys or the CIA. Don't tell me that didn't happen."

"That's classified. I can only tell you that the bureau would never sanction any kind of mistreatment."

"And less than a year after she was arrested, she was sent back to Russia in an exchange of agents. I found that out through other sources."

"I can neither confirm or deny what happened after she was detained."

"Detained. What a polite word for what you did. She was never heard from again. Probably froze to death in Siberia."

"That was the life she chose."

"Chose? Or the one the Russians forced on her? She was probably brainwashed as a kid. Learned to speak perfect English and sent here to pose as an American. You really think she had a choice?"

Huey's was starting to come alive as the churchgoers came flooding in. Jason's volume had increased as the conversation became more heated. Gilmore could see that it wasn't going as he had planned but he knew that all the vitriol from the past had to be flushed out if they could ever hope to work with Jason Black again.

Gilmore said, "Jason, you served your country. The war was over a couple of years later and the movement went on, free of communist influence. That fool Carter got elected. The country healed."

"You're leaving out the part where fifty five thousand Americans lost their lives for nothing, not to mention the mental and physical toll on the survivors. The shirt I'm wearing was made in Vietnam by our former enemies. Maybe if your beloved bureau had been more concerned with exposing Johnson and Nixon's lies instead of busting the protestors and covering up the truth, some of those lives would never have been lost."

"Mistakes were made. Shit happens."

Gilmore was asking for his help, but had nonchalantly shrugged off all the lives that were ruined by an unwinnable war. For the second time this morning, Jason's temper flared. He'd heard enough.

He said, "A damn casual way of dismissing all those families who lost their sons for nothing. You know what, keep your damn beignets."

He hurled his half eaten one at Gilmore, powdered sugar cascading over the man's immaculate suit. The table rocked and almost tipped over as he stood.

Loud enough so that everyone in the place could hear him, he said, "Fuck off, Richard, with your filthy propositions. I'm outta here."

4

Jason hurried back to the hotel lot and started his pickup truck. Gilmore had infuriated him with gauzy recollections of Jason's greatest regret. The FBI agent seemed to have no misgivings about the lives that he and his kind had destroyed.

He knew friends who had been drafted. Some didn't come back. Those who did preferred not to talk about it. He never met a soul who regaled him with colorful stories about the wonderful time they spent in Southeast Asia.

But what made it personal for him was what had happened with Wendy. It wasn't until he met Wendy Walton in his junior year that he knew love for the first time.

He had learned to play guitar as a boy and had tinkered with writing songs, using the few chords he had mastered. His lyrics were simple odes to love, a subject he knew nothing about except what he'd seen in the movies. His first college sociology class was a shocker, when the young professor shattered his romantic notions by calling bullshit on Hollywood. He mocked the G-rated romantic comedies Jason had been allowed to watch, exclaiming, "They ask us to believe Doris Day. A fifty year old virgin. Never been screwed."

Neither had he.

Then Wendy entered his life. She persuaded the policeman's son to distrust everything he had learned growing up. Railing against the establishment and pointing out American hypocrisy at every turn, she radicalized him. He started writing sharper songs of outrage that resonated with the protesters. He honed his guitar skills. Before long, he was a BMOC. His talent was in demand at campus protests nationwide, of which there were hundreds.

The antiwar movement had burgeoned on campuses and despite McGovern's defeat at the hands of Nixon in '72, it grew to the point where there were millions of active followers. The administration had promised "peace with honor" but the protesters sought peace, period. As the casualty figures continued unabated, the peace talks argued over the shape of the table. Both sides of the debate hardened their positions. Flags were burned, Nixon was hung in effigy. Four Kent State students had been killed by the National Guard during a protest, which only made the movement stronger and more determined.

The powers in Washington needed to fight back and they turned to tactics they had employed and honed during the cold war. If they could discredit the movement in some way, the country might become more united. The administration believed the war was a just cause, preventing the spread of "godless Communism".

Jason Black caught the attention of a young Richard Gilmore. The fed attached himself to Jason after a rally where he had performed and plied him with drugged beer and sympathetic conversation at a local pub until he passed out. When Black awoke, he was at a boutique hotel in New York.

Gilmore and his team went to work. The FBI had come to the conclusion that Wendy was a Soviet sleeper agent, trained at an early age in American ways. She'd been tasked with fueling the fires of the antiwar movement, recruiting others along the way. If she could encourage enough dissent, America might lose the political will to prosecute the war. Vietnam would join the growing ranks of Red nations.

They believed she had attached herself to Jason, seeing him as a *polezni dvrak*, or useful idiot. He had talent and charisma and an ability to write songs that furthered her cause. In return, she gave him the love of his life.

When Gilmore and his team revived Jason in the hotel room, they laid out their case. His captors were unrelenting, no matter how much Jason resisted. His passion for Wendy Walton was strong. He would have married her if they both hadn't considered it a bourgeois institution, unnecessary to cement their love. The feds chipped away at her story until he began to have doubts. They had a circumstantial case but wanted verification before they would arrest her. Maybe she could be turned. That's where they needed his cooperation.

He remained unconvinced until they played their final card --- his dying father.

Jason had not been particularly close to his dad. The elder Black's police work demanded all his time. Days, nights, and weekends. Missed Little League games, school plays, PTA meetings. When a father's strong hand was needed, Jonathan Black was seldom there.

A lifelong smoker of unfiltered Chesterfield Kings, his father paid the price for his addiction. But that night, he wheezed his endorsement of the bureau's agenda and pleaded with his son to go along. Jason, in large part out of pity for his old man's fate, gave in and agreed to work undercover.

He was sure that they were wrong; that Wendy was an American girl who was a true believer in world peace and only wanted what was best for the country. Maybe if he could convince the feds of that, they'd leave her alone and pursue their paranoid fantasies elsewhere.

He allowed the FBI to bug his rental in Long Beach. He held out hope that it would lead to her vindication.

After two weeks of monitoring, Wendy had done nothing to further their case. Richard Gilmore's patience was wearing thin. He decided to force the issue. He told Jason to confront Wendy with what they had compiled. He refused. To do that, Jason would have to reveal he was working undercover. She'd never forgive him if it turned out she was innocent.

Gilmore came up with another approach. It would shield Jason from ruining their relationship if he was wrong. It involved Jason telling her that his father had compiled the evidence, and that he was tipping her off so that she could escape or better yet, defect.

The memory of the fateful evening was burned into Jason's brain. He liked to imagine that she had returned to the Motherland to great fanfare for her courageous deeds and had married a Russian count. But of course, they no longer existed. Maybe a poet like the fictional Yuri Zhivago.

Brezhnev and Kosygin weren't given to pay tribute to failure, which is how Wendy must have been perceived. They wouldn't trust that she hadn't compromised other sleepers or divulged important secrets to the CIA. Worst case, she may have become a double agent. They'd had to trade valuable assets for her return before she might reveal any more.

No, it was more likely that Wendy was dead or rotting in some Siberian prison or gulag.

This was the fate he had consigned her to by collaborating with Gilmore and his FBI cronies. Now the old man wanted him to do another dirty deed. He didn't care what it was. There was no way that was going to happen.

5

Jason's eyes misted up at the remembrance, as he drove north through the Lowcountry toward Charleston. After Wendy's arrest, he had severe recriminations, drank to excess and wasted the remainder of his college days. When he finally got himself together, his songs focused on lost love and betrayal. The wretched experience from those days had helped Jason find his voice as a songwriter. The post Watergate generation responded to his pain. Jason Black became Cat Stevens by way of Joni Mitchell.

That's what the critics said anyway.

He'd made and spent a lot of money and as Billy Joel sang in *The Entertainer*, 'laid all kinds of girls'. He was never a big druggie but had smoked his share of weed. He'd opened for the biggest bands in the seventies before headlining sold out tours of his own. For a half a decade, he was at the top of the pops.

Then it faded away as he was slow to adapt to changing musical tastes. He knew that he was repeating himself, but he stayed in his wheelhouse, never venturing outside of his personal safe zone. He was that way with women as well. He stayed away from long term commitments, choosing those beauties who made him feel good at the time. If a woman challenged him on any level, he ran away. As his looks and spot on the charts faded, the groupies sought greener pastures. And largely because of what had happened with Wendy, he could never develop a stable relationship.

These days, the most lucrative music jobs he'd had were on cruise ships, but he recently swore to himself that he'd never do one of those again. The problem being that he was captive on the vessel and couldn't get away from intrusive fans. They were in his face, day and night. Once in a great while, it led to a stimulating conversation with an accomplished person from another world. He had made a couple of nice contacts and if nothing else, they helped make the time between shows more tolerable.

But in the main, his fellow passengers felt entitled --- they had forked over big money to sail away with one of their musical heroes, and that gave them purchase to the star's attention 24/7. Most wanted to bore him with mundane stories of where they had been and what they were doing when they first heard his music on the radio. Others asked prying personal questions as to which particular lady had inspired individual love songs. Many wanted to hear shade about his illustrious peers.

His last attempt at a relationship had stalled a year ago when he realized that if he married Katrina McCann, he'd be settling for comfort and companionship, as opposed to what he still held onto as real love, whatever that was. He knew it was unlikely that he'd find that one true love at his advanced age, just like he'd never be able to rekindle the Christmas spirit of his boyhood.

He walked into his house just past noon, tiptoeing past the sleeping figure in the rocking chair. He shushed Jasper, his ten year old mixed breed, who scrambled to greet him as he walked in.

"I'm awake," the figure in the rocking chair said. "Hard to sleep with that damn dog running to the front door every car that goes by. Misses you. Can't say I do that much. You eat yet? There's pancake batter in the fridge."

The man in the chair was Jason Black's best friend. Aaron Hendricks was seventy something years old, rail thin, and slowly dying of prostate cancer. He had the disgusting habit of chewing flavored tobacco and despite Jason's constant pleas, never relented.

Jason said, "The place stinks, Aaron. Between whatever that vile crap you insist on killing yourself with and your refusal to turn the fan on after you've used the bathroom. Ugh."

"Cold outside. No point in sending heated air out just 'cause I used the crapper. Must've been the chili last night."

"Too much information, old man. Has Jasper been out?"

"Out and fed. Damn mutt knows it's Sunday. Was hovering around the griddle second I took it out. Loves my pancakes."

Aaron loved the dog and as much as he complained about Jasper watching his every move as he cooked, he was delighted that the dog appreciated his hotcakes. He was offended if Jason had the nerve to suggest that they breakfast on something else Sunday mornings.

Jason had to admit that the man had perfected the art of pancake making. Hendricks refused to share the recipe. Even shooed people away while he was mixing so they couldn't get a look at the ingredients.

"You staying for the football or are you headed home?" Jason asked.

"Ain't got a reason to move away from your big screen unless you got a lady friend comin' over and need some privacy. You catch any of the Falcons last night or were you too busy with your hootenanny?"

"Heard the recaps on the radio driving back. Sounded like they played well."

Jason was a latecomer to the NFL. During his school days, it was jocks versus hippies and Jason fell into the latter category. That conflict had long since passed but old prejudices die hard. His enthusiasm for the sport was largely inspired by one of his employees, Julius Truman. The massive black man shared a surname with the ex-president, but that was about all they had in common.

Aaron said, "Julius'll be by later. Says he'll bring a bucket of KFC. He prefers Chick-Fil-A, but they're closed on Sundays."

"Don't go teasing him about being a black man who likes fried chicken. He tolerates it from you, but I bet he doesn't like it."

"Trash talk and he dishes it right back. Ain't got nothin' to do with his color. Boy that big needs fried foods to keep up his size."

"Calling him boy won't cut it either."

"You see him around now? I'm not totally dumb to that PC shit. Julius can take it. Shame he couldn't cut it in the pros or we might be watching him, 'stead of him watching them with us."

"Yeah well, don't encourage him. I talked to some folks who know. They say Julius isn't a good fit for the NFL. He was too small to play line, too slow to be a linebacker. Don't be giving him false hope or it'll hurt him in the long run."

"You notice I ain't encouraging you to do concerts."

"I'll ignore that. Julius is learning the trades. Someday, I can see him taking over the business and flipping houses on his own."

"Shame I won't be around to see it."

"Hold up, Aaron. Your doctors telling you something you haven't told me?"

"Same old, same old. Prostate cancer's like that old Taj Mahal song about cocaine. They say *it'll kill you, but they don't say when.* No new problems now, 'cept I have to get up to take a piss every couple hours."

"Join the club," Jason said. "I did miss breakfast actually. Long story but if you're not glued to that chair for the rest of the day, maybe you could rustle up some of those hotcakes. I need to check my email. I'll be out in a few minutes."

"Glued to my chair? Hah. Take you in a fight any day of the week, pussy."

There was a host of junk mail cluttering his computer's in-box. No amount of spam filters could weed out all the pleading solicitations and phony sales pitches. Not much in the way of fan letters these days. But there *was* an email from the College of Savannah with an .edu suffix.

I was hoping we could have breakfast together. I wish we could have said a proper goodbye. I thought the show went well and the crowd really liked it. I'm afraid when I got the final numbers they didn't look so good. I know my boss. We can't put on concerts unless they at least break even so a return engagement isn't likely.

However if you would like a return engagement on our post concert activity, you know how to get in touch if you're down this way again. Keep on truckin'.

Deirdre Collins.

Keep on truckin'. How romantic. So that was her name. Deirdre. After the old Beach Boys' song, maybe?

He couldn't draw enough fans in a tiny venue to make it worthwhile for a small college to even showcase his old stuff. The housing rehab business was subsidizing his musical journeys. Years ago, it had been the other way around.

He was about to hit the delete key, but Aaron called him from the kitchen to let him know his food was ready.

6

Richard Gilmore prided himself on his ability to bend others to his wishes, making them think it was what they wanted all along. He had long since realized that constructing logical arguments in hopes of changing anyone's position didn't work in this day of entitled egos who were cocksure of their misguided views.

Wendy Walton was his first big bust and although he achieved his goal, he knew the endgame was poorly executed. As a young agent, he was taking no chances. Yes, he'd promised Jason that he'd handle her with care, but he couldn't take the chance that she'd somehow escape his grasp. She was athletic and a trained operative. The only way he could be sure to catch her was the way he had ordered it. And if she and Jason didn't mate like bunnies every chance they got, he might have found a more decorous way.

Now the ham fisted arrest had come back to bedevil him. He hoped that his intercession with the record company would have been enough of an apology. He gotten Black a three album deal with a major label, guaranteeing the company that the government would reimburse any losses they might incur. It was a hollow promise --- his superiors had given him no such authority.

It had proved academic. Jason Black sold a lot of records and paid off the label's advance many times over. His road to stardom might have been hastened with Gilmore's aid, but it likely would have happened on its own.

He'd have thought after all these years, Jason would appreciate the boost to his career. But he had underestimated the trauma the man had suffered when his woman was ripped from their bed in such humiliating fashion.

Now as fate would have it, Gilmore needed him again. He had hoped that the college gig would appeal to Jason's ego, cause him to believe that feds had the power to boost his music career again. But Black was past all that. Gilmore needed to find another lever to bend the old folksinger to his will.

~~~~~

"I'll have another Jack if you're getting up." Aaron had seemed to be fast asleep but started awake when Black reached over to pet his dog.

Jasper had stayed in the kitchen when Jason went to his study to check his mail. Not that he didn't appreciate his master coming home, but when Aaron reignited the griddle, he figured there might be more pancakes in the offing.
~~~~~

Jason said, "I wasn't getting up but since those pancakes were so good, I'll fetch your lazy ass another drink. Did you miss that interception just now while you were dozing off?"

"What interception? A little more ice if you will."

Jason got up to get the bourbon. Aaron had been falling asleep more and more these days, drifting off just hours after waking up in the morning. His old friend needed purpose in his life and Jason considered it important to keep him engaged and motivated, even if it consisted of busy work. He'd seen others slouch toward oblivion out of sheer boredom. He sometimes felt himself pulled in that direction, but he fought it --- hard. He was damned if he'd let Aaron go down that road without a fight.

"Thanks, pal," Aaron said as he accepted his Gentleman Jack. "You took me a little too seriously about the ice. Ain't much booze in there."

"Just trying to keep you awake. That stuff knocks you out colder than Nyquil. Wouldn't want you to miss any more of this exciting game."

"Exciting, my ass. Pats'll win easy. I was just dozing off a little, is all. Even had a dream."

"If it's about a woman, don't feel you have to share."

Aaron was a Vietnam vet. Upon coming home, he worked for thirty years at a local utility and retired with a modest pension. He then hooked on with Jason who gave him a small stake in the business in return for his electrical work and managerial expertise, which cost far less than employing a younger man with equal skills.

At his advanced age, Aaron did almost no hands-on labor, but he was a great mentor for young Paco Compaña, the third member of Black's little rehab team, who was training as an electrician with plumbing skills on the side. Paco did the work; Aaron signed off on it as if he had done it himself.

Aaron sipped the last of his drink and placed the glass down emphatically on the side table. "Actually, kid, you were part of my dream. I've been reading that book you gave me for Christmas, that biography about Joni Mitchell. Man, did she ever get around. Cat Stevens, James Taylor, Jackson Browne and about a hundred others."

"You're talking about *Reckless Daughter*. Figured you'd like it."

"What I can't figure is why your name isn't mentioned about the guys she schtupped."

"Where'd you pick up that expression?"

"I'm a man of the world, lad. Don't duck the question. You ever do Joni? You opened for her, I know that. What I want to know is if she opened for you."

"You know I don't kiss and tell."

"Come on, make a geezer happy in the winter of his years. I won't tell anybody. Not likely anyone's gonna do a bio on *you*, that's a fact."

"Nice. Okay, just to satisfy a dirty old man, I'll tell you."

"See, that's just wrong. Young man wants to get some poontang, it's fine. Just raging hormones. An older gentleman still appreciates the fair sex, he's dirty. He should get credit for being able to function in his golden years."

"Got no problem with an old dude like you doing it. It's talking about it that turns people off. Anyway, no. I did not sleep with Joni Mitchell. I did open for her early in my career. She was already a big star by then. There were two opening acts. Was me, some hair band, then Joni. Variety. Good seats cost seven bucks, believe it or not."

"I went to the Fillmore in San Fran before I shipped out to 'Nam. Saw three acts for two fifty. Allman Brothers and Jethro Tull, I think, were the main attraction."

"It'd be two hundred and fifty now. Anyway, Joni and I traveled separately. She had a big tour bus. I had a VW van I drove myself. She had a nice dressing room. Roses, grass, coke, whatever she wanted. I got ready in the men's room on a bunch of stops. Or a closet."

"Poor you."

"She barely spoke to me. I love Joni's music, she was the best ever. Thing I most remember was that I thought I did a killer version of her song, *Urge for Going*. She came out one day during my sound check. Took me aside and asked me to stop doing it. Said she liked Tom Rush's version much better and that I didn't understand the song. I guess I really didn't know clouds at all."

"I guess that's why my little insults roll off your back. After that, ain't nothing I say is gonna sting much."

"Well, I did stop doing that song in concert, but I wrote a song about cruel people making mean judgments. People thought it was about the rock critics, but it was about her. My first hit."

"That'd show the bitch."

"Now, now. Years later, they did a tribute to her on television on TNT or someplace. Before she had her stroke or whatever it was. She insisted that I be invited, and she covered my table and travel."

"Apologizing for treating you like shit back in the day, I s'pose."

"Nope. When I brought it up, and I was just joking about it, she said she didn't remember saying that. Said she'd heard my version of that song on Sirius/XM a few days before and thought I got it just right. Admitted she was so coked up during the tour she didn't remember much except that I was this kid she hoped to get to know but she was too caught up in the star making machinery."

"That didn't make the book."

"I wasn't interviewed for it. Besides, with all those big stars she hooked up with, nobody would care about a little story about Jason Black."

"Hey fella, don't be so down on yourself. You didn't tell me about the concert. I figured you'd be home last night, though. Too tired to make the drive?"

"The school booked me a hotel room and it was foggy. I don't like driving at night much anymore. Don't see as well as I used to. So I stayed over."

They were distracted for a moment by Tom Brady's third touchdown pass. The Pats were up 24-0 before halftime. The sound on the TV was down so as not to interrupt their conversation, but they both were impressed by the perfect throw.

Jason said, "That number 12 never ages, does he?"

"Yeah, but peddling that avocado ice cream shit? I think I'd rather die young than eat that crap."

"Dying young isn't an option for you. But if you're thinking of checking out, give me some notice so I can hire another electrician to okay Paco's work."

"Great to know you care. So, did you stay in that cozy hotel room all by your lonesome? Fog rolled in at two this morning so I ain't buying that excuse."

"FYI, that hotel room wasn't so nice. Old steam radiator kept me up half the night."

"That all that kept you up?"

7

"Julius just texted. He ain't coming. I'm gonna have to take a switch to that boy." Aaron was pissed.

"Stop calling him 'boy'," Jason said. "It's too cold and he said he'll see us in the morning at the Wagener house. No chicken for you."

"Want to see what little Paco's up to?"

"I'll call him and see."

Paco answered on the first ring. "Hey, Jefe. What you need?"

"Just seeing what you're up to on your day off."

"No days off for me. I was at the house this morning. Making sure my wiring is good for the inspection tomorrow."

"I'm sure it is. Hey, you really didn't need to do that. You deserve some down time, hard as you work."

"The job is more important."

Jason smiled. Paco was the most dedicated worker he'd ever dealt with. The lad double and triple checked everything, and that was before Aaron gave it the once over. Black said, "Reason I called is that Aaron and I are watching the NFL playoffs. Do you want to come over and join us?"

Jason could barely hear Paco over the noise. "I don't like American football much, Jefe. I'm into real fútbol, the one you call soccer. There's World Cup eliminations going on today."

"Gotcha. Just thought I'd ask. Enjoy the games, kiddo. After the inspection, we'll start working on the sheetrock. See ya tomorrow."

He rang off and turned to Aaron. "No Paco. He's watching soccer at a sports bar that caters to that kind of thing."

"Better hope the ICE men don't cometh."

"Not funny. Clever though, I'll give you credit. I really admire the kid, with what he's been through with the immigration situation and all."

"Good kid. But big Julie let us down. Anyway, looks like just you and me and no chicken. Damn."

Jason liked Julius and Paco a great deal. They were family as far as he was concerned. The management books he had read when he started his rehab business all cautioned against becoming too close to your employees. It makes it hard to discipline them if they think they are your friends. And what if you have to fire them? You let emotion enter into your business decisions and the results can be disastrous.

It was difficult to keep them at arm's length since his natural inclination was to let his affection show. There were times he had to make it clear that he was their boss, but it was becoming harder as he bonded with them.

Jason wasn't all that hungry but he said, "How about this? This game is a blowout and I don't need to see any more. If it turns into a miracle finish, it's on Sirius and I can hear it in the truck. Why don't I go to

D'Allesandro's down on St. Philip for one of their hand tossed pizzas. Or Monza's for a wood fired one?"

"Ain't into those fancy artisan pies, my lad. Guess I was spoiled, time I spent in New York. Can't beat the ones in Brooklyn or Staten Island. Yeah, go ahead, I don't care which one. I'll just catch up on my sleep 'til you get back. Woke up at 4:30 this morning."

"How's that different than any other morning? I'll be right back. Sure you don't want special toppings?"

"Surprise me. Later."

Jason grabbed his coat and hopped into his pickup. As he adjusted the rear view mirror, he caught a glimpse of himself. *You're getting old*, he thought. His long hair was still thick, tied into a pony tail, but almost all steel gray now. His lantern jaw was starting to meld into his neck. So far, he had resisted the temptation to grow a goatee to mask it.

Aaron had been after him to "ditch the hippie shit" and cut his hair to a more conventional length. But something in him compelled him to, as David Crosby once sang, *let his freak flag fly*. Perhaps it was hanging on to the last vestige of hope that his music career could be resurrected. Hell, Hall and Oates were back on the road. Cat Stevens was appreciated anew. Van Morrison never left. At one time, he was more in vogue and had sold more records than any of them.

Richard Gilmore had brought these memories bubbling to the surface and he became angry all over again. He'd be damned if he'd ever work with the man, no matter what the stakes.

8

Richard Gilmore had other ideas. He needed to convince Jason to be part of his plan. The circumstances of this new case mirrored the experience from decades ago. No one could fit the bill like Jason Black. There was nothing he wouldn't do to convince him to go along. No pressure he wouldn't apply, no reward he wouldn't promise if it accomplished his goal.

He was waiting in Black's driveway when he got home with his dinner. When Jason saw the elegantly turned out man smoking an unfiltered cigarette, he gave him a look of disgust, as he would if a snake crossed his path. Had Gilmore spoken to Aaron?

Obviously, the fed had not gotten the message. He wasn't interested. Period.

He needed to emphasize that now. He got out of the truck with the food and told Gilmore to wait for him outside. He'd be right out.

He set the meal on the kitchen counter. Aaron was asleep and didn't hear him come in. Good. He'd dismiss Gilmore and settle in for an evening of football and beer.

When he came back out, Gilmore said, "Sorry to interrupt your dinner Jason, but I can't let you think you can blow me off like that with no consequences."

"So you follow me home to harass me? You really think that's going to change my mind?"

"Jason, I tried to do this nicely. I admit, I helped get you that gig at the college. A gesture of good faith that you threw back in my face."

"The answer is no. Nothing will change that. Just accept it and move on."

It was cold and Jason was shifting his feet impatiently to keep the circulation going. Gilmore's cologne was cloying. *Women I know rarely use perfume these days, men never*, Jason thought. *If he thinks it's covering up the tobacco stench, he's mistaken.*

Gilmore said, "You made it very clear you hate me for what happened to your Russian girlfriend. I get that. You think I condemned her to death, or a fate worse than that."

Jason fumed. "You did. They have an expression in Central America which translates to 'the disappeared ones.' A man might be a humble worker and a devoted father one day, then he disappears without a trace or a reason. Government, drug lords, nobody knows. I wrote a song about it."

"The Russkies weren't like that. They wanted to make an example of anyone who went against the politburo. Not public hangings per se, but the disappeared ones as you call them, well, everyone knew what happened to them."

"It's cold out. What's your point?"

Gilmore said, "What if I told you your Natasha or whatever name she was using, isn't dead and might even be up to her old tricks."

"You're despicable."

"Why won't you hear me out? I think once you hear what I have to say, you'll want to do the right thing. By the way, is everyone you have working for you here legally? Be a shame if one of your crew was to get deported one day. Might remind you of what happened to Nastasha."

"You know Gilmore, I may have agreed to give you the benefit of the doubt. Maybe you changed over the years. But right away, you show your true colors. You know my weak spots and damned if you aren't trying to exploit them. Her name *was* and always will be to me, Wendy. Wendy Walton."

He turned and walked back into his house, leaving Gilmore in the driveway, shaking his head.

~~~~~

Richard Gilmore had caused Jason to feel a small amount of guilt at the way he had treated Deidre. He regretted almost deleting her email without the courtesy of a reply.

That's not who I am, he thought.

At the very least, he should answer her email and thank her. Yet, he wouldn't be seeing her again and didn't want to encourage her to think that they had any kind of future together.
~~~~~

And why was that?

She was not a trollop, like many of the others he had been with over the years. They had talked music and although she wasn't hip to his generation, she knew a lot about what was happening now and had some good insights. She had a good job at a respectable profession, and saw the world pretty much as he did. She wasn't as conventionally pretty as some, but she didn't work at it very hard, either.

So why wouldn't he consider her a candidate for something more than a fling? Maybe for the same reason he hadn't let himself commit to *anyone* over the last forty years.

Wendy Walton.

She was his first and only love. The scent of Shalimar, her favorite perfume, still thrilled him whenever he encountered it. Their love was perfect, until it wasn't.

He had sold Wendy Walton out. It was an act of cowardice that had made him hate himself and ruined him for any other woman. He had recurring nightmares about that night, her naked body brutalized by the feds. He had been the cause of that.

He had agreed to entrap the woman he loved. It didn't benefit the anti-war movement to have her purged from its ranks. It didn't bring democracy to Southeast Asia. It didn't restore the lives lost or ruined by the war. It served no purpose other than to put a notch in Richard Gilmore's gun.

Even though his head told him that circumstance was unlikely to ever reoccur, his heart wouldn't let him take that chance with another women. The pain he had inflicted was too great. Wendy Walton was probably dead and he was to blame.

So whenever he met someone that he thought might be a potential mate, he pushed her away, opting for shallow, physical relationships that risked little. As a pop star, there were countless women available to serve his needs. He drifted along for years with these sporadic couplings.

Then he met Katrina McCann. She owned a restaurant on the outskirts of town, and he found himself frequenting the place, at first for the food and then to chat up the proprietor. She was so much like Wendy. In her mid fifties, she was beautiful, vibrant and extremely intelligent. Her devotion to progressive causes sparked a renewed political interest in him.

He resisted seeing her as more than a friend until she finally called him on it. He didn't tell her about Wendy, but let her know that he was a rambling man, who couldn't be tied down. She accepted him on those terms, but their relationship deepened until they became exclusive lovers.

It tore at his heart to break it off with her. He explained that he was denying her the opportunity to be with someone more permanent and committed. She saw through that excuse. They would remain friends, dinners at least monthly, and if those nights led to her bed, it wouldn't be the worst thing.

Try as he might, he couldn't heal the scars he inflicted on himself over Wendy. He sought therapy for his temper, but never let his shrink know about what had ruined him with women. He had reached the point where he could accept that he was destined to spend the rest of his days alone. His past made him unsuitable for any decent woman and now even casual flings troubled his conscience.

Kat was too great a lady to walk away from. But someday, he'd need to do just that. For her sake.

9

Gilmore sat in his Charleston hotel room, watching *Ray Donovan* on Showtime, and contemplating his next move. He had to refine the tactics.

Getting Black booked to a concert at the College of Savannah was his first outreach. A call to an old classmate at his Alma Mater and a small donation had done the trick.

What he didn't count on was Black's hatred lingering from over forty years ago. Wendy Walton was a Russian beauty, along the lines of Maria Sharapova, but Black had had decades to get over her and realize the truth --- he'd been played by Wendy Walton.

Instead of trying to damage Black's music career, which had already tanked of its own accord, attacking his current livelihood might be a better alternative. Black had been a successful homebuilder over the last couple of decades. The occasional weekend concert he performed was a lark. An ego trip, not a lot of income.

Gilmore had enlisted a computer geek to find out where Black might be vulnerable. Even though it was late on a Sunday evening, he called the man in hopes of pursuing a different tack.

“So Charles, what do you have for me regarding Black’s construction company?” Gilmore said, sparing superfluous greetings.

“Really wasn’t hard to come up with. Black Renovations LLC, has building permits out on two properties at the moment. Both in Charleston. One awaits only its final inspection for its CO, that’s certificate of occupancy.”

“I don’t need the technical jargon.”

“Sorry. Anyway, the final inspection on the almost finished project hasn’t been scheduled. The other one has an electrical rough-in inspection booked for tomorrow. Black has two employees.”

“Tell me about them.”

“One is a twenty six year old black man. Interesting name. Julius Truman. Big man, almost made an NFL team a few years ago. Seems he does a lot of the physical labor. Black himself does finish work. Then there’s an illegal, named Paco Compaña. Maybe 19, records aren’t easily found. From El Salvador. Looks like Black’s taken him under his wing. Teaching him plumbing, electrical work, stuff like that.”

“He’s definitely here illegally?”

“Yes. In addition, I think Compaña is doing things he’s not licensed to do, because the electrician of record is an old man called Aaron Hendricks. But Hendricks is 70 years old so I doubt he’s actually doing any work. I see no payments from Black to Hendricks, so it’s likely cash, off the books.”

“That’s promising.”

"You probably can use that situation as leverage against Black. That's where I assume you're going with all of this."

Gilmore said, "Don't assume. So wading through your gobbledygook, I take it that Black will be at the electrical inspection tomorrow. Is there a time?"

"When you call to get your cable TV fixed, do they give you an exact time? No, inspectors just give you a window and from what I gather, it's pretty wide and they miss it quite often. Morning is all I can get. They start at eight."

"Does Black need to be there?"

"Someone needs to let the inspector in and I would think if it was this Paco kid, the guy might be suspicious that he was doing work he wasn't licensed for. Now there's a lot of corruption in that business and it's possible that Black has paid the inspector to look the other way, but ..."

"Give me the address."

The analyst read off the address, then said, "Are you thinking of contacting immigration about this Compaña boy?"

"Thanks for your efforts."

Gilmore had kept things on a need to know basis and this fellow didn't need to know. But when he had asked for a précis on Black's business and finances, the analyst had correctly assumed that Black was a target, either into his own wrongdoing or that of someone else.

Gilmore couldn't acknowledge that. He wanted to keep the circle as tight as possible. He figured that once he explained the mission to Black, the man would see its importance and sign on. That hadn't happened.

The threat to Compaña was promising. Black was the type to be loyal to his acolytes. Deporting Compaña, which could be accomplished with a phone call, would be a powerful incentive for Black to cooperate.

He had considered one other approach, the nuclear option. If he could threaten to expose Black's role in outing Wendy Walton, the folksinger's reputation in the music community would be destroyed. No one from that era would touch him with a ten foot pole. He imagined that it would hurt his home building business as well.

Despite how effective the threat may be, it had to be a hollow one. When it came to actually revealing that information, there was no way he could follow through. If he did expose the betrayal of Walton, it would kill *this* mission. Black had to be seen as a burned out hippie singer turned carpenter. That was essential for this job to have any chance of succeeding.

Gilmore wasn't one to give up without exhausting every possibility. This could be the biggest case of his a career, a fitting way for him to go out, not to mention a huge service to his country.

He didn't want to strong arm Black at his residence again. Better a neutral site. A vacant house with rudimentary wiring fit the bill perfectly.

~ ~ ~ ~ ~

Jason could see his breath inside the house on Wagener Terrace. Usually at this time of year, working conditions weren't draconian. But the forecast was for unseasonably cold temperatures in the early part of the week, before it hit the sixties by Thursday.

He had three choices. The first was to tell Paco to bundle up and work through the cold. He knew that the young worker would comply without complaint. The second was to postpone work until the following week. That meant a delay and additional carrying charges. The third choice was the one he opted for: buy a salamander, a propane gas heater that could bring the place up to comfortable levels within an hour.

He picked one up at the professional section at Home Depot, but now had to find fuel to power it. He couldn't think of any place open that early, so he headed back home with the bright idea of using the tank from his backyard grill. It was nearly full and should tide him over until he could gas up the tank that came with the heater.

Problem solved, or so he thought. Upon unloading the tank and heater at the house, he discovered that the fittings were slightly different.

He said, "Damn it. Why can't they standardize this shit?"

There was no one in the house to hear him. Paco was doing some clean up at the other project. Julius was tardy, continuing a disturbing trend of late. Jason fiddled with the couplings with some tape and odd plumbing parts he had in his truck, but feared that a jerry-rigged solution could blow up the house. He called a local hardware store and the old man who answered told him that there was an adapter he could buy that would work. Or he could just bring the tank in and fill it there.

He hadn't thought of the old fashioned hardware store as a place to get propane. It was a ten minute ride on the other side of town. He got to within two blocks of the place before traffic came to a dead stop.

"Water main break," said the cop who was detouring traffic.

"Could anything more go wrong this morning?" Jason mumbled to no one. He felt his temper rising, but luckily, he was tuned into NPR. They were airing an interview with Pete Townshend that made the time pass without pain. Ten minutes went by before he was able to circumvent the flooding and reach the store.

What should have been a ten minute ride from his house to the jobsite had turned into an hour and a half comedy of errors. The whole affair reminded him of something that would happen on an "I Love Lucy" episode, except that there was no Ricky Ricardo to bail him out.

He thought he had his anger under control when he reached the house. Still no Julius. On the front door was a red tag note from the electrical inspector. "Owner not present. Must re-schedule."

Jason lost it. He kicked the front door hard, almost breaking his foot. His rage continued after he limped into the building. He threw anything he could get his hands on, mad at the world. Plastic outlet boxes, bundles of wire and buckets of tools crashed into the walls, narrowly missing the windows.

That's all he needed now. Broken windows. Fortunately, the front door was a temporary steel clad one, otherwise his anger would have ruined the antique oak and glass door he had salvaged especially for this house.

He knew the way things worked. The inspector would be pissed. Out of spite, he wouldn't come out until later in the week. Jason had arranged for spray foam insulation to be installed Wednesday, and that couldn't happen until the rough electric was approved. The insulation company was busy, and they wouldn't be able to reschedule for at least a week.

He felt like crying. Where the hell was Julius? He was supposed to be there at eight to let the inspector in. There would be a reckoning to come with the big man and it wouldn't be pretty.

10

Julius Truman arrived at the Wagener Terrace house close to ten, unprepared for the shitstorm that awaited him.

Jason started calmly, “Glad you could make it, Julius.”

“Yeah, boss. Hardly a full day’s work here. Frame up a couple interior walls. Clean up the place some. Do some work in the kitchen. Hey, what happened? Shit’s strewn all over the place. Was there a break-in?”

“No break-in, Julius. I did that. Wanna know why?”

“Not sure as I do. But I guess you’re gonna tell me, whether I want to hear it or not.”

“Damn right I am. Long story short, I had to run around this morning to get a space heater so you and Paco could work without freezing your butts off.”

“Sorry to hear that, boss. We woulda worked anyway, no matter how cold it was.”

“Uh huh. Let me finish, please.”

“Sorry.”

“So today was the rough electrical inspection, right? You know that.”

“Surely do.”

"And they start at eight. You knew that, too. Well, guess what? He came just after eight and no one was here to walk him through it. You know what that means?"

Julius slapped his forehead. "Oh, shit. Yeah. Means they can't start spraying the place Wednesday unless we can get the inspection done tomorrow."

"Now refresh me, what time were you supposed to be here this morning?"

"Said I'd meet you here 'round eight."

Jason raised his voice for the first time. "God damn it Julius, there's no *around eight* in this business. There's eight and then there's late. You coming rolling in after nine, we miss the inspection and now we have to postpone the whole project. Another week or two that my money'll be out there. I should dock you for it. By rights, it should come out of your check."

"Hey man, no reason to go all Ebenezer Scrooge on me. You were supposed to be here at eight and you weren't here either. Don't be blaming me."

If Julius didn't have five inches and eighty pounds on Jason, he would have decked the kid. As it was he said, "That's not the point. I had to chase down equipment for the job, or should I say for your comfort on the job. I assumed that you'd be responsible enough to show up on time. Instead you come waltzing in over an hour late, no apologies. No excuses. And then you have the balls to try to turn this around on me. No wonder the Falcons cut your ass."

Now it was Julius' turn to hold back from punching out his employer. "That ain't fair and you know it. It's a freezing morning and I was up late. The alarm didn't go off and so I slept in some. Big fucking deal. And I was never late for training camp. Not once, for your information."

"Again, missing the point. It's about responsibility."

"Yeah, well you can stick your responsibility up your white ass. I been working with you for years now, and you still have me doing grunt work. Move those bags of cement, Julius. Lift up them beams, Julius. How much responsibility does it take to do that menial shit?"

Julius was breathing hard and Jason knew he had to back off. The kid had a slight asthmatic condition. That and his "tweener" size and speed were why the NFL couldn't find a spot for him. It had nothing to do with his lack of responsibility.

Jason was panting as he said, "Okay, let's calm down, okay? I told you from the start, I wanted you to learn the business so one day you could go out on your own or maybe even take over this one. But you've been late a lot. Even yesterday. You didn't show up to watch football. No big deal there, but it just tracks with the way you've been behaving."

"You hear yourself? Behaving? Like I'm your slave or something."

"That's not what I meant and you know it."

"Do I? You let that old cracker make nigger jokes about me and you just go along like."

"I thought you two were friends and were just trash talking to each other. You call him an old redneck, he teases you about watermelon. Seemed like neither of you minded."

"Shows what you know. That racial shit ain't funny, no matter who it comes from. I got a college degree from Georgia. Not a fake one either. Earned me top grades. Yet you just see me as this big old hulk, carrying things your skinny white ass ain't able to."

"Didn't I trust you to handle the electrical inspector if I wasn't here? That's what started this. Didn't I spend a couple of hours this morning making sure this place was warm enough for you to work in? Haven't I shown you the books, taught you how to spot places that were candidates for rehabbing?"

"Sure, between toting that barge and lifting that bale, sure you did."

"I'm sorry you feel that way, Julius. I only wanted the best for you. Okay, while I was teaching you, I had you do things a man your size could handle better than me. Manual labor. But in case you hadn't noticed, I do plenty of that myself. I'm over sixty years old. I've got a college degree too, from a good school on Long Island. You think I want to be up at dawn on a frigid cold morning, lugging around a propane heater? It's part of being an entrepreneur, kid. You do what you have to."

"Don't call me kid. I'm a man, same as you. I get that you think you're taking me under your tutelage and training me for this business. But did you ever stop and think that's not what I want?"

Jason was struck by the word 'tutelage'. He'd never checked Julius' grades in college. He just assumed he was a typical jock who got by on his athletic abilities and cruised through basket-weaving courses. Tutors took tests for him or slipped him the answers. Like the jocks when he was in school.

Even given these assumptions, Jason knew that Julius was really smart. Knew things a dumb jock wouldn't. Read the papers, watched the news. Made literary and cultural references most guys his age wouldn't understand.

Jason had never considered himself a racist in any sense of the word. He didn't see color; thought it didn't matter. If Julius were white, he wouldn't have treated him any differently. But would he still be counting on him to do heavy lifting?

He clasped his hands together. "Julius, I wish we had talked about this sooner. We've invested a lot of time with each other and it looks like we're headed in different directions. It's your move."

The big man shrugged. "I'll finish this project with you. Ain't right to leave a man in the lurch, no matter what he says to you or how he treats you. I do need this job, but when this shack is done, we'll see where we're at. Maybe it just wasn't meant to be, you and me. Chalk it up."

"Yeah," was all Jason could say. His anger had passed into resignation.

II

"Mr. Black, it's Davis Webster, town electrical inspector. I was by your place on Wegener Terrace this morning and no one was there to let me in."

This man was a recent hire that Jason had yet to form a working relationship with. Was he calling to reprimand him? He felt bad enough at missing the appointment and the headaches it would cause. And he was mad at himself for screaming at Julius, when a quiet reprimand might have had the desired effect. This was the last thing he needed.

Jason said, "My apologies. I'm sorry for the inconvenience. I'd like to reschedule as soon as possible."

"Actually that's why I'm calling."

This was a departure. The few times Jason had blown an inspection, it took days to reschedule and the inspector wasn't very accommodating. He suspected that they dragged their feet as punishment, not giving him the next available opening. For an inspector to call him was unheard of.

The inspector said, "As I was leaving, your neighbor told me about the misfortune with your dog."

What? Jasper was at Black's house, likely asleep on one of his seven dog beds or on Jason's king sized mattress. His house was five miles away from Wegener. Something strange was going on. There was no way Jasper could be in any danger. Something smelled funny but he decided to listen rather than correct the man.

Webster said, "I have two dogs myself. Thank the Lord they've never gotten into anything that could hurt them, but I get your priorities. I'd have done the same thing myself."

"Thanks for understanding."

"No problem, sir. Is he all right?"

"Yeah. Minor scare. Just a bit of doggie indigestion."

Jason was going along with the charade. Was this guy the real inspector or some friend of his playing a prank? There would be hell to pay if this was someone's idea of a joke.

The inspector said, "I'm glad to hear that. Thing is, I have an opening in my schedule today. A contractor called to postpone an inspection and I'm free. Is it convenient for me to do your inspection in say, fifteen minutes?"

Despite his battle with Julius, the big man had vowed to finish his work at the house. "I'm about ten minutes away but one of my carpenters should already be there."

"That'd work fine."

"Thanks. I really appreciate this. Just out of curiosity, I don't know any of the neighbors well and I wasn't aware that anyone knew about the dog. Did you catch his name? I'd like to thank him and I don't want to go knocking on all their doors to ask."

"Uh, I think his name was Ron. No Richard. Yeah, Richard. Older gent, dressed nice, suit and tie. Last name started with a G or J. Sorry, I can't tell you more."

"Wouldn't be Richard Gilmore by any chance, would it?"

"Could be. Yeah, that sounds like it. Didn't see which house he came from."

"I know where he lives. Thanks, inspector. I'll see you shortly."

He dialed Julius and told him that the inspector was on his way. Julius agreed to let him in.

Richard Gilmore. *A higher up in the FBI, personally shadowing me. In any case, he'd done me a favor. Saved me time and money with a pretty inventive story. The wily bastard was pulling out all the stops. Whatever this was, it must really be important to him.*

Jason wondered how he came up with the dog story and gleaned that the inspector would be sympathetic. He expected that this was a prelude to Gilmore accosting him again. The veteran fed didn't surrender easily, he'd give him that.

The inspector's call was followed by another, two minutes later. This one came from Aaron.

"Hey, Jase. What ya up to?"

Black told him about the missed inspection and the fortuitous rescheduling. He didn't go into detail on the story of how it went down and how he'd yelled at Julius.

Aaron said, "Sounds like Julie's got it covered. It's almost lunchtime. Why don't you pick up some sandwiches and meet me at your place? Roast beef on rye, lettuce, tomatoes, sounds good. Hold the mayo."

~~~~~

There was absolutely nothing wrong with Jasper, not that Jason was concerned that there was. The forty pound mixed breed leaped onto his master as he came through the front door. Jason rarely came home for lunch, especially carrying a bag that smelled oh-so-good.

"Down boy," Jason said. "That goes for you too, old man."

Aaron was in his usual spot --- the rocking chair in front of the television, now tuned to the NFL network.

"When you hear what I did, you'll serve me right here on a tray table and fetch me a Bud Lite to wash it down."

"Yes, my liege. Dilly-dilly."

"Julius texted me. We're clear with the rough electric. Paco's getting real good at that stuff. I only found two little boo-boos that we coulda been flagged on and he fixed 'em right away."

Jason unwrapped the deli sandwiches in the kitchen and set Aaron's food on the counter. "Get your lazy ass out of that chair and sit up here with me, grandpa."
~~~~~

"Keep talking like that and I might take back the good deed I did for ya. I ain't your grandpa. Bad seed hippie like you, I woulda disowned years ago."

"Yeah, well. I need some good news. Tell me."

Hendricks rose slowly from the rocker and walked over to the counter bearing his lunch. "Where'd ya get this? They were a little chintzy with the roast beef, don't ya think?"

"I tore off a strip for Jasper. I knew you wouldn't mind sharing."

"I love that mutt but that doesn't mean he gets part of my lunch."

Jason looked around at his house, his pride and joy. Years ago, he had stripped the old decaying building down to the studs. People said he was crazy, that he should have bulldozed the place. There were times during the rehab process that he was tempted to follow that advice. He'd found rot and termite damage in the sills. Old knob and tube wiring throughout. Lead solder in the plumbing.

But the basic structure was in good shape. The roof was slate, good for another fifty years. The Cypress siding had stood up to the elements well. The architecture was classic Lowcountry and the size was just right for his needs. The bank sold it to him for under land value. Other developers were interested but the expense of razing and disposing of the house's remains didn't add up when land was still relatively cheap.

When Aaron finished eating his sandwich, Jason said, "Okay, you've had your fun. Tell me this good news."

"Maybe after I eat my cookie."

"Come on. I know you love drawing this out but I've got work to do."

"Okay, okay. Don't worry about a glass for the beer. I'll drink it out of the bottle."

"Running out of patience with you, Aaron."

"Never one of your strong suits, boy. Here's the deal. I charmed the pants off the widow Sanders. The one who was giving us shit about replacing the kitchen cabinets that she custom ordered and then decided she didn't like."

"The ones we told her wouldn't work in the first place but she insisted on anyway."

"Right. Her old man told me how vain she was so I flattered the shit out of her. Sometime before I pass I'll show you how to do that so you won't be jerking off on your own at night instead of having a nice belly warmer."

He spit into a plastic cup, disgorging a sickly brown chaw of tobacco.

"Classy as always, Hendricks."

"I try. Anyhoo, I convinced her that you could take those flat doors and make 'em look authentic Shaker style in your workshop. Paint 'em up a dark blue-green. Period correct. Told her that waterfall granite will be out of style in two years and her friends will be laughing at her. Said you could make up a nice live edge island out of walnut. Take out the upper cabinets and build her some sweet looking shelves."

"How is that good news? It's a lot of extra work. Probably take me a week to do all that."

"And you wouldn't take fifteen grand for a week's work in your shop? 'Cause that's what I got her to agree to paying."

"I take it all back, Aaron. Good job."

"But wait, there's more. Got that line from those late night ads on TV. They always give you another gadget, two for one, just pay additional shipping and handling."

"Which costs more that the crap they're selling."

"Got that right. But I ain't pulling any of that shit on you. You know those upper cabinets and granite we're taking out? More than enough for the Wegener house and much higher quality than the shit you were planning to use. All you need are base cabinets to match or you can go with ones that contrast. Saved you at least six grand right there."

"Aaron my friend, you just earned yourself a bonus. Dinner at the best place in town, your choice.

Hendricks relished every opportunity he had to let Jason know who was the more savvy. His friend saw only the side of him he wished to reveal, but there was so much more.

Aaron said, "But, wait, there's another piece of good news I haven't told ya yet. Guy came by a few minutes before you got here. Dressed real sharp. Looked like moneybags. Wanted to talk to you. I said you weren't home and he asked when you were expected. Hot to trot. I bet he's got a big-ass place that's rundown and needs work. Could tide us through the spring. I told him to come back after lunch and he agreed."

"And did he give you a name?" Jason asked, already knowing the answer.

"Better than that. Left a card."

He handed Jason a plain white business card which bore just the name Richard Gilmore and phone number.

The bastard did think of everything. Oh, well. He'd eat lunch first, then deal with Gilmore.

12

After lunch, Jason was in the place where he was most happy, other than performing onstage. He was alone in his workshop. One of his original attractions to his current house was the large shed grafted onto the garage. The previous owner was a hoarder who had filled it to the rafters with worthless junk. Jason had the disagreeable task and expense of disposing of all the debris when he took over the property.

After he was finished clearing out the shed, he was left with a plain unheated room, 24 feet square, perched on a rough concrete slab. It took him three weeks to render it suitable. He sprayed in insulation, installed a heating and cooling unit and coated the floor with an epoxy resin. He added a dormer with a stained glass window which added character to the roofline and let in northern light. The final exterior touch was a six foot wide, glass paneled garage door.

He had a copy of the plans for Sanders' kitchen. Aaron had asked Julius to remove the doors and drawers from the lower cabinets after he was done with his work at Wegener and drop them off.

He set up his joiner to plane down some reclaimed lumber he'd hoarded to create the countertop for Sanders' live edge island. He'd glue and dowel them together, book-matched, so it looked like they were one seamless piece. While working with the noisy machines, he wore protective headphones that also played music.

Jason jumped at the light tap on his shoulder, startled that someone or something had entered the building without his notice. "Nice job, Jason. Always enjoy watching a master craftsman at work."

Jason said, "How long have you been there? With the headphones on, I didn't hear you come in."

"Just a few minutes. Didn't want to take your attention off your work. What's that going to be?"

"The top of a kitchen island. So, what do you need, Richard? A table? Bench? A window seat, maybe?

Richard Gilmore said, "You've picked up a sense of humor over the years. It'll come in handy on the job."

"I don't think the lumber will get my jokes, Richard. I did appreciate you talking that inspector into coming back today. Saved me time and money. What made you think he'd respond to your dog story?"

"Dog hair all over his pants. Golden retriever from the look of it. Never had one myself but I know that dog lovers take care of their own."

"Sort of like cops. As much as I *am* grateful, I'm not interested in working for you again."

"Let me try to explain this one more time. We're talking about a matter of national security. It involves an old friend of yours, Brand X. A great deal of harm could come to this country if we don't do something soon."

"Betray another friend for the good of the country? That's what you said back in the seventies. It was bullshit then and it's probably bullshit now."

Gilmore opened his coat and Jason flinched. He thought for a second that his old handler was about to pull a gun on him, but he merely was making himself comfortable in the heated space.

"So appeals to your patriotism don't light your fire? I understand your cynicism, I'm not totally insensitive. I'm human, too. Did you know that I'm retiring? I've put in my years, got a pension coming. I might do some private sector work. Part time, just to have something to do."

He paused and his throat grew thick. "My wife died a couple of years ago. Don't know if you'd heard."

"I'm sorry."

"It's something you never get over. I grieve every day. Well, I'm not looking for your pity. It's just that I'd like to go out big and this would be a great sendoff."

Jason saw through the act. This was a deliberate tactic designed to elicit his sympathy. As an artist, he had a deep well of compassion, although he was smart enough to understand it could be easily misplaced, especially at the hands of a clever manipulator.

He said, "Listen, I'm sorry about your wife. I'm sure you've done some great things for your country, but I can't help you. There must be somebody else who can. Someone who does this for a living, not an amateur like me."

Gilmore spread his arms in a pleading gesture. "Like I told you before, you're perfect for this job. No one else comes close. Look Jason, I didn't realize how much that Wendy thing still bothered you. I'm sorry about that. I was young, I made mistakes. And believe me, if I had another candidate who fit the bill, I wouldn't be bothering you."

"The answer's still no."

Gilmore figured he'd give the music career one last try. He'd stood in the shadows the other night at Black's concert and he could see that the man still enjoyed the limelight. "Think about this. It wasn't hard for me to get you booked in Savannah. I could do that in a lot of different places. Like a real tour, get you noticed again. I saw your show the other night. Your new stuff was good. You've still got it, man. I think with a little push, you could be, I don't know, Gordon Lightfoot?"

Jason shook his head in disbelief. He had once toured with the hard drinking Canadian. He admired his work. Lightfoot was almost eighty but still active these days. The problem was Jason didn't have any songs with the radio staying power of Gordo's maritime disaster epic.

Black said, "Richard, give it up, please. I do a few shows a year, just to keep the old juices flowing. I'm not looking for any big comeback. I'm realistic about that. At my age, my appeal is nostalgia. All the audience wants are those ten songs that made me semi-famous. I don't even have to sing 'em anymore. I could just hold the mic up and they'd sing along."

"But you didn't do that Saturday."

"No, I figure they pay to see me do it, as best I can nowadays. I'm like a novelist, who keeps writing the same stories with different characters. Thanks for saying you like my new stuff, but I'm afraid my well has run dry. I'm better off fixing up old houses. That way, I'll be leaving something behind that lasts. At best, my songs are as disposable as the sawdust on the floor."

Gilmore gave a long and dramatic exhale. "Jason, I didn't want to do this. You've got a problem brewing. I can make it stop or I can add fuel to the fire. Your call."

"Your sweet talk didn't sway me, so now you're bringing out the hammer, is that it? It's a shame you can't trot out my dying father to convince me like you did the last time."

Jason turned his back to Gilmore and picked up an extra board he didn't need for the countertop. Meeting over.

Gilmore said, "That was uncalled for. Your dad was a real patriot and he happened to be right. You made him proud before he died. He told me that after you agreed to work with us."

"He never told *me* that. He said he felt used, by you and your cronies in the bureau. He regretted his part in making me do that after I told him how it went down with Wendy in the end. Just go away, Richard. Please."

Gilmore's face morphed from kindly persuader to the hard-boiled bastard he needed to be when all else failed. "Okay Jason, I'll lay it out for you. It seems that the building department has gotten wind of the notion that you're using unlicensed contractors to do electrical and plumbing work. Maybe even workers who are here illegally."

"How would they suddenly get that notion?"

"Think about it. They start looking into code violations now and everyone you've ever sold a house to will start wondering whether they have a case against you. Even if they don't, I'd imagine it'd be hard to find new work."

Jason deflected the threat as if he had it covered, but he knew that he was on thin ice. "If a licensed sub signs off on the work and it passes inspection, they're allowed to use apprentices and interns to do the actual labor. In fact, there's a shortage of tradesmen in all phases of building and the locals are encouraging programs that teach kids how to do that kind of work. Nice try, Gilmore."

"Oh, I know all about selective enforcement. I'm sure that ICE doesn't deport everyone they suspect is working here illegally. But sometimes politics takes precedence. They got Capone on tax evasion."

"Get out of here, Gilmore."

"And if I were you, I'd think long and hard about the way you've treated women over the years. You've heard all about Me-Too, I'm sure. Got to be someone who's not real happy about the way you dumped her. I'll go now, Jason. You think about it. That Paco seems like a nice kid. Going back to El Salvador or whatever shithole country he came from wouldn't be good for him. A life avoiding the drug cartels, or maybe even working for them. And for your sake, it'd be a shame if you have to find a new boy who's willing to learn the trades. This can escalate, or it can just go away. Your call."

13

"You ain't never sought my advice comes to women before," Aaron said.

"This isn't about women. It's about blackmail. I figured that's more up your alley."

"Why's that? I never blackmailed anyone my entire life, much less you. Come to papa, what's wrong, boy?"

Jason sat in the great room on a loveseat. Aaron was on the rocking chair that he had appropriated for his personal use. The old chair didn't fit in with the decor and Jason had threatened numerous times to get rid of it, but Aaron had said that if the rocker goes, so does he. To Jason, that was blackmail, but now wasn't the time to argue the point.

He gave Aaron a quick summary of the previous forty eight hours with Gilmore. When he was finished, Aaron asked, "I know that you smartass liberals say that brevity is the soul of wit, but you left a lot out, seems to me."

"Smartass liberals, eh? You told me you hadn't voted Republican in four decades."

"Fact is, I haven't voted, period. Why bother? Gotta say though, I'm surprised you worked with the FBI once upon a time. How come you never told me about that till now?"

"Because I'm ashamed of it."

"What did you do that was so bad that you can't you tell me? You don't trust your old buddy?"

"Aaron, you know I trust you but I just can't now. Maybe later. The thing is, it's why I won't get involved with the feds anymore. They screwed me over bad, that's all I can say."

Aaron spat into a plastic cup. His teeth were getting to the point where Jason was considering drugging him and hauling his ass to a dentist. It might be too late to save all his teeth, but the yellow and brown rot was getting more disgusting each passing day.

Aaron said, "Okay. I'll let it slide for now. So bottom line is, this Gilliam dude is blackmailing you, saying if you don't play ball, he's gonna wreck your business. That about the size of it?"

"That's it in a nutshell. But his name is Gilmore."

"Whatever. Why not just hear him out? Maybe what he's asking you to do this time ain't so bad. What do you have to lose?"

"He won't stop at that. You're into those spy novels. Even thought of writing one someday, you told me. You give into blackmail once and it never stops. I mean, the guy says he's retiring so it maybe it ends with him. I don't know."

"So hear him out, at least so you know all the options. From what you're saying, he's not above destroying the company. What he's asking you to do can't be worse than that."

Jason hesitated. Confessing to something he'd done over forty years ago might elicit no more than a shrug from his friend. Maybe what he considered a gutless betrayal would be seen by others as his patriotic duty, as Gilmore maintained.

He said, "Aaron, I don't know what this new assignment is, other than it involves spying on an old friend I once toured with, a guy calling himself Brand X."

"So you toured with Brand X. Whoop-de-do. That must have been a wild ride."

"Well, you were alive in the seventies. You can imagine what it's like backstage. There were a ton of women available at the snap of any musician's fingers. And if they looked old enough, we didn't ask for ID. This was before AIDS and most of us didn't use protection. There was a lot of shit going around back then. 'Ludes, acid, coke. Can I swear that a roadie, trying to do me a favor by greasing the skids with a lady, didn't slip her something?

"Ah, those were the days, my friend. Really? A rock star screwing chicks on drugs. I bet there were plenty of groupies, ready to do whatever your pervert's mind could come up with. I read a story about a band that used to cover those chicks with melted chocolate and sprinkles. Then they all take turns licking them off. Yum."

"And you're calling me a pervert, old man. I never was into the group thing. Well, once with two girls, twins. Damn, you've brought me down to your level."

"*You* should write a book, man. Glory days."

"I'm not in a confessional mood, Aaron. You may laugh, but the way sexual offenses from decades ago are ruining people's lives today, I'm thinking my secrets should stay secret. I may be desperate but I'm not that hard up for cash to write a book about it."

Aaron had had a light hearted expression on his face throughout the jibes, but it darkened. "You're desperate? What's going on, Jason? We got other problems with the business?"

This was not a conversation Jason wanted to have, now or ever. But Aaron wasn't the type to let things go once he had a bone in his mouth. He was worse than Jasper if you tried to take away one of his toys.

Jason said, "Desperate's the wrong word, but I need to build up a nest egg. I can't count on a pension like the one you have. There might come a time when I physically won't be able to do what I'm doing. Can't get by on Social Security, and my royalties are down to a trickle."

"You need one of them young hip-hoppers, some rapper like, to cover one of your tunes. Make a fortune. But I don't get it. You musta made big bucks back in the day. You got them gold records hanging on the wall upstairs. You're anything but a big spender. Where'd it all go?"

"You really want to know?"

"Yeah, I do. I'm in business with you, bubba. You ain't paying me a big percentage but I figure I earn my keep. What's going on?"

"Nothing earth shattering."

"Don't duck the question. Where did it all go? Don't tell me up your nose."

"No, I was never into that. Rolled my share of J's but nothing more. What happened was my manager hooked me up with a can't-miss deal."

He stopped pacing and sat across from Aaron's rocker, his shoulders slumped. "I was making good bread, so much that I needed a tax shelter. My guy found this deal where you invest in movies. They had a great list. Big stars, major motion pictures, all tax sheltered. And there'd be big payoffs when the films hit."

"Yeah, but what about the flops?"

"They seemed honest about that. Said there were bound to be a couple of those but the big ones would more than make up for it."

"And they didn't?"

"They did, at least at first. But I didn't read the fine print like I should have. Just took their word. The plan was supposed to be for five years, but the managing partners had the option to roll it over twice. Bottom line is they kept making movies with the profits for fifteen years."

"Why was that bad?"

"Because it was designed to lose money on paper. They took a big chunk as producers on each film. When the cycle ended, the books showed a loss, which they wrote off on taxes against their fees. They lost paper, we lost real money. Everything we put into it, and in my case, it came to millions. I plowed almost all I had into it. I thought it was like putting money in the bank but with better interest and a tax break to boot. It kept showing a nice profit for years. Right up until the end."

"And you never got any of it back?"

"Not a penny."

"So you got fucked over by Hollywood. Sorry. I always heard they screwed around with the books. Made it look like even the big pictures lost money."

"Yeah, just like the record business. I got hosed on both ends."

"That's another reason why you need to listen to this dude from the FBI. See what this guy wants. Can't hurt. Even if all it does is get him off your back. And hey, might even be some money in it for you."

"We'll see. Hey, I'm running late for something. Gotta go. We can talk more about it later."

14

When Jason emerged from his bedroom a half hour later, Aaron gave him a wolf whistle. He was dressed to the nines, by his standards. Clean shaven, no scruff. Hair freshly washed and neatly tucked into a pony tail.

Aaron said, "Hey, why all duded up?"

"Dinner with Katrina. We missed last month because of the holidays."

"Ah, keeping that flame alive. I don't know why you didn't marry that girl. She's some cougar."

Jason knew that Kat would resent anyone calling her a cougar. At this point, he didn't know what to call her.

A friend? A friend with occasional benefits? An ex-lover? All of the above?

They had been together for two years before Jason backed off. They still had dinner together on the third Monday every month. The unusual schedule was dictated by Katrina's work. She owned a restaurant whimsically named *The Frog and Peach*, after an old comedy bit by Peter Cook and Dudley Moore. It was closed Monday and Tuesdays, open only for brunch on Sunday.

"Aaron, cougar means an older woman on the make. Katrina is hardly that."

"She's on the make for you, boyo. And damned if I can figure out why you don't go with it. I was you, I'd jump at that."

If anyone came on to Katrina McCann, he'd object, not that he had a right to. When they broke up, he understood that she was free to do whatever she wanted. But he *would* be jealous. Even though marriage wasn't in the cards, he had a great deal of affection for her. In many ways, she was his best friend, more so than even Aaron.

Aaron said, "She is a catch. What is she, 55? Body of a chick twenty years younger. And those green eyes. Reminds me of that Shirley Eaton broad in *Goldfinger*. You know, the one painted gold? Ash blonde hair, that's thoroughly authentic."

"And how would you know that?"

"Uh, I never told you this back when you two were going hot and heavy. Surprised she didn't. One morning I came here to pick you up for work, didn't know she was staying over. She came out of the bedroom in the altogether. She saw me and beat a hasty retreat, but I caught sight of all the goodies. Only a fool would leave that behind, and I do mean behind."

"You're a funny man. No, she never mentioned it. But Aaron, even you would admit there's more to marriage than just looks. You're a three time loser, after all."

"And I learned me a thing or two from them. But I gotta admit, none of them had what Kat has going for her. She's whip smart. Got money, her own business, doing better than you, I bet. Sweet as all get out. I guess there's that feminist thing that's a little strident with her but I'm sure you could tamp that down a piece if you got hitched."

"Uh-uh. She's big into women's causes and that doesn't bother me one bit. I'm there with her. I don't expect you to understand, but the problem is, I don't think I love her. I respect the hell out of her. Admire her. But the feeling just isn't there."

"*You've lost that loving feeling*," Aaron crooned, his off-key impersonation of Bill Medley. "Though from what you say, you never had it for any woman, have ya? Ever think maybe you're really a homo?"

Even today under duress, Jason had never told Aaron about how he'd betrayed Wendy Walton. All these years later, he couldn't bring himself to confess his role, even to close friends.

Jason said, "Never had that inclination. Look, when it comes to marriage, I want it all. And besides, if I did go that route, what wife would tolerate you being around all the time? Hell, you should move into the guest room, save time and money."

"Nah, I need my privacy and I wouldn't want folks to start thinking we're queer or nothing. Although, I'll tell you, you sink a few bucks into that room, wire it up for satellite, put a big screen in there. Fancy up the loo. I could be persuaded."

~~~~~
~~~~~

Katrina McCann liked taking Jason to nice places. From a business standpoint, she justified it by saying she was checking out the competition. And she was a great businesswoman. She took notes on her competitors' presentation, their menus, even the music they piped in. She never missed a trend, and was good at picking the ones that had staying power versus those that were fads.

She had another reason for selecting the places where they dined every month. She opted for romantic settings --- water views, soft lighting and great wine lists. She hadn't given up on him, even though she had seen a couple of others since they had split. But Jason Black was the man she wanted. They just fit together. Everyone who knew them said so.

They were a handsome couple. Same taste in food, clothes and friends. Both loved baseball, although she rooted for the Braves and he was a Mets fan, but not to the extent that it caused much strife.

And they were honest with each other. No hidden agendas, no minor deceptions in the cause of sparing feelings. She told him about her past loves, including her rocky first marriage. He had less to share on that level because he hadn't taken any woman seriously in years. He never could bring himself to tell her about Wendy.

This night's journey took them to the seaside village of Beaufort, a forty five minute drive south of Charleston. She picked him up in her BMW 335i. It would hardly be fitting to show up at a fine restaurant in his beat up Ford pickup. They caught up with day to day stuff on the drive down, holding more personal matters for their candlelit dinner.

He wore his one pair of designer jeans and a wool navy blazer, both purchased at an outlet, a season past their prime. She was elegant in a simple black dress. Cut low, pearl necklace. Lots of leg on display and she had a lot more where that came from. The aroma of her honeysuckle perfume pervaded the small booth. Much nicer than Gilmore's cloying cologne. As he took in the lovely vision, he had to agree with Aaron --- she had it going on, big time.

After they were seated and had ordered a bottle of wine, Katrina said, "So Jason, something's on your mind. You seem preoccupied. I did most of the talking on the way here."

She always made the wine and food selections. She knew far more about these things than he did and he was glad to defer to her greater expertise.

"It's nothing, Kat. This place is really cool. I like what they've done with the ceiling. It looks like it was built in the eighteen hundreds but I Googled it after you made the reservation. Built in 1973. They got all the details right. Heavy trim. Whitewashed shiplap on the walls. Brass gaslight chandeliers. This looks like it could have been here since the Civil War."

"The War of Northern Aggression, you mean? That's what they call it here." She came from Bucks County, Pennsylvania, but had been in Charleston since the eighties.

"Don't be sly. I doubt there's a civil rights demonstration in the last ten years you haven't marched in."

"Hardly. Most are on weekends and it's hard for me to get away from the restaurant. We did succeed last month in getting them to take down those Confederate statues."

"Yeah, I heard. Wondered if you had anything to do with that. I missed your December update. Holidays good for you?"

"Yes. Would have been nicer if we spent them together."

Jason felt awkward. Part of him thought that their monthly dinners were cruel and unusual punishment for her and that it was selfish of him to keep stringing her along. It kept her hopes alive. It wasn't fair.

By rights, he should have broken the ritual. He had been blunt --- there was no future for them as a married couple. He was afraid his monthly presence in her life was impeding her from finding someone else. But whenever he came close to cutting it off clean, he couldn't let go. He'd never told her he loved her, but the fact he couldn't walk away said something, didn't it?

But something was missing.

It had been like that with every woman he had met since Wendy. The electricity just wasn't there. The bar only grew higher as the years passed. He forgot about all the bad times with Wendy --- the arguments, the suspicions toward the end. He just remembered the good.

He needed to cut Katrina loose someday, for her own good. He would miss her company. They both enjoyed the food, wine and the sex that sometimes capped one of their perfect nights out.

Katrina said, "You ducked my question, Jason. That's not like you. What's bothering you?"

He didn't want to lie to her, but he had hoped that tonight would be a respite from his worries. "I'm sorry. I can't really talk about it, but I'm kind of being blackmailed."

"If you can't talk to me about it, who can you talk to?" She gave him a mock serious look, then laughed. "Oh, Aaron, that's right. I bet you've told him everything. No offense, I know you love the guy but his take on things is usually to the right of Attila the Hun."

"Yeah, it's funny. When I told him we were meeting, he said your only flaw was that you were a hard core, bra burning, feminist."

"Well, he's right about that. Although at my age, I consider bras my friend. Thanks for not pointing that out. But let's not get sidetracked."

The waiter approached with the wine and gravitated toward Jason's side of the table to pour a sample for his approval.

"I'll take that, young man," Katrina said. "Don't assume the man is the one who knows wine."

"Sorry, ma'am," the waiter said, pouring a dram into her glass, which she sniffed, swirled and tasted. She nodded her approval. He poured them both a glass and said he'd return shortly to take their dinner order.

Katrina said, "I shouldn't have corrected him, I guess. But it's something I tell my wait staff. Even though most of the time it *will* be the man, don't assume. And don't assume he'll take the check, either."

"Well, Kat, *I* assume our deal is still on. Alternating checks, right. Tonight is your turn. I got it the last time. So order large for me, girl."

"Girl, eh. I suppose a woman of my age should be flattered. Not."

"*Don't call me girl*. Is that offensive nowadays?"

"God, Jason, you are a master at diversion. You tell me you're being blackmailed then lead me off into wine and feminism. Cheers."

They clinked glasses. He said, "I didn't do it on purpose, really. In fact, you started talking about Aaron, then the waiter and..."

"Stop right there. You're doing it again. Doesn't matter who's to blame. Blackmail. Out with it, Black."

"Somebody I once worked with wants me to work with them again. I don't want to. I can't say why. So he's trying to blackmail me into doing it."

"Can't you go to the authorities?"

"He *is* the authority. There, you've tricked me in saying more than I wanted."

He looked out the window. Although the sun had set on the side opposite of the river, the colors of the sky were reflected in the water. The pastel shades were stunning in the early evening, adding to the romantic ambience. It was bad timing for them to be discussing baser matters.

Katrina followed his gaze and drank in the exquisite setting. Her restaurant boosted no such view. She hoped her food made up for it.

She said, "You *want* to tell me. You know you do. And you know you can trust me to keep your secrets."

"I know that, Kat. It's just that I need to work this out by myself. Don't be mad, it's got nothing to do with trusting you."

"I'm not angry. We have no rules, you and I. I've told you about men I've been with. Not in great detail. I didn't think that was appropriate to cite chapter and verse."

"God, you make it sound so clinical."

"That's all it is with anyone other than you. So what's with the blackmail?"

"You won't quit, will you? The man who wants me to do something for him has the power to hurt my business. He said he could keep that from happening if I go along with him."

"And why is that?"

"Okay. I give up. You know Julius and Paco aren't licensed and Paco is here illegally. His parents brought him here as a baby and then left him with friends when they went back to Central America. He's what they call a Dreamer."

"He's a great kid."

"He is. He's a hard worker and very responsible. And it's hard to find good tradesmen these days. A lot of native born Americans aren't into working with their hands."

"Tell me about it. I'm in the same boat. Wait staff, sous chefs, hard to find. All these Gringo kids want to start at the top for big money. Aren't into working their way up the ladder. I admit I'm not too careful about checking citizen documents and such. I probably have Dreamers working for me. I don't ask, they don't tell."

"Right. If we kicked everyone out of the country who came here illegally, I'm convinced the economy would collapse. Regardless, this man has the power to get Paco deported and restrict Julius to grunt work. My whole business model would collapse."

"You can't go to the police?'

"He *is* the police."

"What the hell is this country coming to, Jason?"

"It's nothing new. Maybe worse now than the last few years. Thing is, I have a history with this guy. That's something I really can't get into with you, but the last time I did his dirty work, it didn't turn out so well. And I'm afraid if I give in again, the same thing will happen."

"And you can't tell me what happened before?"

"Kat, it's something I'm not proud of and on top of that, it's probably still classified or some such nonsense. If it got out, it might lead to even more trouble for me."

"God, Jason, you're scaring me. It sounds like you were involved in Iran-Contra or something. Like that Barry Seal guy who got involved with the cartels. Tell me it's not like that."

"I saw that movie too. No, my life isn't in danger, not now anyway. I just don't trust this guy. He knew about something I did after the concert the other night and I'm starting to think he set the whole thing up to use against me."

"Oh. What was that?"

"I know we made an agreement that we're both free to do what we want but I'm not really comfortable talking about it. I was on a natural high after the show.

Still get off on it. I was weak and made a mistake. That's all I'll say."

"Do me a favor. If you ever get that horny, just call me. Don't go sleeping with women young enough to be your daughter."

15

It was two in the morning and Richard Gilmore couldn't sleep. This next day would be pivotal. He needed to rest. He'd have to be at his best to negotiate the perils that lay ahead but his regrets kept nagging, nagging, nagging. The relentless tick tock in his brain kept hammering him about the stupid mistakes that could undue a lot of the good he had done in his forty plus years with the bureau.

Despite the acknowledged dangers of smoking in bed, he'd already gone through half a pack. He kept the window open a crack to air out the room, hoping to avoid penalties for violating the hotel's smokeless policy.

This could be the crowning achievement of a distinguished career. He never thought that recruiting Jason Black would meet with such resistance. He had reasoned that over coffee and beignets at Huey's, a mutually beneficial arrangement could be worked out. He had no idea how Black had carried his bitterness about their previous encounter through these many years.

Gilmore reacted emotionally to Black's intransigence, something he rarely did. *No one walked out on him. No one had the balls to do that.*

But in front of others, Jason Black had done just that, in an extremely embarrassing demonstration.

He was feeling low about his campaign against Black's business and the threat of deportation against an innocent young worker. Why had he stooped to this now, so late in life? Maybe he *was* losing it.

It was about his legacy, he thought. Around the shop, he had been considered a relic of times gone by, old and in the way. His language was dated, his values archaic. There were a few who respected him for his past accomplishments, but most saw him as an old curmudgeon who just didn't get it anymore.

Then there was that unpleasantness in the office when his dry sense of humor wasn't appreciated by some of the younger people on the staff.

He wanted to go out on top, head held high, like his boyhood idol Joe DiMaggio. The Yankee Clipper didn't want some kid, upon seeing him for the first time, to pity a broken down ballplayer getting by on past accomplishments. When he realized he no longer had it, after one last moment of glory, DiMag hung it up. Gracefully.

Richard Gilmore believed he had one more such moment before the final inning. But now he had two strikes against him, and the pitcher had a nasty curveball.

~~~~~
~~~~~

Jason Black couldn't sleep either. His evening with Katrina didn't end with a rustling under the sheets, as she playfully liked to put it. She was willing, but he begged off. That constituted a first.

At this point, he wasn't sure he ever wanted to have sex again. Wasn't the *heyday in the blood* supposed to be tame by now, according to Hamlet?

What an irresponsible fool I've been, all my life, he thought. Implying to Kat he'd been with another woman made him uneasy, even if he hadn't spelled it out in detail. He didn't know Deirdre well enough to know if she in fact, had used him, and not the other way around. These younger women were different. Would she brag to her girlfriends that she had slept with a pop star? Was this just *another notch in her lipstick case*, as Pat Benatar once sang?

Maybe today's women weren't so different, after all. He wondered how many others back in the day had been attracted to his music and/or his money but not really to him. He was now full of regret for his treatment of women. He had been callous, using them to service his needs, casting them aside like yesterday's newspaper. He'd never forced anyone into something they didn't want to do. And regardless, he wasn't the same person now, was he? Could he declare a statute of limitations on his conscience?

Sure he'd lied some in the past, misleading his lovers to believe that he'd call the next day. He'd persisted after getting negative signals initially, but he knew when to stop. He never masturbated into a potted plant or exposed himself like some of the fallen notables had. He considered that sick behavior and couldn't understand why any man would think a woman would find that stimulating, no matter how famous you were.

Back in his youth, good girls were supposed to resist. Boys who gave up after the first try never got any. He realized that was wrong by today's standards. But short of a woman coming on to him, how was he to know that she didn't want what he did, but had been told that *good girls don't*?

Now he was kinder, gentler, to coin a phrase. He tried to be honest with his intentions, as he had with Kat. But something still kept him from committing himself to a lasting monogamous relationship.

Maybe he should contact his therapist again and open up about his past with Wendy. She'd be honor bound not to reveal any of the sordid tale, and he could finally unburden himself. He'd set up a session, first thing.

He was a mess. His mind was going in a million directions and each was fraught with doubt as to who he was. He'd always considered himself a good man. But Gilmore had planted a seed that was growing exponentially. Maybe he was cutting himself too much slack. Maybe he *was* a bad guy at heart.

He was breaking the law with Paco and Julius. He'd betrayed Wendy, the woman he'd loved. He was inflicting pain on Katrina, selfishly using her for her company and as an outlet for his carnal desires. He'd laid into Julius and injured their relationship over a missed inspection.

After lying awake in bed for an hour, he got up and went into the kitchen for a glass of water. *No, make that a scotch.* Jasper followed him. He patted the dog on the head and gave him a cookie.

"That's just for being you," Jason said. "You don't think daddy's a bad man, do you?"

Jasper lifted his paw and placed it across Jason's arm. Black didn't know if that meant he agreed, or if he just wanted another cookie.

"Dad's going upstairs to the studio. You can come or stay down here, pal."

Jasper followed his master up the stairs. Jason had taken the room over the garage on the far side of the house and converted it into a recording studio.

He selected a Martin DC-16e cutaway Dreadnought and spent a couple of minutes tuning it by ear, even though it had a built-in tuner. Jasper scampered over to the dog bed that Jason kept for him in the studio and started digging at it until it met his standards. Jasper seemed to like Black's guitar playing, found it soothing. He lay down quietly in the corner, paws outstretched, ready to resume his interrupted slumber.

His master booted up his desktop computer and started writing lyrics. He kept writing until he had a rough outline of where he wanted the song to go. He played around with some chords. Minor key. Slow tempo.

He hadn't written anything of substance lately. His last record consisted of cover versions of others' hits. His uncomplicated life hadn't given him anything deep to write about. He was content just to keep on, keeping on, do his thing with the houses and live his life modestly. Not exactly fodder for new material.

But now, he was inspired. His angst over his relationships or lack thereof gave him something to explore. It was therapeutic. Rather than pour his heart out to a shrink, he could do it through his music.

The final mix might just be multi tracked guitars and vocals, perhaps a rudimentary bass line that he could handle himself. He'd decide on whether to use percussion later.

He'd decide on a final title later, too. For now, he'd call it "*For Deidre*".

16

Jason awoke to the sound of a jet engine in his kitchen. It took him a moment to orient himself. What time was it? Where was he? Jasper was nowhere to be seen.

The brain fog lifted and he realized he was at home and it was just past seven. He'd worked until almost five, completing basic tracks for the two new songs he'd written, *For Deidre* and *Trapped.* Both would need new titles. The first because he couldn't admit his misgivings from the other night so explicitly. The second because it was the name of an old Jimmy Cliff song that Springsteen had done a great cover of.

He'd gotten just over two hours sleep. He longed to drift off again but it wasn't possible. He was awake now and Aaron was in the kitchen.

When he came out from the bedroom, tousled and groggy, he said, "You could at least close my door when you fire up that Grind n' Brew. Damn thing sounds like a friggin' gas leaf blower. It's a rude awakening."

"My intentions, exactly, although I was hoping Kat had spent the night and might stumble out nekkid again. But I see you blew it on that score."

"Sorry to disappoint you. Kat's pissed at me."

"Do tell."

"Pour me some coffee first. Go high test on the real cream. What the hell, something's got to kill you."

Aaron handed him a mug and he drank deep from it. "Coffee's good. You see, Aaron, it's like you were saying last night. She's hard core when it comes to women's issues."

Jason took another sip. "Katrina and I are honest with each other. It's been almost a year since we quit seeing each other exclusively. She's had male friends. I kind of told her about what happened after the concert Saturday. I slept with the woman who booked the venue."

"I knew it. I knew it. What a fucking idiot you are. You tell Kat about your conquests but you can't tell me. I suppose you think that's a healthy modern relationship, but there're some old rules you just don't mess with. Kat still has designs on you, man. You don't tell a fine lady like that that you've been a bad boy. Can't blame her for not putting out for you last night."

Jason stopped himself from saying it had been his call. Aaron would harangue him for the next ten minutes over that. But he did question himself for telling Kat about Deidre.

Changing the subject, Jason said, "I take it you fed Jasper and let him out?"

Aaron nodded. "He came bounding out of the bedroom when he heard me come in."

"Why are you here so early anyway?"

"I brought the cabinet doors from the Sanders house. Figured you'd want to get an early start on them."

"I thought Julius was going to do that. After work yesterday."

"He called a little after Kat picked you up. Didn't have time. I wasn't busy so I went over and pulled them out. No bother."

He felt his temper rising again. "That's not the point. He said he'd do it. If I'd wanted you to do it, I'd have asked. Another fuck-up from Julius. How many more am I supposed to put up with?"

"Calm down, Jase."

"No, I'm pissed. I have a lot of shit going down and the last thing I need is someone who isn't pulling their weight. I've got a mind to fire him right now."

"Stop. He told me about how you yelled at him yesterday. He was still shaken up."

"He should be. I gave him a chance to learn the business. I was grooming him to take over someday, have him run things after I retired. And this is how he repays me?"

"You sound like his dad."

"That's how I saw it, damn it. I treated him like a son."

"Jase, I'm stuck in the middle. I promised Julius I wouldn't tell you something I've known about for a while. He's got a legit reason for what you think is him slacking off. But he needs to tell you himself."

"Why hasn't he, then? Look, if he's got a drug problem or something, I'm here for him. All he has to do is tell me."

Aaron laughed. "The other day, you were on my case for calling him boy and saying how he likes fried chicken. You just did worse than that, man. You assumed because he's black and comes from a bad part of town that he's got a drug problem."

"I didn't say he did, just that if it was something like that, I'd support him."

"King White Man, coming to the aid of a poor back kid. How noble of you."

"Come on Aaron, you know me better than that. Shit, I can't do anything right anymore. I sleep with a grown woman and I'm a sexual predator. I offer to help a black kid and I'm a racist. I work with you, an old man. Am I guilty of age discrimination too? Just add that to the list."

"You *do* call me old man and that hurts my delicate sensibilities."

Jason looked stricken before Aaron burst into laughter. "Just joshing with you, Jase. Lighten up fella, nobody's calling you anything, least of all me. I done much worse than you in my time, take that to the bank. Just don't let that temper get the best of you. You already got a problem if that G-man follows through on deporting Paco."

"So I should just let Julius run wild? Screw us over in case we lose Paco?"

"I'm just saying that Julius is a great kid and when you find out why he's missed a couple of deadlines lately, you'll be proud of him."

"A sick mother he's taking care of?"

"When he's ready, he'll tell you. Just don't be too tough on him. He's under a lot of pressure."

"Something's got to change with him. Doesn't matter how valid his reasons are, he's not getting it done."

"Tell you what. Forget what I said before. Put me in the middle. You tell me what you need done every day. I'll get Julius to do it or I'll do it myself. Either way, it'll get taken care of. You can count on it. Just back off Julius. In time, you'll understand. That's a promise."

~~~~~

Jason had buried the lede with Aaron. Last night, while working on his songs, he had decided to contact Gilmore and tell him that he agreed to listen. He didn't feel very good about it. But he had assessed his options and concluded that each presented a unique risk.

He could engage an attorney to contact Gilmore's superiors. That would pit the word of a lifelong fed against a long haired radical folksinger. The odds of winning that battle were infinitesimal.

Aaron, Julius and Paco were all he had for family now. His parents were gone. He was an only child. He'd never married or had kids of his own. The tight little work group he had fostered over the last few years meant everything to him.

But it was slipping away. He'd alienated Julius. Aaron was old and slowly dying. And now Paco might
~~~~~

be deported. He couldn't live with that. Another betrayal and forced exile, courtesy of the FBI.

He told himself that maybe what Gilmore wanted *was* the right thing to do. He hated himself and Gilmore for how it had gone down with Wendy, that would never change. But was an old grudge from the Seventies worth ruining Paco's life?

After Aaron left to check on the Wegener property, Jason called the FBI agent.

"You win, Gilmore. I'll listen," was his terse greeting.

"Black, I didn't win. We both win. America wins. When you hear what I have to say, I think you'll understand."

"Look, don't wrap this up in any patriotic bullshit. Dylan said, *patriotism is the last refuge of a scoundrel.*"

"Actually, it was Samuel Johnson, but who cares?"

"I suppose it doesn't bother you that you had to resort to blackmail to make this happen."

"I want to explain the mission in person. I'll text you with a time and place." He hung up.

Gilmore suspected that Black was recording their conversation. *Typical amateur ploy*, he thought. Recording a phone conversation without the consent of the other party was on shaky legal grounds. But he knew that if it reached the right ears in the bureau, he would be censured. He didn't trust that Black had suddenly come to his senses overnight. But he had to let it play out.

Jason began working on the cabinet doors that Aaron had brought. Even though it was a few degrees warmer than it had been the previous morning, he still had to wait for the heating system in the workshop to kick in to get the place up to a bearable working temperature.

In all, there were twenty four doors and drawers to address. He had an adequate supply of poplar strips that he could fasten onto the doors to achieve the Shaker effect he was after. Poplar did not take stain well, but since he was painting the faces, it wouldn't matter.

He expected that Gilmore would pop in on him to fill him in on the mission, but the fed hadn't specified a time. So he set about making a jig he could use to cut the vertical pieces since most of the cabinets were the same height. He estimated that he could get all the pieces cut by lunchtime and then spend the afternoon securing them.

He placed his cell phone on a counter a few feet from his work bench. He checked it periodically, since it would be easy to miss a call or text under the earsplitting din of the blade, especially since he had donned protective headphones.

He didn't even hear the rap on his door when Julius came by at mid morning. He'd already completed half of his millwork, and was contemplating a coffee break when his charge stepped into his field of vision. He knew better than to touch him while he was concentrating on heavy machinery.

Julius said, "Boss, how you doing? Thought I'd come by and clear the air. Don't like you being mad at me."

"I'm not mad at you. I was about to make coffee. Like a cup?"

"Sure."

Jason had a small pod coffeemaker in the workshop along with a compact refrigerator stocked with water, soda and milk. He started the coffee and laid out two cups, old promotional mugs from his former record label. He still had a few boxes of similar memorabilia that he often thought of disposing of, but the mugs came in handy. Once in a while, he'd give one to a client who remembered him from his days as a working musician.

Jason said, "I'll be straight with you, Jules. I love you like a son. I've never been a real father, but I've talked to a bunch of them. They tell me about their hopes and dreams for their kids. How they want them to have things they never did. I sympathized but I also thought it was kind of selfish, because it was what *they* wanted, not necessarily what the kid wanted."

"That's what I was saying yesterday."

"I know. I was in a bad frame of mind yesterday for a bunch of reasons you don't know anything about. Things just built up and I took it out on you. For that, I'm sorry."

"I spoke out of turn too, boss. I'm sorry about that."

"Be that as it may. Thing is, I understand if you don't want to be a rehabber all your life, if you don't see that as a career. But we should have had that conversation a while ago if that's the way you felt."

"See, that's it. I don't know exactly what's in store for me. I know what I'd like, but fact is, I do enjoy working for you and I do like doing what we do."

Jason had to tread lightly. Aaron had told him that Julius had a secret. If he told Julius he knew about it, the younger man might feel that Aaron had betrayed him when he had taken pains not to. It was a family affair and Jason had done enough damage to his little work family lately.

Black said, "My problem is that while you're working with me, I need to know I can depend on you. This is a small business. You and Paco are my only employees. Aaron told me that if I had assignments, I should give them to him and if you didn't come through, he would."

"Wow." He sighed and his eyes took a shine. "That old dude's a real friend. No matter what he says to me when he gets to trash talking."

"But Jules, he's a seventy year old man with cancer. I don't want to put a lot of demands on him. You need to level with me. What's going on with you?"

"Boss, I need this job. I need to make a living. I was afraid if I told you about what I was up to, you'd let me go. And truth be told, I didn't want to disappoint you neither. If my other thing doesn't work out, I'd be happy to be doing this forever. And that other thing you wouldn't ever have to know about."

"You know what that sounds like? Sounds like a wife telling her husband that she's having an affair that could work out. If it does, she'll be leaving him. But if it doesn't, she'd stay with him. I call it 'better dealing' and

I don't like it. Especially if you hid the affair in the first place. You see where I'm coming from?"

"I do. I guess if you fire me now when I tell you, I'll have to live with it. Maybe come crawling back at some point and hope you have pity on me."

"Let's not overdramatize this. That's my fault by saying it's like a marriage. Coffee's ready. Take your mug and tell me what's going on. Unless you're doing major felonies on the side, firing you now is not in the cards."

"Well boss, it's like this. I always wanted to be a lawyer. Wasn't sure I could measure up and I surely didn't have money for law school. When you hired me, I put those ambitions aside. You remember that house we did on Hilton Head a while back? Anyway, that's where I ran into the man who owns the Falcons. He has a place on the island. We got to talking. Said he always liked me and was sorry I didn't make the team. Then out of nowhere, he said that if I wanted to take legal classes, he'd pay the tuition."

"Wow, what a great thing to do. Always admired that man, starting Home Depot and all. But why didn't you tell me then?"

"See, I wasn't sure it'd work out. I started going to classes at night, heavy schedule after working on houses all day. I didn't want you to think I was two timing you. I was handling it pretty well till this last semester. Things got rough and I was studying into the night for exams, burnin' it on both ends. That's when I started missing work. Calling in sick when I wasn't. I'm sorry about that, I truly am."

"So where does it stand now?"

"Got the bar coming this summer. If I pass, well, that *is* what I want to do. If not, I don't know."

"Meaning you'll try again or you'll give up and work for me?"

"I don't know. Can't be sure. I mean, if I come real close, maybe I keep trying. If not, I give up."

"Wrong answer. Julius, I don't want you to give up on your dream. If being Perry Mason is what you want, keep at it until you get it, man. Don't ever give up. Don't be like me."

"Be like you? What're you talking about?"

"I'm a musician. I don't know how good I am or was, but that's all I ever wanted to do."

Jason looked around his workshop and thought about how it had become his shelter from the turbulent world outside. In it, he felt safe. No one could harm him while he was working with his hands, crafting things out of wood. His refuge from the cruelties of the music business that had used him up and cast him aside.

He said, "But the record business changed. I was being squeezed out and I let it happen. I wasn't ruthless enough. I wouldn't compromise. I could have started throwing some synths and hip-hop shit into my songs. Could have listened to new stuff and moved more in that direction. But I didn't. My generation considered that selling out. I thought the new music was crap and I said so in interviews. Made me sound like a bitter old man. So after a while, I quit even trying to adapt. Kept hoping that someday, the cycle would turn, that my music would be relevant again. But, it never happened."

"I never knew that. That's bad, real bad."

"Not so bad. I rehab houses for a living. I like doing it. And you and me and Aaron and Paco are a family. I love you guys. So even though it was Plan B, it's worked out fine. Like when I had my own band. Tight knit group."

"I thought you were big time into fixing them old places up. Never thought it took second place to what really got you off."

"And I thought it was that way with you, too. Difference is, I'm an old man and even if I did sell out now, there wouldn't be any buyers."

"I'm not sure that's true, boss. Your tunes ain't exactly my taste, but a lot of older folks still dig your sound. You oughta take your own advice and not give it up."

"That's my cross to bear. But you're still young. You get to my age and you're not Harvey Spector, *then* you have my permission to quit. But now, you take that exam and you keep taking it until you pass. Then it will give me great pleasure to fire your ass."

17

Jason had seen Doctor Hannah Melrose a dozen times over the years. He had originally sought out the psychiatrist's help when he admitted that his temper was becoming a problem. He'd viewed her counsel as a last resort, having tried to resolve the problem himself, but having little success.

He was looking for a quick fix. She offered no simple solutions. After a half dozen sessions, he eventually accepted his outbursts as part of his DNA and terminated the therapy.

Gilmore had stirred up an unhappy chapter of his past and he didn't know who he could talk to about it. Aaron's advice on women came from the Paleolithic Age. Julius and Paco were young, not to mention that he was their boss. Sharing any personal angst with either of them would be unseemly. Katrina McCann would hate him for what he did to Wendy, knowing her political leanings. He called Melrose, hoping that a session with her might at least give him some comfort.

Although she was semi-retired, she agreed to see him that afternoon. She lived close by and worked from her home, a classic Charleston beauty that he had restored for her.

Melrose was married to a real estate attorney who Jason had done business with on occasion. He liked both of them, but they never socialized. They occasionally saw each other at parties and at restaurants. The good doctor would discretely ask how he was doing with his problem, and he would routinely reply that he was fine, even though he wasn't.

They sat in her parlor, which looked exactly as it had the day he finished the work. It was furnished with tasteful antiques and reproductions. He knew very little about painting, but the portraiture displayed looked old, authentic and perfect for the decor. Once they were situated, he complimented her on how she had taken his blank canvas and made it feel homey and comfortable.

She accepted the praise and said, "I was surprised to hear from you. I thought you'd given up on me."

"Not at all. You helped me realize where my anger issues came from. I've been better, although lately things have flared up again."

"And you're looking for a little mid course correction? Is that it?"

"No, actually, it's something different this time. It's something I've never told anyone else about, even with you in our sessions back then." He related the whole story about Wendy. How he believed that it had sabotaged every other relationship he'd been in, including the most recent with Katrina.

When he was finished, she stared straight ahead for a moment, lost in thought. She said, "You've held that in for over forty years? Told no one about it?"

"My dad knew how it went down. But he died shortly after she was arrested. I couldn't tell any of my friends. I'd have been shunned. Then later, after I became kind of a public figure, I had to keep it a secret. If I told the wrong person and it came out, my career could have been ruined. Even now, I think that if the truth comes out, my business might be hurt."

"So how does it feel to finally unburden yourself? And why now, after all this time?"

"The man who got me into that wants me to work for him again. It got me thinking. I've never been married, never really came close. I push women away before things get serious. I feel so guilty over what I did to Wendy that I can't have a normal relationship. There's a woman I've been seeing that's everything a man could want and yet I push her away."

"And you think it's because you betrayed this Wendy person that you're not fit for anyone else?"

"Basically, yeah. I condemned her to the gulags or worse. I'm probably responsible for her death."

"You came to me for a simple answer to a complex problem. Jason, as an artist, even though you seem well adjusted on the surface, there's a certain amount of narcissism going on. It goes with the job. Everything's all about you. Your art is who you are. Your feelings, your thoughts, are expressed in a way to get others to relate. It's the world seen through your eyes, your perspective."

"I checked my ego at the door years ago, doc."

"That's not where I'm going with this. You think your problems with women are because *you* betrayed the love of your life and you're not worthy of a real relationship. So you chase them away when they venture into that territory."

"That's what I'm saying."

"Try this on for size. What if you're afraid, not of hurting them but of them hurting you?"

"Why? I dump them, they don't quit me."

"Jason, you understand the way it works. I don't provide the answers. You do. Hopefully, I help lead you to the proper conclusions."

"I get that. But much as I like you, this isn't the start of another bunch of sessions. For a number of reasons, I don't have the time to beat around the bush. Just tell me what you think. If it's wrong, I'm not looking to hold you accountable. It's just that there's no one else I can talk to about this."

"That's a problem in and of itself." She thought for a moment and then exhaled in resignation. "I'll agree, but understand, this is not generally the best course. My take is this and I warn you, it's based on incomplete information. Wendy betrayed *you*. You fell head over heels for her and she was using you. It's likely she never really loved you."

"I'll never believe that. She *did* love me."

"This was your first love and it was based on a counterfeit premise. The rejection issue with other women is not because you treated *her* badly. It was because she wronged you. She betrayed *you*."

"But I might have signed her death warrant. I don't know what happened to her when she got sent back to Russia."

"Some other men would feel satisfied that she was punished for what she did to them. Don't you see? She was a spy. She got caught. You're not the bad guy for turning somebody in who tried to destroy your country."

"But I loved her and because of me, she lost her life."

"You don't know that. She might be in Moscow feasting on caviar and drinking champagne for all you know. Her reward for deceiving you."

"I doubt that."

"Doubt it all you want, but whatever happened to her was of her own doing. She accepted the risk that she'd be caught and imprisoned or hanged. I can't speak to her motives. Might she have been forced into it? It's possible. But that's not anything you could control."

"You're saying that I pushed women away and treated them like crap as a defense mechanism? So they couldn't hurt me? That's not the way I see it. I didn't want to hurt anyone else like I did with Wendy. You're telling me it was the total opposite?"

"I don't know any people who are that saintly. That would give up their own happiness for forty years in service of others. It's actually narcissistic to think that you're sacrificing your own well being so that others won't suffer. You're a good man Jason Black, but no one is that good. Again, I don't believe in quick tune ups and if you don't buy into what I'm saying, I'm not looking to convince you. But think about it. Sessions over. No charge."

18

After his session with Doctor Melrose, Jason felt more confused than ever. She had called him a good man. He wasn't sure he agreed with her assessment, but it counted for something.

Either way, his life was about to change. Even if he saved Paco, Julius was halfway out the door. Aaron was old, sick. His little family would be broken up, one way or another. But maybe the relationship with Kat had a future, now that he had Melrose's insight to think about.

Gilmore had texted him that he was on his way and due at any moment. He would pass the time with his music, tinkering with the new songs he'd written.

Very often his art helped him sort things out. When you distill your complex feelings into words on a page or notes on a scale, they become binary. You remove the emotion and evaluate the issue as if it's happening to a theoretical 'someone else', a character in a song. This method had worked for him in the past when crises arose.

He had left the front door unlocked with a note telling Gilmore where he'd be. Jasper lay in the corner of the studio on his dog bed, a far more effective sentry than any security system. The moment anyone came close to the house, his ears would perk up and he'd give a quick yelp.

Jason had tailored the recording studio to his needs. He'd injected foam into the wall cavities adjacent to the rest of the house. He replaced the standard interior door with a thicker, more soundproof model with a laminated glass panel. He fashioned a custom threshold for a tighter seal and wired up a *Recording in Progress* sign that he could switch on when he needed quiet. Rather than glue foam rubber panels to the wall, he made up a series of portable baffles that he could draw around him while singing and recording acoustic guitar parts.

He had a 16 track mixing board which combined with his Pro-Tools software, gave him the ability to make an album that would please the most discriminating audiophile.

Jason was laying down a bass line for his *Trapped* song when Jasper stood at attention and cocked his head. Someone was here. Sure enough, a few seconds later, he heard feet clomping up the old staircase. It had to be Gilmore. Aaron never came upstairs any more.

He said, "Afternoon, Richard."

"Nice little studio. Did I ever tell you I've toured some of the biggies? The Record Plant in New York. Sun Studios in Memphis. Hitsville, USA in Detroit. Never made it to Abbey Road. Some day."

"I didn't know you were such a music buff."

"Lots you don't know about me, Jason. That's why I'm on this case. I've seen some things in the evidence that others haven't."

"Aren't we chummy now? Shame you had to resort to blackmail."

Jasper hadn't greeted the visitor in his normal fashion. When Gilmore came into the room, he slinked back to his dog bed and cast a wary eye at him. Jason thought the dog was a good judge of character.

Gilmore looked around for a place to sit and found an old pleather office chair shoved into a corner. He slid it closer to Black.

He said, "Jason, I tried to smoke the peace pipe with you. Offer you some incentive to help me out. I'll admit I overreacted when you told me to buzz off."

"In slightly more explicit language, yes. So if I hear you out, you guarantee me that Paco's in the clear?"

"I do. But I want you to do this for me on its merits. I think when you hear what I have to say, you'll oblige."

Jason wondered how he would have responded if Gilmore had approached him in this manner to start with. Maybe he had. But he was so tied in knots over Wendy Walton that he wasn't amenable to anything Gilmore proposed. His session with the good doctor might be paying dividends. Or be leading him into a quagmire, he wasn't sure which.

Jason said, "Well, out with it, man. This is like the Macguffin in those Hitchcock movies. The big secret that really doesn't matter. Who was James Mason working for in *North by Northwest*? In the end, who cares?"

"Very nice movie reference but totally off the mark. I wish this was a Macguffin. I believe it's a matter of national security. You're the key to finding that out."

"Do tell. I'm like Dumbo, all ears."

"Still taking it lightly. Okay, I'll read you in. You have any water up here?"

Jason went to the mini-fridge he kept in a former clothes closet. He fetched two bottles of water, and handed one to Gilmore. Jasper perked up again, so Jason reached into the cookie jar and tossed a dog biscuit his way.

"Everybody happy? Good. Tell your story, Richard."

"A few months ago, a junkie was arrested in Savannah. He was on that big bridge over the river, raving about how he might jump. Cops talked him down, put him in a holding cell for forty eight hours. The next day, one of the drunks sharing the cell told a young guard something interesting. Said that the junkie was saying some weird shit, something about Russians and suitcases full of cash. Well, the place wasn't crowded and the young guard didn't have a lot to do, so he went to talk to the man himself."

Jason said, "Stop right there. I've had a lot of experience with folks on drugs. They'll say and do anything for their next fix. Zero credibility."

"I didn't come down with yesterday's rain, either. I know that. But the guard said the guy was cogent. Gave details. Not some wild rambling. So the kid told his supervisor, who laughed at him. Said, if you believe this asshole, call the FBI."

"Let me guess, he called you."

"Nope. But a low level agent wrote it up. The big bosses didn't buy it for a second. I try to read all that stuff, not like the young ones in the office. Too busy deciding what they want for lunch. Something about it struck me, so I called the guard myself and he filled me in."

"This is why you went to all these lengths to get my attention? Really?"

"Let me finish. I flew down to see for myself. Of course, we had to locate this junkie and see if he repeated the same story when he was sober or if it was all made up. Good luck finding him again, the guard said. He'd tried and failed."

"I take it you had better luck."

"Yeah. Found him the next day. In the morgue. O.D.'d."

"So all you're going on are the ravings of a lunatic dead junkie? Any chance you'd consider moving up that retirement date?"

"Yeah, I get it Jason. I haven't always been like a big brother to you, but everything I did, I did for good reason. So if you'll put your cynicism aside for one more minute, I think you'll see the light."

"Fair enough. I'm waiting for what this has to do with me."

"I went through the junkie's possessions and look what I found."

Gilmore reached into his pocket and pulled out a small piece of canvas. It was a remarkably well preserved backstage pass from the Capitol Theater in Passaic, New Jersey, stamped June, 1976. Jason's eyes widened when he saw it.

It had his picture on it. It said, **Jason Black/Brand X. World Tour**.

He held it in his hand for a moment. He probably had a few of these from that tour stashed away in the memorabilia boxes in the attic.

He said, “Odd. But so what? Is this why you think me and X have something to do with Russians and suitcases full of cash? Thin gruel, even for you, Gilmore. Why didn’t you just show me this two days ago?”

“I was going to before we got sidetracked and you stormed out of that restaurant. The junkie had said he was a huge Brand X fan. Tried a few times to crash his compound and succeeded once. That’s when he saw the Russians and the cash. What do you remember about Brand X?”

“Brandon Xavier Murphy. Not so cool name for a rocker, but Brand X? That was way cool. That’s what he called himself.”

“You did that tour and even cut some sides with him a few years later. You keep in touch?”

“Not since forever. I mean, to be honest, he was nuts. He started out kind of eccentric, but as time went on, he got really wacko. You think *I* was some kind of radical hippie, this guy was to the left of Mao. Or is it to the right? I get confused these days.”

“Do you have any idea where he is now?”

“Actually, he’s down here somewhere. Not sure exactly, as long as it’s far away from me. I have enough crazy in my life without inviting more. But he wasn’t a *bad* guy and we got along fine. And in spite of all the weirdness, he does have a certain charm.”

"He's in a town called Hardeeville. You know it?"

"Yeah, it's south on I-95. On the way to Hilton Head."

"Your old touring partner has a compound there. Small gated community that went under in its early stages. He bought it for pennies on the dollar. It's surrounded by a tall brick wall. Was supposed to be a high class enclave for the rich."

"I know the place. The developers were fools. Hilton Head is twenty miles due east. Why would anyone want to buy in a development like that if they could have a place on Paradise Island a few minutes away?"

"What if they were Russian oligarchs who didn't want it to sell? If it was a front for a cyber attack and money laundering operation."

"Brandon was wicked crazy, granted. But a Russian spy? Come on Gilmore, don't you know any other songs? I'll admit, you were right about Wendy, but I know X. He doesn't have the smarts."

"How do you know that? Apologies again for how I handled your girl, but she was working for the bad guys, even you have to admit that. So how do you know if Brand X hasn't fallen under their spell as well? You say you haven't had contact with him in years."

"Scientists do say that brain cells can regenerate. In your case Ricardo, they've *de*generated. Tell me what paranoid Commie scheme you've dreamed up now."

"I hoped you'd grown up and it would be easier to talk sense to you. Let me spell it out for you. You lost all your dough from your glory days."

Here we go again, Jason thought. *This guy knows everything about me. More than Aaron, Kat and my boys combined. How did I get to this place?*

Gilmore went on. "Don't look so shocked. I know about that movie deal. We busted those guys but the money was gone so there was no restitution. Can't get blood from a stone."

"So what's your point? I didn't do anything illegal. I was a victim."

"Not saying you weren't. But Brandon, for all his eccentricities, put most of his money into this wacky scheme out of some California hippie's garage. Little venture called Apple. Maybe you've heard of it. He's loaded."

"Well, bully for him. Maybe I *should* be in touch for old times' sake. A few of those dollars might come falling out of his VW bus or whatever he's driving these days."

"That's kind of what I had in mind. Even after making a fortune in the market, he's still an anarchist at heart. He's using his wealth to do everything he can to disrupt things. And when the Russians got wind that there's a rich American who hates his country, they helped him along."

"Steer me straight on this. The FBI thinks the Russians *did* try to influence the presidential elections?"

"No doubt about it. Not just the last one either. They've been at it for years. And it's not just presidential campaigns."

"So because you tricked me into betraying my lover all those years ago, you think I'm the perfect guy to entrap an old friend, a harmless airhead that I used to tour with. That pretty much it?"

Gilmore grabbed Jason's arm and wouldn't let go. He was stronger than the FBI agent but he didn't want to get physical. That wasn't his bag. Never had been.

Gilmore's eyes burned with the fervor of a true believer. "Jason, get this betrayal thing out of your head. If Wendy was innocent, nothing would have happened to her. She was a plant. We proved that. You helped prove it. I know you loved her or thought you did. We know she took advantage of you to push the anti-war movement forward. But not to help the cause of peace. The intent was to destroy America from within."

He still couldn't allow Gilmore to disparage Wendy. He said, "The Wendy I knew was a sweet peace loving woman who loved me."

"Jason, it's time you faced facts. She wasn't being tortured when she told *you* she was an enemy agent."

Jason's voice was faint. "She did it to save lives. End the war, stop the killing. I let you put a damn bug in our bedroom. She trusted me and I turned her in, didn't I?"

"And you did the right thing. I understand it was hard. She was good at what she did. She identified your vulnerabilities and played into them. You were an uncomplicated kid who'd never had a serious lover. She was a gorgeous girl who seemed too good to be true. Jason, you need to face facts. There's evil in the world. I deal with it every day. Not everyone has a good heart.

Some people want to do us harm for reasons we can't understand."

"Even if I accept that, you lied to me about the arrest and then you made it worse, didn't you? You promised to tell her the place was bugged without my knowledge. She was never supposed to know my role."

"Damn it, this wasn't some high school dating game. This was war. We had to use every tool in our bag. I'm sorry it happened the way it did, but we couldn't risk letting her get away."

"You had the place surrounded. You didn't have to humiliate her the way you did."

"Jason, I'm going to tell you something that I've told no one except my late wife. I've come full circle on the war in Vietnam. We were wrong. We should have listened to you instead of trying to stop you. We wasted over fifty thousand of our best young men and women plus countless numbers of wounded. It was one of our biggest mistakes as a nation. So that forty years later, like you said, we'd be wearing cheap clothes made over there."

Jason sighed. He would never trust Richard Gilmore. He'd lied so many times. But he'd never stop harassing Jason and finding ways to hurt him and his friends if he didn't go along. He was boxed in now and had little choice but to play the game.

And he held out the hope that there was a chance Gilmore was telling the truth. Maybe his former touring partner really was doing something that could cause harm to the country and Jason could do something about it.

He said, "So what do you want me to do?"

"Get back in touch with Brand X. Regain his trust. Get us proof that he's helping a foreign government muck up our political process. No doubt, he's got computers, iPhones, probably a ton of those with all that Apple stock he owns. Find the ones he uses to contact the Russians. SD cards, SIMMS, hard copies. Dead trees. Whatever you can get your hands on."

Jason Black was back in bed with the FBI. He didn't relish what lay ahead. He'd experienced a lot of Brandon's craziness back in the day and didn't look forward to revisiting Colonel Kurtz.

Jasper whined in the background. Jason gave his dog a pained look. "Can't bring you along, buddy. Uncle Aaron will take care of you. Daddy's off to join the circus."

19

Richard Gilmore was pleased with himself. His plan hadn't gone off without a hitch, but now everything was falling into place. He congratulated himself on his doggedness. He had finally overcome all the barriers, some of them self imposed, to advance his goal.

He wasn't there yet. This bust could be the crowning achievement of a notable career, or it could be a sad dénouement for a tired old bureaucrat. Either way, he'd earned the steak dinner he was about to enjoy. Too bad he was alone and there was no one to share it with.

He sat alone in the restaurant he'd been told served the city's best steaks, in a town noted for fine dining. *Hall's Chophouse* was on King Street. It was old, family run and pricey. Tonight's meal, with one glass of wine, would set him back well over a C-note, but he'd earned it.

After a series of misfires, the final stratagem that sealed Jason Black's commitment was the truth. It wasn't the whole truth but it *had* set him free. What was it David Lee Roth had once said about sincerity being the key? *Once you learn to fake that, you're on your way.*

That saying had to originate with someone else. Oscar Wilde? Whatever. It had worked.

After finding the backstage pass amongst the junkie's possessions, he set about researching Brandon X. Murphy. The rock stuff was easy. He'd made four records, had a couple of which were 'turntable hits.' In other words, they had gotten a lot of airplay on FM underground stations but never really sold. Offstage, he had the reputation of a wild man rivaling the Who's Keith Moon --- tearing up hotel rooms, overturning backstage banquet tables, presiding over orgiastic celebrations with participants of both sexes.

He recorded for the same label as Jason, and some coked-out exec thought a tour featuring the two of them would be a great idea. Brand X opened the shows. His fans were rivet heads, into the loud, electronically distorted riffs his band employed to cover for their lack of virtuosity. His lyrics were crude, misogynistic, and trite. He did look the part --- tall, skinny, long jet black hair.

His cult following traveled far and wide to see him perform. They followed their rock god across the country in multiple cities, leaving devastation in their wake.

The tour lasted three months before the record company came to its senses and split them up. X ran out of gas and checked into rehab a few weeks later. Jason drew more appreciative audiences without the burden of Brandon X. Murphy dragging him down.

Murphy did stage a mild comeback in the eighties, using his real name. He was clean and sober and had honed his chops to the point where he could make a decent record without bringing in veteran session players to play the parts he couldn't. He even co-wrote a couple of songs with Jason during that period, giving Black a couple of cool lines and a basic chord structure that the more talented writer refined and recorded.

By the mid eighties, Brand X was off the radar. Gilmore could find no record of where he was living or what he did to sustain himself, until he discovered the Apple portfolio. X was worth millions, but like a hippie Howard Hughes, he was a man of mystery. Did he own a private island somewhere in the Pacific? Or a villa in the south of France, or maybe Lake Como? Was he in Tibet, in some Buddhist Monastery or in India with a guru?

The trail had gone cold and frankly, nobody cared. But a few years ago, he resurfaced in South Carolina, buying the failed development that now housed his compound.

The junkie's story sounded credible enough for Gilmore to monitor the gated entrance himself for a few days. He saw a couple of suspicious rental cars entering and leaving the community. His computer geek tracked the credit cards used to procure the vehicles and found them tied to a shell company that the Russians often used. Gilmore suspected that something was afoot but didn't have anywhere nearly enough to convince anyone. His best bet was to somehow infiltrate the compound.

That's when he hit upon the idea to get Black involved. It would be strange karma. Jason Black would be the linchpin in his first and last big case. Even though he hadn't had any ties with Murphy since the eighties, they likely still shared a musicians' kinship. Black would need to redevelop Murphy's trust but Jason had charisma to spare when he deigned to show it.

One of the obstacles he anticipated was convincing Black that his earlier undercover work had proven worthwhile. That betraying his lover was a small price to pay to rid the movement of a corrupt faction. It wasn't true.

The Communist influence on the anti-war movement had proven inconsequential. Yes, there were a few sleepers scattered about, but the Kremlin wasn't sinking big rubles or hopes into the project. Black was correct that the bureau wanted to discredit the whole movement by implying the Soviets were behind it.

Even with Wendy Walton, their trophy arrest, the scenario didn't have legs. No other agents were exposed. It was the first big arrest of the young Gilmore's career but it didn't yield the hoped for results.

It had come full circle. The young, ambitious fed was now an aging veteran, grasping for one last shot at redemption. So he helped arrange for Black to do a concert in Savannah, just a few miles from the X compound. He hoped it would garner the attention of his old touring partner. Maybe X would attend, out of nostalgia for his old mate.

That didn't happen. So his next move was to approach Black after the show when the performer's endorphins were sky high and convince him to perform an encore in service to his country. It should have been an easy sell.

Gilmore's scheme was disrupted by Deidre Collins, who attached herself to Black after the show. He followed them to the hotel, booked the adjoining room and listened through the thin walls.

Between the show and the night of pleasure, he felt that Black would be even more primed for his entreaties. He didn't count on the man's resentment about Walton persisting as strongly as it had. When Black stomped out of Huey's, embarrassing him in front of the other patrons, Gilmore got mad.

The waiter interrupted his thoughts. Gilmore had finished his she-crab soup. It was excellent and he told the man so. His filet mignon and steak fries were delivered and he had to admit, the restaurant's reputation had not been overstated. The meat was perfectly cooked, blackened on the outside, hot pink inside. The peppery glaze was superb and he rated it among the best he'd ever had.

He had a small pang of guilt as he ate since such a rich meal was diametrically opposed to his doctor's advice. He had a mild cardiac issue and had been prescribed medication to thin his blood and reduce his cholesterol. A better diet and exercise regime were definitely on the agenda. The stress of his current mission was not helping matters, either. He'd been through a lot over the past few months.

But tonight, he deserved a celebration. Recruiting Black was a struggle, but he was finally on board. They'd meet at his studio the next afternoon to go over strategy, based on some ideas Gilmore already had developed.

Richard Gilmore had taken risks, but he felt that he needed to be proactive regarding his legacy. He was acting as a lone wolf now, but if Jason Black brought home the bacon, he'd have all the support and reinforcements the bureau could offer.

If he was wasting his time exploring a dry hole, no one had to know. Black certainly wouldn't go public about a failed mission to betray another old friend. He'd worry about that later. Right now, his main concern was if he would have enough room for dessert.

~~~~~

Less than five miles away, Jason and Kat sat in her empty restaurant, lights down low. They hadn't seen each other for two consecutive nights since they had broken up, but Jason couldn't resist the invitation.

Katrina had been puttering around her store on her day off, tweaking the menu and tidying up some paperwork when she noticed it was getting dark outside. There was food remaining from Sunday that they couldn't serve to customers, so she called Jason and asked if he'd help her eat it, rather than see it go to waste. It was a thin pretext, but after his session with Gilmore, he needed to get out, so he walked and fed Jasper and drove the ten minutes to her restaurant.

Kat would never just heat up leftovers for him --- she added her own twist to the dish and paired it with a nice cabernet. She made a fresh Caesar salad and
~~~~~

checked to see if there was any Italian style cheesecake left to accompany cappuccino later.

After the salad, Jason said, "Milady, you are just what the doctor ordered. That situation I told you about is coming to a head and I might be away for a while."

"Away? As in out of the country?"

"No. Not far actually, but I might be incommunicado for a bit."

"It all sounds so cloak and dagger, like some kind of spy novel. Can't you tell me anything?"

"You know I trust you with my life. Although after last night, I wouldn't blame you if you poisoned my food."

"Why would I do that? What are you talking about?"

"I had no business telling you about what happened after the concert Saturday night. Got me all wound up and I couldn't sleep. Actually wrote a couple of new songs. Best thing I've done in years."

She said, "That's one of the reasons I wanted to see you. I acted like it didn't bother me. But it did."

"Exactly. Why did I tell you that? I never wanted to hurt you and I did. I'm sorry."

He was about to expand on that when she said, "Hold that thought. The main course is ready."

Rather than just microwave the eggplant dish, she had insisted on heating it slowly in the oven to retain its original texture. She added more asiago, fontina, and rubiloa to spice it up. A dash more sauce, or gravy as some Italians called it.

Upon returning with two platefuls of her latest improvisation, she said, "Sorry. You were about to make a point, Jase."

"Don't apologize for this. It smells heavenly. Look, I can't excuse men who use their power to force women into something they don't want. But because I had a few hit records I had power over this woman the other night."

"Okay, you understand the power that stardom gives you. Are you thinking it wasn't consensual?"

"I told you I was being blackmailed. That made me start thinking about it. The way I treated women back in the day. Am I still doing it?"

"You're a public figure, I assume she's not. She may have felt powerless to turn you down."

"So I'm only supposed to be interested in women more famous and powerful than I am? How about you? You have a certain cache in town, being a successful restaurateur and all. You've been written up in the papers and magazines in this city more than I have. Do you qualify? Should we compare press clippings before we sleep together?"

"Shut up and eat your pasta before it gets cold. You're being ridiculous now."

"I *am* playing a little Devil's Advocate but I'm telling you how men like Aaron feel."

"You and Aaron aren't seeing it from a woman's point of view. Men have had the upper hand forever. Women were supposed to just put up with it. If a woman used sex to get ahead, she's a slut. A man fucks an underling? Hey, it's a fringe benefit of being in a powerful position. It's not so easy to say no when your career depends on it. What if the woman reports it to HR and nothing happens? What does she do then, kick him in the balls?"

"That usually works. Look, I'm with you on this. The bad guys need to get their comeuppance."

"Well, we agree on something. Come on, I didn't want tonight to turn into a debate. The rules are changing and you're uncomfortable with it."

"No Kat, I get it. I shouldn't have done what I did the other night, but not because of her. Because of you."

"Jason, we've talked about this and we agreed --- no strings. We're both free to do what we want."

"It's becoming academic with me anyway. Not many women are even willing to flirt with a faded old folksinger their parents grew up listening to."

"That old folksinger is still mighty attractive to a discriminating woman, which I consider myself. You like the melanzane con linguini?"

"I like the company more."

"Even after we've just been arguing?"

"I like a woman with spirit. Gable said that in a movie, I think. Or is that sexist?"

"Coming from you or Gable, it's kinda sexy actually."

"Does that mean I might get lucky later?"

"There's a chance. But there's cheesecake and cappuccino first."

20

Jason didn't get very much sleep. Katrina had stayed over, but that wasn't why he lay awake most of the night.

He'd called his crew over for a nine a.m. meeting, asking Aaron to arrive a half hour earlier. Kat had taken the contents of his refrigerator and whipped up an incredible omelet. As he sat waiting for his men to arrive, he decided to tell her about what lay ahead. He didn't name names or get too specific, but he outlined the mission. She deserved to know.

He said that he'd be going undercover to expose what could amount to a traitorous scheme involving someone he once knew. When he finished, she said, "This sounds dangerous. Can't the FBI find a professional to do this? One false move can be fatal when you're working undercover."

"You conveniently forget that at heart, I'm a coward. Things heat up and I'll run, tail between my legs."

"Don't spoil my illusions. You were against the war all those years ago when it wasn't exactly a popular opinion. I would have thought the FBI would disqualify you because of that."

"They're willing to overlook my misguided youth."

"I don't like the idea of you working for the feds. I don't trust them. Call it a hangover from the bad old days, but all I see when I think of them is that bulldog mug of Hoover, blackmailing the Kennedys."

"You're way too young to remember him, Kat. You just saw the movie. Trust me, he didn't look like Leonardo DiCaprio. Look, my handler thinks that our target is sowing chaos. Undermining American institutions."

"Are you saying that he's in league with the president?"

"No, silly, but the effect is the same. It's dividing the country."

"I trust you, Jason. I think you and I believe in the same things and you'd never sell them out, no matter what. I'm just worried about you, that's all."

Had he betrayed the values he shared with Wendy when he turned her in? Or had he upheld them? Over forty years later, he still struggled with that one.

He said, "Thanks for breakfast. You'd better get going, start your day. I know you wanted to get to the markets early."

"That way I have my pick of the best seafood. Fresh ingredients make the best meals."

"Sounds like a Papa John's slogan."

"Don't get me started on that asshole. Denies health insurance for his workers rather than charge a few extra cents for that crap he pretends is pizza. Then says he was tricked into using the N-word. Gimme a break."

"You never stop with the causes, do you? That's what I love about you."

"Love? Are you saying you love me? That's a first." She said it with a smile, but she really wanted to hear him say it.

He rummaged through his cluttered brain for the right answer. "When I get back, we'll talk about it. All I know that an old folksinger is never going to find a finer woman."

She held his gaze for a moment, then looked away. "That's not what I asked, Jason. I'm not getting any younger either, fella. How does that old song go? *If it takes forever, I will wait for you.* Don't take that for granted. It may not be true."

She kissed his cheek, picked up her purse and walked out. Her perfume lingered. Her husky morning voice. Would it be the last time he ever heard it?

~~~~~

She was gone by the time Aaron arrived and Jason saw no reason to mention her visit to the old man. He had a lot of ground to cover and spending ten minutes indulging Aaron's fantasies about Kat wouldn't be the most productive use of time. He told him that he didn't know how accepting the mission would impact his building work for the immediate future.

He said, "So, bottom line is, I'm turning things over to you. The cabinet doors are all glued up. They just need paint and finishing and I've arranged for a friend to take care of that. He'll do it for two grand and
~~~~~

that includes the live edge countertop. Once you approve the work, cut him a check."

"What should I do on Wagener?"

"Your call. You've got the plans. It's not as high end as the Sanders place, but make it nice. It's an up and coming area. If you have trouble with any design elements, Kat will help. She has a good eye."

"That ain't all that's good on her. Maybe working close with me, she'll see what I've got to offer and ditch your ugly ass."

"I'm in no position to object."

Aaron hadn't gravitated to the old rocking chair as he usually did. He stood in the kitchen the entire time. He seemed energized by the added responsibility.

He said, "What I'm not liking about this is you sound like you're not coming back. There's no chance of that happening, is there?"

"I'm going to be dealing with a crazy man named Brandon X Murphy. Brand X. He might be doing some seriously bad shit with the Russians. I'm just taking a while off to settle some old business is all."

"I don't like this kind of talk."

"Neither do I. But just in case, I don't want the state to take everything. I have no heirs, no living relatives. Katrina will get my portfolio, such as it is."

"Maybe you'd better rethink this, boyo. I know I told you that you should listen to what this guy wanted you to do, but I didn't say you should do it. Shit, you're in great shape, should have another twenty years minimum. You sure you want to throw that away?"

"Hey, I'm not planning on dying. I'm probably exaggerating but I want to make sure my people are taken care of if things don't work out."

"I think you're crazy. You got a good thing going with this business. Why risk all that? You say this guy dropped his threats about deporting Paco and such. Then why do it? What do you have to gain?"

"Doing it for King and country I guess you could say."

Aaron was adamant. "You don't believe that and neither do I. Seriously, I'm saying this from the heart. Don't do it."

"Thanks for the concern. Right now, I need to push ahead."

Paco and Julius arrived. He explained to them that he had to be away for a while and that Aaron would be in charge until he returned. He didn't want to panic them with talk of wills and letters of intent, so he just said to keep doing their jobs until he returned.

Paco took it hardest. He said, "Boss, you sure there's nothing we can do to help? You can't tell us any more about what this is?"

Paco's Dreamer status was shaky since the politicians in Washington couldn't agree on what to do. Gilmore had used this against him. But since Jason had committed to helping him, he said he would guarantee that deportation would never happen.

Jason said, "No, guys, everything'll be fine. I shouldn't be away long, it's just something I need to take care of. I'm lucky to have you guys around. You won't even notice I'm gone."

Paco said, “Are you sick, Jefe? Is that what this is all about?”

“Nope, I’m fine. When this is over, hopefully I’ll be able to tell you all about it. But for now, just trust me.”

“But there must be something more we can do to help. Anything at all.”

“Just keep working on the houses. Keep your focus on the job. Surprise me with how much progress you’ve made when I get back.”

“Vaya con Dios, boss.”

Jason felt his eyes moisten. He loved all three of these men, each in a different way. They were his family. He hoped that this wouldn’t be the last time he saw them.

21

That night was another sleepless one for Jason. He didn't smoke grass these days and was wary of any medication, prescribed or over the counter. But if he didn't doze off in the next five minutes, he'd head for his bathroom to find something that could knock him out.

Jasper lay snoring in the bed beside him. It seemed that the dog could be in a deep sleep one moment and then fully conscious and sharp a second later if he sensed danger. He envied Jasper for that.

The meeting that afternoon when Gilmore laid out strategy had given him more concerns. And Aaron had never opposed him this strongly about anything. *Why am I doing this? Is it penance for Wendy? Am I putting myself in harm's way as punishment for what I did decades ago? Can I trust Gilmore?*

The answer to the last question was the easiest. He didn't trust the man at all. Yet he was putting his life in his hands. *Again, why?*

Something was amiss with this whole process. When the FBI recruited him to spy on Wendy, it had been a group effort. He had detailed instructions from several criminologists, each with a different area of expertise. One explained the psychological angle, hints on how to detect lies with facial tics, etc. Another taught him the tradecraft side --- planting undetectable bugs, dead drops, codes and such. They planned an escape route if things went awry. They schooled him on indications that his mark was onto him and when to bail.

Gilmore had provided none of these experts this time. There was an SD card in one of his shirt pockets, to be used to download evidence from Brand X's computer or phone if he couldn't just steal the device.

So much of this seemed improvisational. There was little in the way of specific instructions. Jason had to talk his way into the compound, gain Brandon's trust and smuggle out any incriminating material he could lay his hands on. He needed enough to persuade a judge that a search warrant was called for. He might just be there one day, or it could take a month. The commitment was open ended.

What would come next? Back in the seventies, no one else in the antiwar movement knew Wendy had been exposed due to his efforts. Jason told the others that she had lit out for the West Coast, where she had family. Although they found it odd, they didn't pursue it. Protest leaders came and went. It wasn't as if they were running a business with a tight organizational chart. Sometimes other priorities took them away.

He got out of bed but instead of searching for an insomnia remedy, he went to his office. Jasper cocked his head when his master stirred but didn't follow. The dog decided that Jason didn't need his help.

Black wrote a letter for Kat, and this time he named names. He described the mission ---- he was to infiltrate Brand X's compound and attempt to develop evidence that could prove he was committing acts of treason in collusion with a foreign power. Just putting it in writing made him realize how ludicrous it all sounded. *Why him and not a skilled undercover operative?*

Gilmore had explained that Jason would be the last person X would suspect, a fellow musician with a shared past. If the treasonous acts were merely the ramblings of a desperate junkie, no harm, no foul. But if there was a there *there,* he could be performing a valuable service.

But again, why him? *Trusting the fate of the democracy to a faded folksinger?*

He closed the letter by telling Kat that in the event of his death, Richard Gilmore of the FBI had instigated the operation. She should hold him accountable in any way she saw fit. She was not to contact Gilmore unless they had reason to believe that something had gone wrong. He needed an insurance policy in case the fed sold him out, and she was the person he trusted most.

He emailed it, attaching the detailed account as a separate document. He instructed her not to open the mission letter for forty eight hours. He hoped he'd be back by then or at least able to contact them to let her know that he was safe. The timing was guesswork. He might be in and out in one day, or it could take weeks to insinuate himself into Brandon's good graces.

He found an expired analgesic in his medicine cabinet and took a double dose. He had to sleep. It might be the last time he could.

22

It took almost two hours to reach the Hardeeville complex from Jason's house. The ride down I-95 was uneventful, and it gave him time to think more about his approach. He'd try to talk his way in if he was detained at the gate, hoping that the years of drugging hadn't erased his name from X's mental hard drive. He didn't remember the last time they had seen each other, probably in a studio somewhere, laying down tracks. He did remember that there was no bad blood; they had parted on friendly terms.

He'd checked out the aerials of X's complex. There were four buildings on the property. Three were model homes, built by the original developer in the nineties. They were of modest size, and were probably outdated by today's standards.

The newest and largest building was Brand X's private residence. Gilmore had quipped that it was a smaller replica of the Playboy Mansion in Holmby Hills. If it was indeed smaller, the real thing must be enormous. With his experienced eye, Jason estimated the size to be at least twelve thousand square feet. It had a pond and an outdoor pool that emptied into an indoor one, a facsimile of Hef's famous grotto. Built from brick and stone, it looked like it could withstand light artillery fire. No hurricane in God's creation could blow it down.

The key areas of the compound were surrounded by a stout brick wall. Even in Hardeeville, not exactly a prime area, Jason estimated that the wall and structures on the property must have cost a pretty penny to build. As to its market value, it would be anyone's guess. It was such a unique situation that only someone with unlimited funds and a desire for complete privacy would be a buyer. But X was not looking to sell.

Jason and Gilmore had agreed on a low key approach. Jason dressed down --- torn work jeans, bleach stained tee shirt, black leather jacket. He drove his pickup truck up to the gatehouse, where an armed guard sat watching last night's SportsCenter on a flat screen.

"Can I help you?" the guard asked. The man was as tall as Jason but thirty pounds heavier, none of which was fat. Ex-military. He wore a nondescript gray uniform, the tight shirt a couple of shades lighter than the pants. The short sleeves accentuated off his bulging, tattooed biceps. With his close cropped blond hair, he reminded Jason of Robert Shaw in *From Russia With Love*, playing the assassin Red Grant.

Jason said, "I'm here to see Murph."

"There's no one here by that name."

"Brandon Xavier Murphy? Sorry, I'm an old axe buddy. He called himself Brand X back when we were gigging together."

"He still does. I've never heard that other name. Do you have an appointment? Your name is?"

"Jason Black. I'm sure the dude'd dig seeing me. I was in the area and thought I'd stop by and see my old compadre." He laid the hippie schtick on heavy, part of the ploy to come off as a harmless old pothead.

"I'll call up to the house, but he never accepts visitors unless they have an appointment." The guard retreated to his warren and picked up a phone. Jason doubted that the sentry at the gate was the only muscle on the payroll. The great and powerful Oz had to be protected from lookie-loos or fans from his glory days.

While waiting, Jason tried to read the man's body language. It looked as if the guard had been put on hold and shunted around from one number to another. Did X have one of those annoying audio menus that plague you when you call customer service?

Finally, the man opened his Dutch door, a surprised look on his face. "Well, there's a first time for everything. It seems that the X-man *will* see you. You'll have to wait until someone comes down to escort you up to the main house. And I'll need your cell phone."

"Why is that?"

"The boss is a stickler for privacy. He doesn't want pictures of the house to show up on Instagram."

Jason played dumb. "What's that?"

"Old fella like you wouldn't know what that is, I s'pose. Well, rules are rules. I can't let you go up with a phone. If you need to call out, I'm sure you'll be able to use the landline at the house."

Jason made a show of reluctantly turning the device over. Gilmore had anticipated that someone as secretive as X wouldn't allow his guests to have cell phones on the property. He'd provided Jason with a fresh burner.

Black didn't tell Gilmore, but he wasn't about to wade into this without his personal smart phone. He had hidden it in his tool box beneath an assortment of hammers and screwdrivers. If he had to call for help, he needed its directory, since like most Americans, he had few numbers committed to memory.

Black handed over the phone he used for business and waited. The guard stayed in his warm little cabin, watching the screen and occasionally glancing over to Jason in the truck. About five minutes later, a golf cart pulled up, the gate opened and the guard said, "Pull up to the other side of the gate and follow that cart. Have a nice day."

Jason obeyed the instructions, although having a nice day was beyond his ken. The tabby concrete driveway meandered through specimen trees and plantings for several hundred yards. The final passage was through a leafy tunnel of willow oaks that had been trained to overhang the roadway from both sides.

He had to admit the approach was impressive. It wasn't his style, but if someone with unlimited resources chose to build a monument to himself, the aesthetic choices were appropriate.

After emerging from the tree canopy, the main house came into view. It was even more magnificent than the photos. Tall, stately and expansive, with a brick and limestone facade, it was a perfect billionaire's mansion. The lawn was lush and green, even at this time of year. The grounds reminded him of the Pinehurst Resort in North Carolina. Pristine, meticulously maintained, nary a stray leaf or fallen branch to mar its beauty.

The golf cart stopped at the front entry where the concrete gave way to a vast sea of cobblestones. A shiny silver Bentley sat in a shaded corner. If the intended effect was awe, it achieved it. Jason wondered how many workers would need to be employed to keep the place shiny.

His escort stepped out of the golf cart and signaled him to leave the truck in front. In the cold morning sunlight, it was obvious that he was the original guard's twin. Like the gatekeeper, he was built like a battleship, dressed in the same garb. His bearing mirrored the other: blonde crew cut, square jaw, thick tatted biceps.

The man said, "Please give me your keys. We'll park it out back and it'll be brought around when you're ready to leave. Follow me."

Can't have an old Ford pickup parked anywhere in sight around here, Jason thought. *Stand out like a turd in the punchbowl.*

The arched front doors were made of bronzed iron and leaded glass, twelve feet tall, weighing nearly a half a ton. Black's escort ushered him into a lobby that would befit a five star hotel. It featured soaring coffered ceilings, Italian marble floors and intricate plaster trim, topped by five piece crown molding.

His guardian said, "You wait here until the boss or the boss's secretary comes down. Stay put and don't roam. There are video cameras in every corner. Not saying you'll steal anything, but there are some priceless things here and we can't be too careful."

"That's cool, bro. I'll just chill."

"I'm sure it won't be long." The guard retraced his steps out the front door.

Video cameras, Jason thought. Gilmore had given him a primer on how to spot them but he was far from an expert. He had to assume his every move was being monitored.

He imagined that one of X's minions was squirreled away in a secret room, observing Jason for tell-tale signs that his motives weren't pure. He felt small and vulnerable in these surroundings. As Tom Petty once sang, *The Waiting is the Hardest Part*.

23

Gilmore had moved his headquarters from Charleston, encamping at a chain motel off Fording Island Road in Hardeeville. It was less than a mile from the X compound. The nearest FBI field office was minutes away in Bluffton. He hoped that his mission would bear enough fruit to warrant their assistance.

He sat in his Ford Explorer, watching the front gate of the compound. Equipped with binoculars, coffee and two jelly filled Dunkin' doughnuts, he observed Jason sweet talking the guard. He hadn't even wiped the last crumbs from his mouth when the gate swung open and Jason's truck pulled in.

There was no reason to watch much longer but Gilmore was thorough. He stayed for an extra quarter hour, in case Black's proposed meeting with X was quickly turned aside. X was a known unknown and therefore unpredictable.

If nothing else, Black could report on the security measures at the compound. Gilmore didn't have nearly enough to obtain a court order for a search of the place. Despite his promises that he had Jason's back, if something went south, the singer would be left to his own devices.

He went back to the motel. He hated to be in this position, waiting for something to happen over which he had no control.

~~~~~

Jason waited in the lobby for ten minutes. No Brand X. For a house this large, he figured there would be a lot of comings and goings from a sizable staff. But the place seemed empty, almost abandoned in its quiet. He was alone with his thoughts, and each passing minute created new fears, new scenarios on how this could blow up in his face.

He tried to take his mind off his plight by surveying the architectural details of the lobby. It was a one of a kind space. The valuable items the guard had spoken of were guitars, hung from gold hooks on the each leg of the split staircase leading to what he assumed were the living quarters.

He was too far away to read the signatures they bore, but he recognized the different styles and scoured his memory for musicians who favored those particular models. He saw a Fender Telecaster that might have been used by Jimmy Page. There was an old Gretsch, Chet Atkins model, that Clapton once spoke of playing in his early days. A Gibson Les Paul that Peter Townshend shredded in the seventies. If these were authentic, they would be priceless. They belonged in a museum, which this house might become if the government seized the property.

Finally, a stunning blonde woman in a tight fitting yellow pantsuit came down the stairs. Her eyes
~~~~~

had a vacant quality that didn't meet his when she spoke. He recognized the signs of a habitual pot smoker, and as she neared, one whiff confirmed his suspicions.

She said, "Jason Black. X tells me that you once toured together. Anyway, he apologizes for the delay. He's on a very important call at the moment and he has a yoga session right after that. He would love you to join him for dinner this evening, if that will fit your busy schedule."

She gave him a scornful look, as if she couldn't imagine such a wastrel having anything important to do. But Jason already had a hint that Gilmore might be onto something big. The woman's accent. He wasn't an expert linguist by any stretch, but she did sound Russian.

He said, "I'd dig that. Righteous. So come back, when?"

"We normally eat at seven. I should mention that we don't serve meat. We're vegan. And X drinks no alcohol, either. Will that be a problem?"

"I'm cool with it."

"I'll have one of the twins escort you to the gate and we'll buzz you in this evening."

"Thank you. I look forward to it."

She nodded and glided back up the curving dual staircase, straight out of *Gone with the Wind*. Now that he'd been given the official seal of approval, he felt free to wander around the lobby, inspecting the paneling and moldings. The detail was impeccable. He'd never taken on anything so ambitious. The enamel on the trim was as smooth as the finish on a Mercedes. Meticulous and time consuming work. Big bucks in a normal sized house, unimaginably expensive in one of this size.

One of the twins (he wasn't sure which) came in, and grunted that Jason should follow him to the main gate. As he followed the golf cart out of the compound, he felt more at ease. Brandon hadn't detained him or objected to the unannounced visit. The dinner invitation was surprising. He doubted that a man with something to hide would be so gracious.

He retrieved his business phone from Twin One. Exiting the compound, he pulled into a nearby parking lot and called Gilmore. "Richie? I'm out now but he invited me for dinner."

"Really? That's good. What was he like?"

"I didn't actually see him, he was busy. Just saw his secretary and a couple of guards. Armed."

"Only two?"

"There must be more but that's all I saw. I'm sure he has a whole army of people working for him. The grounds are like Augusta National."

"I've booked you a room at the Holiday Inn Express. Prepaid under the name of Dick Grayson"

"And who are you, Bruce Wayne? I'll use the room to shower and rest up. Talk later."

Gilmore sounded tired, Jason thought. He was way behind on his sleep and imagined that his handler was in the same condition. A nap this afternoon was in order. He'd need to be sharp tonight. There was no way Brandon would have invited him for dinner if he had any inkling that he was working undercover, was there? But who knows what was in store for him after the veggies were served?

There was a message on his voice mail, a number he didn't recognize. He checked it anyway in case there was a crisis Aaron couldn't handle and was calling from a jobsite.

"Jason, Hi. It's Deidre Collins. I need to talk to you. Please, please, please. Call me back."

24

Jason wasn't sure he should be seeing Deidre, even as he sat across from her at the Skull Creek Boathouse.

The boathouse was at the northern end of Hilton Head Island. This time of year the place wasn't crowded, but during the summer, you could wait for hours to get a table or a seat at the bar.

It wasn't because of the food, although it was fine. The view was incredible, especially from the huge outdoor deck. Giant fans kept it cool in the summer and space heaters in the Tiki bar made winter days tolerable. It was next to an actual boathouse and every so often a large forklift would roll by, bearing a pleasure boat ready to launch.

Jason knew that Gilmore wouldn't approve of any contact with Deidre Collins.

"You're taking your eye off the ball," he'd say. *"You have to focus on X."*

But Richard Gilmore wasn't here and Deidre Collins was. Seeing her in the flesh, he remembered how much he'd liked her. She was smart, really knew music and although she wasn't a beauty, hey, she was all right. Didn't Springsteen take heat for that line in *Thunder Road?*

It was too windy to sit outside, so they took a booth at a window facing Skull Creek, which linked the Atlantic Ocean and Port Royal Sound to the Intracoastal Waterway. The water sparkled like diamonds as the brisk breeze stirred it into a light chop.

After they were seated and served coffee, Jason said, "Deidre, I agreed to see you with some misgivings. I can understand it if you have regrets about the other night, I'm sorry."

"I have no regrets about that night with you, Jason. There's some weird stuff going on and that's what I want to clear up."

It was past the lunch hour and the early bird diners were still hours away. The wait staff didn't seem to mind that they were just hanging out, drinking coffee.

He gave her a blank look. "I'm listening."

"There's something else I need closure on."

"Go ahead."

She said, "Jason, was this whole thing a scam? I'm talking about your concert at the school. Did you trick me into booking you? My boss at the college was pissed at the fact that I spent much more on publicity than I normally do. This whole thing was started by an alum who claimed he was a big fan and was willing to cover your fee. Then he reneged and we couldn't track him down. Did you set this up? Do you know this imaginary alum?"

Damn Gilmore. By trying to approach him sideways instead of directly, he had put Jason in a bind. He couldn't tell Deidre that an FBI official was behind this whole mess. And why did Gilmore skip out on paying for the show?

Why hadn't Gilmore just sought him out at his home instead of manufacturing this concert scenario? The fed claimed that it was to show Jason how with a little boost from Washington, his music career could be reignited.

It was a stupid idea from the start. Black was realistic about his career. No amount of prodding from the government could revive it. If Gilmore had dug a little deeper, he would have understood that. But, looking at the bright side, he'd made a few bucks and spent the night with a nice lady.

Regardless, he had to respond to Deidre and he wanted to do it without lying. At least, too much.

He chose his words carefully. "Deidre, someone wanted to even an old score with me. I'm sorry you got involved. I've been in touch with the authorities and they assured me it won't happen again."

"So this person posed as a rich alum and promised to subsidize the show? Why, if really had it in for you?"

"I have no idea. We didn't exactly have a full house. Maybe he wanted to rub my nose in it."

"I guess I'm making myself look cheap here. A big star sleeps with a groupie after a show. What a cliché."

"Hey, I don't want to hear that. You are far from a groupie. I'm in your debt. This was a crazy person trying to screw me over and I'm sorry you got caught up in it."

She looked out over the water. The sunsets were spectacular from the Boathouse, and given the way the clouds were forming, this was promising to be one of the better ones.

She said, "I don't know how my boss got the notion that you planned this and I was part of it. Maybe the publicity money. The only reason I did that was because you accepted a much lower fee than I thought you would. Being such a legend and all."

"I'm far from that. I don't kid myself that I'll ever be what I was."

"Thanks. You know, that album of cover versions you did a few years ago was really good."

"I don't think too many would agree with you there. But I appreciate that. I hate the idea that I'm a has-been, living on forty year old songs."

She was touched by his admission that he missed the accolades. She pitied him in a way, even though he had had reached heights that few had experienced. Was it Jeff Bridges who said *falling feels like flying until you hit the ground?*

She said, "You're not living on old material. But I do think you're being realistic. Any new songs you wrote aren't going to sell today. That's more an indictment of the market than you. It doesn't mean you aren't relevant or great at what you do. If this generation doesn't embrace you, it's their loss. In a hundred years, I bet your music will be remembered while the hot artists of today are forgotten."

"That's nice of you to say. Too bad in a hundred years, neither of us will be around to see if you're right."

She smiled and again he thought, *she's really quite attractive. Her sweetness shines through when she smiles.*

She said, "Just know this --- there's nothing we did the other night that I didn't want."

"Although seeing you now, it's hard to figure why you'd share a bed with an old man like me."

"It's the forbidden fruit. The idea of it is more exciting than the act itself."

"Did you just insult my masculinity or am I imagining that?"

"I'll tell you in a hundred years."

25

When he got to the motel, checking in as Dick Grayson, Jason grabbed a much needed twenty minute power nap. Gilmore wasn't around and Jason had no idea where he was. Refreshed, he cleaned up and got dressed. He wore nicer jeans and a collared, long sleeved white shirt, untucked. He had let some scruff develop over the last couple of days to cultivate the image of an aging hipster, which he supposed he was.

Until he sat face to face with his old tour mate, he couldn't be sure how to present himself. If he played the fool, X might let some sensitive information slip, figuring that Black was too dumb to comprehend. Or if Jason seemed intelligent and willing, X might try to recruit him to the cause.

He would allow X to dominate the conversation until he could figure out an effective game plan. Gilmore had prepped him yesterday as best he could, but you don't become a skilled undercover operative over night. And even they can make fatal mistakes.

There was no guard at the front gate. He buzzed the house and after identifying himself, the gate swung open. That seemed odd to Jason. Maybe X rarely received visitors after hours. Was there security inside or did Brandon only employ them during daylight hours or for special occasions?

He wondered if the security detail had any inkling of what X was doing with the Russians. Men who had risked their lives for their country weren't likely to join the enemy, unless they were conscience-free Hessians who were extremely well paid.

The sun had set over an hour earlier and Jason was grateful for his Xenon headlamps. They were the only illumination along the narrow winding path --- no streetlights or landscape lighting. It was pitch black; the tree canopy hid even the dim crescent moonlight. Jason's night vision wasn't what it once was and he didn't enjoy driving after dark, especially in the poorly lit roadways.

The main house was a shining oasis in the darkness. Old fashioned gas streetlights mimicking those in Central Park lighted the cobblestones, and the entry portico had hefty copper coach lights on either side of the tall doors.

Jason rang the electronic bell and the iron doors swung open, revealing another stunning blonde woman. She smiled, revealing dimples and the perfect teeth of a supermodel. She didn't say anything in the way of greeting, just asked for his phone.

He had brought the smart phone that he used for business. He'd wiped Gilmore's number from its speed dial and committed it to memory. There was nothing on the device that could give him away.

After confiscating the phone, the gorgeous escort gestured for him to follow. He tried to be an enlightened man, as Kat put it, but he couldn't help but appreciate the sway of her pelvis in the short, tight skirt as she walked in front of him. She navigated a maze of hallways and doors until they reached a generously sized study.

Lined with floor to ceiling bookshelves which were filled with enough volumes to populate a small town library, it projected a strong masculine presence. There was a crackling fire with real oak logs. It gave the space a warm, woodsy fragrance. A huge Oriental rug covered the center of the hand-scraped Brazilian cherry floor. A fourteen foot tray ceiling loomed overhead, and the wall space that the bookcase didn't cover was painted a dark hunter green. It reminded him of the Lord of the Manor's den at Downton Abbey, such was its grandeur. Again, Jason was seeing dollar signs as the contractor in him estimated the cost.

A chunky walnut desk occupied the far end of the room, behind which was a tall leather chair, its high back to the entry. As she left, the escort closed the tall wooden double doors with a loud click, which echoed throughout the otherwise silent room. The leather chair swirled, revealing its occupant.

"Jason, hey man it's been forever, dude. How you hangin'?" said Brandon X Murphy.

~~~~~
~~~~~

Maybe it was the excitement. Richard Gilmore might be close to the biggest case of his career, a crowning achievement that books would be written about --- history that would outlive him by a hundred years. He anticipated a best seller with his own account of how it went down. A nice supplement to his government pension.

And what a tale it would be. A ostracized senior agent who persisted when others laughed and told him he was demented. His cunning in maneuvering a reluctant Jason Black to serve as an undercover operative. His skill in setting up an airtight case against these Commie bastards.

Of course, Gilmore would cloak it all in a veil of modesty so it didn't look like he was blowing his own horn. He'd be generous and share some of the glory with Black, if he survived. Hollywood might come knocking to make a movie. Too bad Efrem Zimbalist Jr. wasn't around to play him onscreen.

At the very least, he'd live out his days as a go-to guy on one of the cable networks whenever a cyber-raid involving foreign governments surfaced. He would be a consultant on retainer, the foremost expert on the dirty secrets of espionage. And he'd be available at a moments' notice to recount his glorious triumph in arresting Brandon X Murphy and his circle of Russkie conspirators.

He was tingling with anticipation. Tonight would be crucial. Whatever happened, he couldn't allow for the possibility that this was all exactly as it appeared on the surface --- an eccentric, drugged out, ex-rocker multi-millionaire who worshipped Russian supermodels.

Gilmore's chest was pounding. He'd been getting very little sleep lately. Eating rich foods in restaurants. No exercise to speak of. His next physical was scheduled a month from now and he knew that he'd better get his cholesterol down or his doc would lecture him again about how a man his age with his numbers should be taking statins. Maybe this time, he'd fill the prescription.

His left hand felt a little numb. Probably from leaning against the steering wheel of the SUV as he sat waiting outside the compound's entrance. If Black had somehow wormed his way into X's favor, they had code words to indicate that the ruse was working and progress was being made. If X refused to return his phone, Black could ask to use a landline to call his partner. Denying that request would mean trouble.

Field work! Gilmore hadn't done that in a long time.

The numbness had now spread to his shoulder area. This wasn't normal. He couldn't be having a heart attack, could he? He felt a twinge in his chest. It wasn't a sharp pain at first, just a dull throb. Then a spasm, that felt like the prick of a cold dagger.

Panic set in. Where was the nearest emergency room?

His whole body shuddered. He was suddenly very cold. Jason Black be damned, he had to get help. He dialed 911 and gave the woman his location and a quick description of his symptoms. He re-started the car and the nav system lit up. *Hospitals*. There was one in Bluffton, five miles east on 278. He gunned the engine and headed to the med center that the system's voice guidance said was closest.

He never made it there. A local cop found him, slumped over the steering wheel. The SUV had come to rest on the shoulder of the highway. The 911 call had come too late.

26

X looked positively radiant, the picture of good health. He was less than five years younger than Jason, but could have passed for twenty. His tanned face was unlined, his voice clear and crisp and his eyes were bright and sparkling.

Those eyes were the most compelling feature. Like David Bowie, X had one hazel eye and one blue one. Jason had thought it a gimmick involving a contact lens because X idolized Bowie, but X had once swore to him that his eyes were natural. It was a genetic abnormality that occurs about six times per thousand live births.

Jason mused that the years of heavy drugging hadn't extracted their price on X, appearance-wise. His hair, now clipped short, looked thick. He was dressed in a black Tommy Hilfiger polo shirt and neatly pressed button fly Levis. He was barefoot.

Before Jason could decide on an appropriate handshake, fist pump or high five, X gave him an awkward man hug. Jason pulled away as gracefully as he could.

He said, "The years have been a friend to you, Brandon. You look great."

"Veggies. No alcohol. Mother nature's son, that's me. Weed, but only the finest. You'll join me later?"

"I'm afraid we've gone in opposite directions, my friend. I'm a carnivore and I drink too much wine. Haven't smoked a joint in years."

X laughed. "Opposites attract, they say. I do keep a nice wine cellar for my guests. Although most of them are into harder stuff. Vodka and shit, no matter how I try to educate them. Red meat galore and unfiltered cancer sticks, too."

"Never picked up the nicotine habit, but I do like a good burger now and then."

"Don't worry, man, it's live and let live with me. Folks wanna poison themselves, have at it. So what brings you here, amigo? Not that it ain't great to see you after all these years."

Jason began his cover story, which like all the most effective ones, hewed close to the truth. "Just coincidence, is all. I did a concert down in Savannah last week and one of the people backstage said you lived close by. I'm up in Charleston, not that far away really, but I didn't know. Asked around a bit and got your address."

"Still with the music, eh? I gotta say, I left that behind years ago, although I still get people telling me they dug my sound. Royalties ain't much, but I get checks every so often. Even from those tunes you and I wrote. You too, I imagine."

"You were better at business than me. Sold my rights a while back."

X shook his head. His eyes danced with amusement. "Who woulda thunk it? You were the stable one. The smart guy. Intellectual. Dumb old me just took a flyer on a couple of California dudes who dug my music and boom. You probably don't know it, but I made a fortune as a big early investor in Apple. Life is so fucking random, ain't it?"

"You don't buy that old saying, *luck is the residue of design*?"

"Nope. Right place, right time, you're an Apple millionaire. Wrong place, wrong time --- you get knifed in the back. No reason why. No cosmic plan. Shit just happens."

X shrugged and raised his right hand in a helpless gesture. "Hey, I'm forgetting my manners. You want a drink? You were partial to bourbon, right? Got some Pappy Van Winkle. They tell me it's good stuff. Never developed a taste for that shit myself."

"It's not good stuff, Brandon. It's great stuff. I'll indulge, if you don't mind. Rocks."

"Coming up. Hey, man, if you don't mind, just call me X when people are around. Brandon's okay when we're alone. I know we go way back, but most people here don't even know who Brandon Xavier Murphy is."

"Sure. How many people *are* here, by the way?"

"Tonight? For dinner, you mean?"

"Well that, and just on a daily basis. Must take a small army to keep up this place."

"Very small. I have about ten guys who maintain the grounds. Four comely eastern European chicks maintain the pad and occasionally the master. Wink,

wink. Security? Just the twins. Front gate gets locked down at six. If people come after that, I can buzz them in. Like you tonight."

Jason's eyes glanced around while he did the math. Just polishing the furniture would take all week for a crew of maids. He guessed that most of the unoccupied rooms were neglected and cleaned only when guests were anticipated.

Black said, "I'm embarrassed I didn't ask before, X. Are you married?"

"Me? Nah. Man like me's got to ramble, dig? I sleep alone, can't stand someone snoring and thrashing next to me while I'm trying to cop Zs. How 'bout you?"

"Never. Guess I haven't found the right girl."

"Ha. That's what Merv Griffin used to ask Johnny Mathis whenever he had him on the show. *Still haven't found the right girl, eh Johnny?* Kind of an in joke between two old queens."

X handed Jason a generous pour of the bourbon in a heavy crystal glass. "Oops, I'm sorry, Jase. Are you gay, man? I never figured that with you but you always were a little sensitive."

"No, that's not it. Shrinks would tell you I had a bad experience with a woman when I was young and deep down, I don't trust any of them as a result. But I still get around some. A man has needs."

"Dig it."

"I'm a little curious about the security. I mean, they took my phone this afternoon. Escorted me up the driveway. Beautiful digs, by the way."

"Thankee. When you have a lotta bread, there's a lot a folks trying to reach into your pocket. No offense, but the cops down here aren't the brightest bulbs in the string. So I got my own insurance. Ain't nobody gonna fuck with the twins, that's for sure. Bourbon okay?"

"Best ever. So, who are we dining with?"

"Just the two of us, man. Catch up on old times. Great to see your face. Not many from our time still around. You making a living with your music still?"

"Not really. I do a few concerts, maybe ten a year. No real demand for what I do anymore."

"I see." A shadow fell across X's face and his pleasant mood turned dark. "See what I mean about money? You come here looking for a handout or something? Is that why you're here?"

"No, not at all. I got into another business, oh, twenty years or so ago. Re-habbing houses around Charleston. I make a good living doing that and I really like the work. I didn't come here for your money, Brandon."

"My bad. Sorry I accused ya. I'm just so fucking used to it. Hard to make new friends. You never know whether they're digging you or your bread. Fucking capitalism. That what's it's all about, ninety nine per cent of the time. Follow the goddam money."

"Say that again. Greed is good, the bastards say. About a hundred eighty degrees off what we were all about when we were making music."

X turned and walked to his desk. He pulled a gigantic joint from a carved wooden box and fired it up without asking. "Normally, I'd wait 'til after dinner but we're old friends and you don't mind, do ya? Take the edge off. Sure you don't want one? It's primo, not like that shit we smoked when we were kids."

"Booze'll do fine."

"Just got me aggravated for a bit, talking money. Sorry. I just fucking hate this system here, even though it's been good to me. I mean, I'm rolling in dough but it don't make me happy."

"Sorry to hear that. Most folks would kill to be you. You live in a beautiful place. You want for nothing. You have all the fame you want although I think we both know what that's worth."

"Yeah. Nothing. I saw through all that bullshit years ago. Assholes loving my music. I was never any good. I admit that now. Just thrashed out raw emotion. Pissed off the establishment. That was the only value in what I did. Told the truth about the government. What filthy whores they all are."

Jason saw his opening but was careful not to overplay it. "You got that right. Look at the idiot they elected president."

"He ain't so stupid. He sees this shit for what it is and he's taken advantage of it. But he's no different than all the rest. Talks a great game, but in the end, he's one of them."

"So what's the solution?"

There was a knock at the door. There was a petite woman in a French maid's outfit, down to the short puffy skirt, stiletto heels and fishnet stockings. A slender girl with oversized breasts, the kind X had liked when they were touring. Another Russian accent.

X smiled in appreciation. "Cool. Jason, we got lots to talk about and the whole night ahead. Let's eat."

27

"Aaron, it's me. Kat."

It was late in the evening and Aaron was at Jason's house, watching a Super Bowl preview on the NFL channel and tending to Jasper.

"Ah, so when the cat's away, eh? Old Jason's gone AWOL and you're looking for a real man to fill your needs."

Katrina was used to Aaron's flirtations and took them in stride. She knew if she ever agreed to one of his bawdy suggestions, he'd scramble away as fast as his ancient legs could carry him. But she wasn't in the mood for his insinuations, even on the phone.

She said, "Aaron, this is serious. Jason left a letter for me."

"He told me he did. Said you weren't to open it unless you hadn't heard from him in two days.

"That's what his instructions were. Sorry, but I ignored them."

"My, my. You *are* a headstrong girl. You might want to reconsider that if you ever want to get a ring. Just saying."

"Thanks for the fatherly advice. How many wives have you had? Three at last count, unless you're holding out."

"Shows I have a lot of experience in these matters. So why the call, if not for booty?"

"Jason is doing undercover work for the feds. It's dangerous, much more than he thinks."

Aaron knew that to be true but didn't want to further panic Kat. "He's a big boy, Kat. He knows what he's getting into."

"I don't think he does. Did he tell you anything specific?"

"Just that he was supposed to dig up some dirt on an old friend of his."

"Yeah, well that old friend is a bad man. Brandon X Murphy or Brand X as he calls himself."

"I've heard of him. Some heavy metal trip from the eighties, as I recall. Harmless enough, unless you're worried about losing your hearing at one of his shows. I thought he was dead, tell the truth."

This is why Aaron and Jason get along so well, Kat thought. They both take life as it comes. But they are hard headed and oblivious to pitfalls. So far, the worst that had happened as a result of their feckless behavior was losing a few grand on a project. The stakes were higher now and Aaron had to take this more seriously.

Kat said, "I ran into a couple of X's boys at a rally last year. It was about taking down those Confederate statues. You can guess what side I was on. There were these twins there on the other side, against us. Big ex-military goons. Neo-Nazis and proud of it. Swastika tats, the works. They got in my face, taunting, calling me names. I thought for a minute it'd come to blows with my people."

"Sounds like them Nazi creeps. Hit a defenseless woman."

"I wasn't exactly defenseless. I have a concealed carry permit. They were bragging about Brand X and how he has their back. My point is, if Jason is working undercover on X for the FBI, these guys would swat him like a mosquito and think nothing of it. X lives in a big compound in Hardeeville. Lots of places to bury a body without a trace."

"Come on, Kat. The feds aren't stupid. They wouldn't send him in without backup. Or some kind of plan."

"That's just it, Aaron. Jason said this was a tight operation and he was going in alone. And he didn't fully trust this FBI guy who sent him in. I couldn't figure out why he'd volunteer for this and now I know. He was blackmailed into it. The man threatened to deport Paco. And dig up dirt on Jason with women he knew when he was a pop star. He's a damn builder, for God's sake, not a spy. He makes one false move and these bastards will kill him."

Aaron Hendricks had his own agenda but he knew that Kat was not one to sit still when she saw something she didn't like. "He told me it was low risk, high reward, was how he put it."

"His letter also said he was leaving his portfolio to me and the business to you. You don't do that unless you're thinking you may not come back."

He needed to find out what else Kat was thinking. "So what do you want to do?"

"He gave me the FBI guy's name and number. I tried calling it. No answer, not even voice mail. Just rang and rang. If Jason calls for help and he gets the same response, he's screwed."

"So I'll ask again, what do you want to do?"

"I think we need to get to the closest FBI branch office or whatever the hell they call it and warn them. Pull Jason out."

"Kat, they ain't gonna tell us about an ongoing investigation just because we're friends with Jason. They'll deny everything. And even if they don't, they'd tell you they know about the danger and they have it covered. Nothing we can do."

"If you won't come with me, I'll go myself. I can't let the man I love walk into a situation like this and do nothing."

He was a fool to let this woman go, Aaron thought.

"I'll go with you, Kat but I'm telling you, it's a waste of time."

"Maybe it is. But if anything happens to Jason and we could have stopped it, I couldn't live with myself."

"Jason told me once you got a burr under your saddle, you never quit. How many brassieres did you burn, back in the day? And what cup size were they? Just curious."

28

The dining room wasn't outsize in proportion to the rest of the house. It could comfortably accommodate twenty people but it was not the grand banquet hall that Jason had imagined. The walls were covered with shiplap pine up to a high plate shelf, devoid of plates. It was nicely done, just not the opulent dining space that a mansion of this magnitude would normally boast.

The room was painted white with dark stained oak floors. Jason expected an Oriental rug to add a splash of color, but the surface was bare. No paintings or tapestries adorned the walls and the space looked rather stark as a result. He sensed that the room was rarely used. There were hints of deferred maintenance.

He hoped that X would give him a tour of the mansion later, where his builder's mind could sketch out a rough floor plan. That would help if he needed a path to the inner sanctum at some point to unearth X's secrets.

They finished the first course, an excellent bisque with a creamy tomato base. It contained chunks of lobster, which told Jason that X's vegetarianism was restricted to mammals not crustaceans. Making conversation, Jason said, "Have you given up on music entirely, or do you still dabble?"

"I just noodle when I'm bored and that ain't often. I keep busy. What about you? I'm curious as to why you even bother. No offense, but playing in front of small audiences must be a little humiliating considering."

"In a way, I suppose it is but even though the numbers are smaller, the ones who do come appreciate it. I guess it's like a hobby these days. Like George W. Bush painting."

"That loser. He's what pushed me over the edge when it came to being interested in politics again."

X had told him earlier he was proud that his music in the eighties trashed the establishment. This sounded like those leanings had blossomed.

Jason said, "You thinking of running for office?"

"No, no, no. Nothing like that. No way do I get into that crooked game. I want to bring the whole system crashing down. Oh, here's the main course. I think you'll dig it. No meat, but I guarantee you won't miss it. Thanks, Alexa."

The dinnerware wasn't fine china or anything formal. It featured a Southwestern motif, lots of cobalt blue and orange, out of place in the hoity-toity surroundings. X did provide an excellent wine for his guest, a Cakebread Cabernet Benchland Select. Kat would probably say that a red was not an appropriate pairing for lobster, but Jason didn't care. He finished the entire bottle over the course of the meal without realizing it.

He waited until the help departed before saying, "Back to what we were talking about before. Are you talking revolution, Brandon? We tried that and it didn't work unfortunately."

"Nothing that simple. What I have in mind is a lot more complicated and will take a lot more time. I really don't want to talk about it. No offense, but my philosophy scares a lot of people who don't understand it. Let's get reacquainted before we go down that road, brother."

"Hey, I hate the system as much as the next guy. You remember our all nighters back when we toured together? The system only works for the rich. No offense to you, but you fit that bill now."

"Yeah, power to the people. I mean Jase, you don't seem to have changed much from our wild and crazy days and you sure wrote some tunes boning the man. But I'm not just some kid fucking around now. A lot of people would consider what I'm doing crazy. That's all I'll say."

Jason tucked into the main course and found it to be as delicious as X had promised. He said so, and between bites, they spent the next few minutes talking about food.

He'd heard enough from X to believe that Gilmore's instincts were right about the man. But loose talk about anarchy didn't equal proof of anything. Brandon had always been prone to exaggeration. Having fabulist ideas about breaking down the system isn't against the law in a democracy, otherwise John Lennon would have been imprisoned for writing *Imagine*.

Coffee was served with an elaborate flan, although in these surroundings, it would be called crème brulee. X suggested they retreat to his study and when they did, he offered Jason another fat spliff.

Jason said, "As tempting as it is, I'll pass. I have to drive home tonight and I'm afraid I've already overindulged."

"You're not driving home tonight, amigo. Cops around here are big on stopping us old hipsters. Talk about profiling. You blow over the limit and you won't be driving for a year. Uh uh, buddy, you're staying over. I insist."

Jason had a high tolerance for alcohol. He functioned satisfactorily when over the legal limit, but X was correct. It wasn't worth the risk and it gave him an opportunity to dig further into his target's psyche.

"Thanks for the offer. One thing though, if I take you up on it, I need to use my phone. I have someone expecting me back home tonight and they'll call out the National Guard if I don't show up. And I do have some morning appointments in Charleston I'll need to move around."

"You can use the land line here."

"Hate to admit it X, but I'm a child of technology now. I don't remember phone numbers. I just have them on speed dial or in my directory. Even my chick's. Pretty pathetic, but it is what it is."

X thought for a moment. He pursed his lips and squinted at Jason, as if evaluating whether he trusted the man. He let out a loud belch and lit his joint.

After taking a long drag, he said, "I guess it'd be all right for an old mate like you. But no pictures, please. And nothing on social media about tonight. Those are my terms."

"Jesus, X, why so paranoid? Your secrets are safe with me, whatever they are. We're old friends, aren't we?"

"That we are, Bubba, that we are. Thing is, if you do what I warned you not to, I'd have to kill you."

Jason smiled at his host's joke, but X did not return the look. It didn't appear that he was kidding.

29

Jason decided not to do anything right away with the phone that X had reluctantly returned to him. Contacting Gilmore was out of the question, since he was sure that his call would be monitored. That would blow the whole operation out of the water. Besides, there was little to report, other than that Gilmore's suspicions were legitimate.

He wanted to call Aaron to let him know all was well. Kat was a worry-wart and would welcome his assurances. He knew that she'd try to pump him for more information and that if he couldn't dance around it, his cover might be blown. Better to err on the side of caution and postpone both calls until he knew the lay of the land better.

Jason doubted that the aging rocker would be capable of murder, but the threat could not be ignored. As he lay on the king sized bed in the mansion's sumptuous guest room, unable to sleep, he contemplated his next move. X had told him that breakfast was served in the dining room at seven thirty sharp, and that he could come down for coffee at seven if he was an early riser.

Jason was certain that the house had elaborate security measures, given Brandon's penchant for privacy. There had to be cameras in the hallways, alarms on the windows and doors. It seemed like overkill if the concern was theft. The guitars were the most likely targets of an *Oceans Eleven* type caper, but they must be insured and numbered. As such, they would be hard to fence, given the plethora of counterfeit items out there. X was never one for jewelry. Black saw no extraordinary works of art adorning the walls, not that he was an expert. The few signed Peter Max posters weren't worth the risk and expense of planning a sophisticated heist. Maybe the man kept a lot of cash or bearer bonds in a safe.

The door to his room wasn't locked from the outside, but he felt like a prisoner nonetheless. He didn't see any obvious surveillance inside the room --- it was either disguised or deemed unnecessary given the other measures in effect. He assumed he was being watched. He was becoming as paranoid as his host and he didn't like the feeling.

~~~~~

Aaron and Katrina were up at dawn and on the road to Savannah. She had tried Gilmore a number of times and gotten the same result: no answer. Aaron told her he believed the trip to be a fool's errand, but there was enough gallantry left in him to insist that Katrina McCann not confront the FBI alone.

The office was located on one of the town's many squares in a nondescript building that could have housed a dental practice. According to the FBI website,
~~~~~

there was one agent in charge and three lesser functionaries. The main branch servicing the region was in Atlanta, a five hour drive. The op could be run from there, Kat supposed, but it made more sense from a location closer to the site.

The receptionist took their names and said that someone would be with them presently. That someone was an attractive young agent named Sarah Bernstein. She wore a crisply tailored skirt and a plain white silk blouse. Her appearance and demeanor suggested a Hollywood actress portraying an FBI agent as opposed to the real thing. She seemed green and eager to please, like a Golden Retriever. Not exactly what Kat expected.

After introductions, agent Bernstein asked, "So, Mr. Hendricks and Ms. McCann, how can I help you this morning? Glad that cold snap finally broke and we have some nicer weather."

Aaron looked over to Kat, who took the lead. She said, "Yes. Let me get right to the point. I'm sure your time is valuable and you're a busy woman."

Bernstein nodded pleasantly.

"A good friend and associate of ours was recruited by one of your colleagues to go undercover against a man named Brandon Xavier Murphy, who lives in Hardeeville. We believe our friend is in danger and was forced to do this against his wishes. We haven't heard from him and we fear the worst."

Sarah looked as if she was paying strict attention and shared their concern. When Kat finished her preamble, Sarah said, "Ms. McCann, if in fact this is an undercover operation, we can't just tell anyone who walks in off the street about it. And in saying that, I'm not acknowledging that any such operation exists. I'm just speaking theoretically. It's not that I doubt your sincerity, but this type of thing would be carefully planned and executed to protect all involved."

Kat was deliberate, trying not to show her contempt for the bureaucratic double speak. "Yes, we figured you'd say that. But I have a letter from our friend spelling out the entire mission and how he was lured into it. It appears appropriate safeguards weren't taken."

"People, that's not the way it works. We're very careful to follow strict procedures when mounting any such activity. We almost never recruit amateurs. If we do, it must be approved at a high level. We don't put civilians at risk without protection. Our agents just don't go rogue, that's the stuff of spy novelists. If your friend wrote you a letter suggesting otherwise, I would question his stability, to be honest."

"My 'friend' is one of the most stable people I know. You may have heard of him. Jason Black."

"The old rock star? That Jason Black? If I'm thinking of the same man, didn't he write anti-government protest songs? Forgive me but that's hardly someone I'd call stable. Sounds more like someone with a grudge against the establishment."

Katrina said, "People change. Jason is a reputable builder who dabbles in music. He's never lied to either of us."

"May I see the letter?"

"We're prepared to let you see it. But be aware that I've made copies and I'm not shy about going to the media with them if you don't respond."

"Again, the FBI doesn't participate in nefarious conspiracies, no matter what you see on television. We have checks and balances every step of the way. I wouldn't think of destroying your letter. Please show me that respect."

Aaron spoke for the first time. "No disrespect intended, ma'am. My friend Katrina is a little emotional at the moment. She's had contact with some of the characters involved on the other side and she's worried that Mr. Black is playing out of his league going against them."

"If I may read the letter, please?"

Katrina handed her a copy, which Sarah perused, her face set firmly. These were not wild-eyed conspiracy nuts. They had evidence to back their claim.

As she read over the pages, it appeared that their fears had substance. She didn't think this kind of operation would have been approved by a responsible superior. Something else had to be going on. After reading the entire missive, she put it aside and stared ahead in silence.

She said, "There are some troubling allegations here. I'm not going to comment any further. I'm going to share this with the agent in charge. I'd appreciate it if you would wait here until he decides on an appropriate course of action."

30

Sarah Bernstein's boss was a man on the rise. The forty two year old Jed Sanford had a law degree from Yale. He had risen up the ranks in deliberate fashion, every step of the way gaining the respect of his superiors, who ticketed him for greater things. His mother and father both had extensive backgrounds in public service and their mixed race marriage had thrived for over five decades. The early years of their union weren't without their issues in the deep South, but they had overcome.

Sanford was an easy guy to work for, unless you thought you could get by with less than your best effort. He had a low tolerance for slackers and career bureaucrats. There was a high initial churn rate under him at every stop until he was able to employ his kind of people. Once you gained his trust, he had your back.

He got things done. His rising star would soon take him another rung up the ladder. Atlanta was the next logical step, then a posting in Washington.

He had an authentic open door policy which Sarah had frequently taken advantage of. They had a solid working relationship: she came to him for counsel and he made it easy for her be honest, even if it made her look bad. His critiques were never mean spirited, his advice constructive. He was clearly her boss, but he guided her with patience of a loving parent, no yelling or personal attacks.

She tapped on his open door and he waved her in. He wore three piece suits, even in the summer. His office was spare, not a paper out of place or a hint of clutter anywhere. Although the offices were smoke-free, he occasionally lit a celebratory cigar after hours, the most serious breach she could imagine him committing. As a result, the place smelled of lilacs, a plug-in air freshener attempting to cover the scent.

He said, “So young Sarah, what’s on your mind? You deal with those nut jobs from Charleston?”

“That’s why I wanted to talk to you, sir. They may not be nut jobs.”

She sketched out their allegations, without using the name of the agent who had originated the inquiry. When she finished, Sanford asked, “And did this high ranking official have a name?”

She had no choice but to tell him. “His name is Richard Gilmore. He’s a deputy assistant director.”

“Stop right there. You obviously haven’t seen this morning’s briefing memo.”

“Not yet, sir. I usually read it first thing but you assigned me these people from Charleston.”

“Interesting coincidence, although I don’t believe in coincidences. Richard Gilmore was found dead in his car late last night.”

“Oh, my God. Was he murdered?”

“Heart attack, at least that’s the pre-lim.”

“I’m so sorry. The two people waiting in the conference room have a letter from a Jason Black, alleging that he was trying to get some dirt on him to get him to work an undercover op. The letter says..."

"Do you have the letter, Agent Bernstein?"

"I do."

"Then let me read it for myself, sparing your interpretation." He realized that sounded harsh to his young charge, so he walked it back. "Which I'll be happy to entertain later."

She handed him the letter and he read it in silence, his only reaction being an occasional raised eyebrow or soft sigh. When he was finished, he said, "So Richard Gilmore was conducting an undercover investigation involving this Brandon X Murphy. Sarah, I'll admit I'm not much of a politician. If I was, my career probably would have advanced faster than it has, not that I'm complaining."

She bobbed her head slowly as he went off on this tangent, wondering where it would lead.

Sanford said, "I find it odd that Washington would authorize such an operation without reading us in first. I'd speculate that there's one of two possibilities. First, that this is so big and so sensitive that they don't trust us --- it's that far over our head. Maybe the CIA and Homeland Security are involved. Or second, that Gilmore did this on his own. I did see a report that a junkie the locals had detained said that something was afoul at Murphy's place. Involving suitcases full of cash and people with foreign accents. I gave it zero credibility. If this letter is real, apparently this Gilmore took it seriously and was trying to gather more evidence. Frankly, I'd never heard of him before the death notice, but that's not uncommon in a big bureaucracy. Details were pretty sparse, it just called him veteran agent Richard Gilmore. No bio or arrangements."

"So what do I tell those people waiting in the conference room? The woman said if we didn't do something right away, she'd go public. She's an impressive lady and I'd think she'd get in the door on her looks alone. Even if the papers and TV don't respond, social media would be her next resort. That could blow any clandestine operation clean out of the water, sir."

"Right. We have no legal avenue to detain them. I could try to get a court order to keep them under wraps, but I couldn't even begin to make *that* case. They'd laugh me out of the room."

"I think that they're really just worried about their friend's safety. Apparently this Murphy character has neo-Nazis working for him."

Sanford came as close to shouting in frustration as she'd ever heard him. "Damn, those idiots again. Sarah, let me make a few calls. See if I can find out if DC knows anything that they can tell us. Maybe they already have agents in place. They may stonewall, but I can try. If I tell them we're ready to jump in, they may fess up to keep us from messing up their plan."

"What do I tell this McCann woman and her friend?"

"Not you. *We* tell them that we're taking them seriously but if they try to do anything on their own, they might endanger Black further. They need to trust us. We're on the case. In the meeting, just go along with what I say. Have I ever lied to you?

"No, sir. Never."

"And I'm not about to start now. We need to get to the bottom of this. We can't risk queering a major op, but if Gilmore was acting as a lone wolf on flimsy evidence, I'm not going to risk the life of an innocent civilian he conned into doing his bidding. Jed Sanford is going to insert his black ass squarely in the line of fire. Count on it."

31

This is starting to become a habit. A bad habit, Jason thought. Like the last few nights, he lay awake until four thirty before drifting off. Combined with the fitful rest he had gotten after breaking with X at midnight, he had gotten about four hours of sleep before he awoke at seven. Not nearly enough.

He took a shower in the luxurious guest bathroom. Marble penny tile dotted the shower floor. Furniture grade his-and-her vanities with glass vessel sinks. He thought he'd seen just about every kind of faucet made, but these were new to him. European. Swedish, he guessed. Even as an experienced contractor, it took him a moment to figure out how they worked. The towels were heated, as were the travertine floors beneath his bare feet. X had spared no expense to make his guests comfortable.

The bathroom was stocked with all kinds of soaps, toothpastes, shampoos, conditioners and shaving butter. In short, anything an overnight guest might need. Jason was grateful because he hadn't brought any of these items with him, since he hadn't anticipated staying over.

When he made his way to the dining room at seven, coffee and cinnamon rolls were waiting. The coffee was served in a large silver urn, containing over a gallon of fragrant Kona blend. Real cream and unrefined sugar were laid out in a similar elegant fashion.

He normally opted for a more nutritious breakfast than sugary pastry, but they smelled so good that resistance was futile. He sampled one of the sticky rolls and it was delicious.

X came down a few minutes later, freshly scrubbed and smelling of Aramis. Was fruity cologne for men back in and had he missed the trend? Dressed in black jeans and a Led Zeppelin tee shirt, X seemed chipper and ready to take on the day.

He said, "Sleep well, Jase? Accommodations up to your standards?"

"I'm getting a glimpse of how the other half lives. Or should I say the other one per cent."

"What can I say? I'm doing my part for the people, man, but that's no reason I can't live large. Let me ask you, how did you get into this house flipping business? Looks pretty easy on TV. One of the chicks I'm with loves that *This Old House* show."

"*One* of the chicks? Lucky man."

"Hey, comes with the territory. So come on, tell me about your business."

"Well, the trick is finding the right properties. It's like the perfect storm. You've got to buy right. Get a place that needs work in a good neighborhood. Find a seller who has to get out and needs cash in a hurry. And you have to make smart calls on what buyers are looking for at any given time. For example, women are big on white kitchens these days. Ten years ago, darker wood was in and you couldn't give white away."

Another supermodel maid came in and X ordered breakfast, too softly for Jason to overhear. When the girl left, X said, "Hope you don't mind. I ordered one of my special omelets for you. I promise you'll like it but if it doesn't light your fire, we'll make you up whatever your little ole heart desires. So back to your biz, you kind of exploit folks when they're in a bad way, no?"

"That's a little strong. I look at it like I give them a way out. A lot of the properties I get are so rundown that nobody other than rehabbers wants them. I buy foreclosures too. So if I'm screwing anybody, it's the bankers and that doesn't bother me at all."

"Right on, brother. Fuck them. You do the work yourself or hire it out?"

"I do a lot of it myself. The more sweat equity I put in, the more profit I take out. I have a couple of guys I work with who're pretty versatile. I rarely have to bring in high priced tradesmen. Why so curious?"

"Dude. This place is cool. I just have to keep it all polished up and stuff. But there are three houses on the property that the original developer built. I use them for my outdoor maintenance staff, you dig?"

"Got it. So it's just the ladies staying in the main house?"

"Right." He wiped his mouth with a cloth napkin and tossed it back on the table. "Those digs were built by what I guess you'd call a hack builder. Not real high quality. Disposable, like a lot of shit in this country. Planned obsolescence. Anyway, things are constantly breaking down in them."

The food came and like the previous evening's fare, it lived up to its billing. Jason couldn't place all the ingredients, but the omelet was even better than Kat's, and that was going some. He told X how much he liked it.

"Beats the shit they served backstage at our shows, that's for sure," X said. "So bro, here's what I'm thinking. How much you pulling down a year, doing what you're doing? Ballpark, like."

"Varies. I don't need a lot. I do three or four projects a year."

"Like in dollars, man."

"After expenses, I net maybe ninety, give or take. Why?"

"Let's say I put you on retainer for one fifty for a year. You get those pads up to speed. Also keep tabs on anything in the big house that needs fixing. No budget, just spend whatever it takes. Then we talk about another position in my organization if things work out. What do you say?"

"What kind of position? No offense, but at my age, I don't fancy being some kind of high paid handyman."

"That ain't what I have in mind. Look man, I don't want to make any promises but I think you and I see eye to eye on a lot of things. We get to know each other better, there's a lot we can do together. My whole operation is in for reorganization. The timing of your visit may be perfect. I'd love to have a right hand man I can trust. You helped me big-time when I was burning out. I'd like to return the favor. What do you think?"

32

"What the hell do you think is going on?" Aaron said.

Kat had noticed that while reading the letter, Bernstein's attitude had changed from that of an underling performing a rote assignment. She was taking them seriously now, but to what end?

She said, "If my instincts are right, they're coming up with a story to cover their collective Federal asses. Maybe even finding a way to shut us up."

"You think we should leave right now and not give 'em that chance?"

"My guess is that Agent Bernstein's boss will be dealing with us now. If this really is a national security issue, he's got to have a handle on it. Too big for a rookie to deal with. He probably figured she could blow us off, but we came prepared."

"Shh. Looks like you're right. Here they come."

Jed Sanford and Sarah Bernstein marched into the room with grave looks on their faces. Sarah introduced Sanford as the agent in charge of the Savannah field office of the Federal Bureau of Investigation.

If the formal title was designed to intimidate, it didn't work. The two feds sat beside each other at the conference table, across from Aaron and Kat.

Sanford began, "I appreciate your concern in bringing this to our attention. However, this puts us in an awkward position. We have no legal standing to enter this man Murphy's compound. There is no clear and present threat to Mr. Black that we can ascertain."

Katrina said, "Gilmore thought that something crooked was happening there. I told Ms. Bernstein about the neo-Nazis. Jason is *not* a professional when it comes to your line of work. His very presence there puts him in danger."

"I understand, but he did enter voluntarily, despite the suggestion that he was, shall we say, persuaded."

"Voluntarily? Blackmailed by Gilmore, you mean."

Sanford shot Bernstein a look. "I'm afraid that this is complicated by the fact that Mr. Gilmore has suffered a fatal heart attack. He died late last night."

Kat said, "I'm sorry about your man but that's all the more reason to pull the plug. What if X found out that this Gilmore was onto him and had him killed? Get Jason out of there. If you don't have enough evidence to go in, we will."

Jed Sanford had modeled his style after "no-drama" Obama. He remained calm, even though he would have liked to lock these prying fools away for a day or two.

He kept his voice calm. "That's not an action I'd advise, Ms. McCann. If there is real danger, at best all you'd be doing is giving Murphy two more hostages. And if the man is just minding his own business and these suspicions are baseless, he could sue you. That is, if you survive a tussle with his security people. If they are neo-Nazis as you allege, they won't hesitate to shoot you if you trespass. Since that state has *stand your ground* statutes, they'd be within their rights."

"So what do you suggest? We're not going to let this stand without doing something, with all due respect." The way she spat out the words, *due respect* was clearly absent.

"Do you have any way to contact Mr. Black?"

"No. I tried his phone and it went straight to voice mail. I just said to call me. I was afraid if they had his phone, they'd know he was there undercover if I said more. If you guys had your shit together, you'd have a another way to get in touch."

"No reason to resort to ad hominem attacks, Ms. McCann. We're on the same side here."

"Are we? Seems to me that your priority is your precious operation and ours is to see that our friend is safe. This letter tells me that you people forced him into doing this and you don't place a very high value on his life."

"Please, Ms. McCann. That is totally against what we stand for. Mr. Gilmore might have merely been emphasizing how important it was for him to cooperate."

Kat bit her lip. Jason hadn't included the specific threat to deport Paco in his letter. He didn't want anyone in authority who might read it to use Paco's situation as a wedge against them later. Aaron agreed they shouldn't mention it unless it was vital to save Jason's life. After a brief stare down, Kat said, "I'm still waiting to hear your plan to extricate him."

"Give me some time. We can't just go in, guns blazing. I think you'd agree with that. I'm sure I will be speaking with the agent next in line after Mr. Gilmore shortly. He or she might already have a backup plan in motion. If not, I'll stress the urgency of removing our asset and we'll go from there."

Kat gave him her toughest look. Powerful men had wilted under less. "You have until noon to come up with a plan to get your 'asset' out. After that, I can't say what we'll do next. All options will be on the table and we won't be consulting the likes of you."

Sanford sighed. "Let me stress that if you're thinking of doing anything extra legal, it'll be my duty to stop you with every means at my disposal. Failing that, I'll arrest you after the fact. As much as I sympathize with your concerns, I can't abide vigilantism."

"Duly noted. Good day. Aaron, we're out of here." With that, they both stood and left the room. After a couple of wrong turns negotiating their way out of the complex, they were back on the street. No one followed them.

Sarah's mouth was agape at this ballsy woman. She had encountered activists before, but none so determined as Katrina McCann. She suspected that she and Jason were more than just good friends.

She said, "Sir, what do we do? We can't have her and that old man trying to break into the compound to rescue their friend. It's a suicide mission. And it sounds like that's what they're planning to do."

"She's bluffing. That lady talks a good game, but I bet the idea of going up against Nazis has her peeing in her pants."

"Forgive me sir, but that's sexist."

"Not at all. That prospect might have me peeing in my pants, although I'd never admit it."

"You didn't tell me before we came in --- do you have the name of the next agent in charge of this operation?"

"That's just it. There is none. Nobody in DC knew anything about this."

"They could be covering it up."

"I don't think so. Before we came in, I made a call up there. I made it clear that something embarrassing and at worst, tragic could happen if this goes off the rails. They insisted that no one had authorized any activity against Brandon Murphy. They clammed up when I mentioned Gilmore's name. Really odd the way it brought the conversation to an abrupt end."

"Are you thinking this wasn't authorized?"

"I think it's possible that Gilmore did go rogue. My man up there said we should stay out of it. But it's on us to clean up the mess in our own backyard. Jason Black's name still carries some weight. If he comes to harm because of this, Washington will have a lot of explaining to do."

33

Aaron and Kat weren't familiar with Savannah, but they found a Starbucks just around the corner from the FBI office. They had missed the morning rush, so there were only a few scattered student-types there using free wi-fi. They were able to settle in without feeling rushed.

Aaron said, "So Gilmore is dead. Only met the man once, when he came by looking for Jason. Didn't look sick or nothing. Goes to show, you never can tell."

"That's an uplifting thought. Look, here's the bottom line for me. I don't trust the feds. That whole scam they tried to play on Jason was dirty pool, whether it was Gilmore acting on his own or someone above him authorized it. We have to make a plan to get him out of there. We can't wait until they do something. I know the way the bureaucracy works. They'll stall and equivocate as long as they can, and meanwhile Jason is out there naked to the world."

"So what do we do?"

"We need a way into the compound. I agree with Sanford that we can't just shoot our way in. But there's got to be a way to get in on some phony pretense. Murphy was a rock star way back when. His music was shit but that's beside the point. There's got to be stuff about him all over the web."

Aaron said, "What are you talking about? Pretend we head the Savannah chapter of the Brand X Fan Club?"

"No. I'm thinking stuff about his family or friends. If he has parents still alive or siblings, we could use them to get in. Some kind of family emergency or something. Worth a try. My laptop's in the car. See what you can dig up and I'll try to come up with something else."

The old man was impressed by her doggedness. "Jason's lucky to have you, Kat. I ever tell you that?"

"He doesn't *have* me. Whatever. He thinks you're pretty handy to have around, too. Let's get to work."

~~~~~

X was laying on the charm, much heavier than he had the previous evening, when he had chosen his words carefully about his ultimate mission with Jason.

They were in a tricked up golf cart, on a tour of the grounds. Eventually, they would reach the tract built homes that needed rehabilitation, but for now, they were enjoying the warming sun and Lowcountry scenery.

Jason said, "You know, I really should be going soon. I'll think about your offer, promise. By the way, thanks for giving my phone back but I can't get a signal."

"Oops, I should have mentioned that. We have lousy cell service here. You need a booster. It runs
~~~~~

through the wi-fi system in the house and some hot spots they've set up around the property. Calls get shifted to the internet, VOIP or some technical shit I don't understand. All I know is it works great."

Jason was suspicious, feeling that routing calls through Brandon's computer system would make it easier to monitor them. He didn't know exactly how it worked either, but he would be even more careful about calling out.

He felt that he had established a small amount of trust with X, so he should be able to leave now and return when he needed to. He'd report his findings to Gilmore. It wasn't enough to obtain a warrant, but the G-man would have some further ideas on what he needed to make that possible.

Jason said, "After this little ride, I'll be on my way then. I really appreciate the hospitality and the offer, Brandon."

"I'd like you to stay until after lunch, Jase. I have some friends coming in I'd like you to meet. Shouldn't be a problem to hang 'til then, no?"

"I'll need to make a call to my rehab partner. We had some appointments today but I think he can handle them on his own. I just need to let him know."

"No problemo, bro. Just so happens we're right near a hotspot now. I'll give you the visitor code and you should be able to call out."

"Thanks."

They pulled up to a maintenance shed. In addition to storing the equipment needed to service the property, it was also a wi-fi hotspot.

After giving Jason the passcode, X sat in the cart checking his smart phone while Jason walked away to make the call. Black assumed that it was being monitored somehow, somewhere. He'd try to speak in code and pray that this S.O.S. worked better than a message in a bottle.

Voice mail. Katrina kept her phone buried in her chaotic purse and rarely picked up in time.

"Kat, it's me Jason. Can't get away now, much as I'd like to. You'll have to work solo. Sorry. When I was at Richie G's a few days ago, I noticed what looked like black mold. You can tell him that it is mold and that we should get it out ASAP. Very unhealthy. Looks like they used unqualified workers, too. Probably illegals. The report's in that envelope I left for you so you can share it with him. I'll try to meet you there but it may be beyond my control. Don't call me back, bad cell service here. I'll try you again later. Thanks."

He didn't notice that X had crept up behind him and had been close enough to overhear. He was starting to feel uncomfortable around X. Something was off about the man, despite his affable demeanor. It seemed false.

X said, "Everything okay?"

"Uh, yeah, I think so. You good?"

"I can't wait for you to meet my friends later. I think you're in for a big surprise."

That's exactly what Jason was afraid of.

34

"I think we have a way in, Aaron," Kat said.

"Good, because I haven't been able to think of anything. You heard Jason's message. It sounds to me like he's being held there against his will. We need to listen to it again and see if he was trying to tell us anything more. He was obviously afraid someone would hear what he was saying, so he was talking in some sort of code."

"Richie G is Gilmore. Illegals means Russians *are* there. He wanted me to open the letter he left. Of course, he didn't know I already had. Black mold?"

"Get it out, ASAP. Might mean get him out. He doesn't know Gilmore's dead, because it sounds like he wanted us to contact him."

They had taken a room at an executive motel in Bluffton, not far from where Gilmore had booked himself and Jason. They had no intention of spending the night there, but needed a base of operations close to the compound. Aaron put it on the company's tab. Saving the life of the LLC's CEO was a legit business expense, he figured.

Katrina said, "I got in touch with Julius and he'll be here later this afternoon. Jules is a computer whiz, and it took him no time to get us a lead."

"Kat, if this really is dangerous, do you want to get those boys involved? One of the reasons Jason agreed to take this assignment was to protect them, especially Paco. Gilmore threatened to have him deported."

She held her palm up. "They both said they'd do anything for Jason. Let's come up with a plan first, then we can assign roles. Paco can take care of Jasper and hold down the fort at home, but we might need Julius' muscle and computer skills on site."

"So what do you have?"

"Brandon X. Murphy, is actually the third. His dad, Brandon the second, is 85 and in a nursing home near here. Mid to late stage of Alzheimers. X is footing the bill for his care."

"Of course."

Kat said, "Not so of course. X hated his father. Don't need to get into all of it now, but basically he had to be shamed into supporting the old fella."

"How the hell did you get all this?"

"Julius made Facebook friends with Murphy's sister, Sofia. She's real active blogging with that social media crap. And he says she's to the left of me when it comes to causes. But she also spills a lot of personal shit, especially about her bro. She's not on good terms with old X. Hasn't seen her brother face to face in years."

Aaron nodded. "Talk about a dysfunctional family."

"That's our opening. If we can somehow convince the sister to help us get into the compound, we can do the rest on our own."

“Not to scare you, but I should give Julius the combination to my gun safe so he can bring some metal.”

“Jesus, Aaron. I thought we weren’t going in guns blazing.”

“Right. But once we’re in, we may need ‘em. You ever handle a gun?”

“This may shock you, but I have a concealed carry permit. A single woman running a restaurant, working after hours on weekends? I felt I needed protection so I took some courses. Proud to say I was best in class.”

“This ain’t a dog show, lady. If we’re dealing with them white supremacist assholes, no telling what we’ll need to do. I’m hoping it doesn’t come down to a fight and we can get Jase out without blood being spilled. Especially mine. Oh, and yours too.”

“So how do we approach the sister?”

“That’s your bailiwick.”

Kat thought for a moment. “Seems like she just does social causes. I’m thinking she’s on her brother’s tab, even though they don’t get along. Jules couldn’t find an employer for her. Maybe if I call and explain the deal, sister to sister, she’ll help us.”

“Or warn her brother instead.” Aaron smacked his lips, a popping sound. “Kat, I have a way with the ladies, but this is more up your alley. You make the call. But be careful.”

~~~~~
~~~~~

Jason had seen worse. "You're right, X. Those houses are in bad shape. But nothing I can't handle. Depends on how much you want to spend and how soon you need it done."

"We can talk about that later."

X gunned the electric golf cart full speed as they headed back to the mansion. The skies had brightened, burning off the morning fog. Jason had taken off his jacket and was starting to sweat. He wasn't sure whether it was the warming temperature or his discomfort about X.

The houses *were* deplorable. There were probably a dozen workers staying in the two shabbier ones. They had started out as three bedroom basic homes, less than two thousand square feet. There were bunk beds in each bedroom. The kitchens were small and outdated, probably original. The paint was faded and the walls were scarred with dents and nail pops. Popcorn ceilings masked the sloppy finish work above.

Jason said, "If you don't mind me asking, how do these people live like that? I must have seen a hundred Palmetto bugs crawling around those first two houses."

"Call 'em what they are, pal. They're cockroaches. These guys are used to it. Compared to where they come from, this is like a luxury spa, man."

"Tell me if it's none of my business, but are they here legally?"

"Shit, no. And if you're going to ask me next what I pay them --- they're making decent bread. I got a way to funnel a big chunk of their paycheck back home, without the U.S. government getting its filthy paws on it. Hey man, tell me about how you got involved in the peace movement way back when. You must have told me but it's been a lot of years."

Here was an opening. If Gilmore had the power to deport Paco, he certainly could call in the troops to bust the illegals on this property. He hoped it would only be a pretense to investigate X further and that the workers might find asylum.

He said, "Not much to tell. I was a regular college kid, tweed jackets, pledging a fraternity and all. My dad was a police chief, small Long Island town. Never gave much thought to politics other than idolizing JFK like the rest of my family. Raised Catholic and all."

"The Donna Reed Show. And you were little Jeff Stone. Or maybe more like Ricky Nelson."

"Nope, not either really. I had a guitar. Took a few lessons but I wasn't real good. My senior year in high school, I actually played and sang at the talent show, one of my own songs. I wanted to be Paul McCartney. Even tried playing bass left handed."

"You weren't bad on bass, man. And you did do all the instruments on that album in '82, as I recall. Cool."

"Anyway, I joined a band in college. That's when I 'woke' to use an expression they're using today. My friends were all into the anti-war thing. I had my college deferment so I was pretty blasé about it at first, but it was all around me. I started to write songs about the war and the bloody changes. I was embarrassed to tell my parents, especially my dad. He was gung-ho on the war. Junior year I came home for the holidays, long hair and beard. He kicked me out of the house. My mom talked him into letting me back in, but he didn't say two words to me the whole time."

"Wow. My dad was like that, too. I hate him to this day. Yours still alive?"

"No, he was a smoker. Died of lung cancer a long time ago. But the way he treated me convinced me I was right. The old guard was closed minded. They believed whatever the government said. They accepted authority, we questioned it."

X sang, imitating Mellencamp. "I fight authority, authority always wins."

"Well, in this case, they didn't, did they? My music started to get a reaction around campus and word spread. Other schools holding rallies wanted me to play. For free of course, but it didn't matter. I wasn't in it for the money. Just wanted our voice to be heard."

"Any of them record company leeches come by?"

"There was some interest. One of the A and R guys said we need a female vocalist. From RCA, as I recollect. Wanted us to sound like Jefferson Airplane. So we auditioned some female singers. None of them worked out, but a couple of them hung out with us for a while. Funny, that's how I lost my virginity."

"Groupies. Gotta love 'em."

"Yeah, this one wasn't a groupie. She was a couple years older than me. Real sophisticated, very cynical about not just the war but the whole system here."

X suppressed a laugh. "Smart chick."

"I guess. I fell for her big time. They say you never forget your first love. True. I think about her every day. She taught me so much. Helped me write songs that were so much deeper. My muse, I guess you'd call her."

X had a strange look on his face, a sly smile like he knew something Jason didn't. He said, "So what happened to her?"

"Uh, she left. Off to where she came from. Haven't heard from her since. But she's the reason I am where I am today. Wrote a lot of songs about her, gave her different names, depending on my mood when I wrote them. Some days I hated her for leaving, others I missed her so much it didn't matter. Why so curious about my protest days?"

"Just getting to know you all over again. Maybe you already told me some of this shit years ago, but those days are a blur. Too much blow does that."

"Never tried it. Nobody believes me when I tell them that but it's true. Saw what it did to others, including you, my friend. I did smoke my share of weed. Funny, my girl never did that. Barely even drank."

"Man, I envy you. I never had that. Always treated girls like subway trains. Always be another one a few minutes after one leaves. Simpler that way. You think more clearly, dude. No sentiment to get in the way. Just give the people what they want. My case, it was metal. Lyrics didn't matter, long as they were macho. Today, I couldn't even tell you what some of my tunes were about."

"Different strokes. I went through a period of keeping things vague. People weren't sure what I was trying to say."

X smiled and shook his head slowly. "But you had those pretty melodies. Didn't matter. Long as the words didn't get in the way. Hey, you taught me a lot. My last record was chock full of smart words. I don't listen to my own stuff much, but when I do, that was my best work. Lyrics were into some deep shit. Problem was, my fans didn't want that. They were into power chords. Wouldn't accept me as Mr. Politically Aware. But by then, Apple was happening and I couldn't give a shit about the music."

Jason had never had much use for Brandon's music. He had considered him a dilettante, not a real artist. A fun guy to hang with when he wasn't on drugs, but not a deep thinker. He liked the guy and helped him with some songs, but like X had said, they didn't thrill the rivet heads.

But listening to him talk now, he had to acknowledge that Brandon had grown. Whether he'd been through analysis or had come to these realizations on his own, he had a pretty accurate view of his legacy in the music business.

Jason said, "So politics is your new thing?"

"We'll get into that later, man. I gotta tell you, I was up most of the night. Lot of last minute prep for our guests. But I did take a couple breaks and checked out some of your newer stuff. Wanna hear what I thought?"

"Sure. Always good to have input from someone I respect." Jason cringed inside as he said it. X may have grown, but his musical opinions weren't something he really valued.

"You've gone soft, man. You used to tell the truth. Now you hide behind your big words, like you say, keeping things vague. Not sure what you're thinking. You're like McCartney, not Lennon. John was totally honest. Listen to *How Do You Sleep*? Macca does *Silly Love Songs*. You're missing that edge you used to have. For what it's worth."

"Paul *was* my favorite Beatle. Sorry you feel that way. I try not to preach. Make people think. My stuff takes work to unravel but I think in the end, it's more rewarding. Like I said, different strokes."

Brandon was distracted by his phone, which Jason welcomed. He didn't really enjoy having his lyrics dissected by someone so out of touch.

X said, "Text coming. My visitors are at the house already. I gotta get back and greet 'em. These peeps don't like to be kept waiting. I had one of the maids pick up some nicer threads for you. They're in your closet. Not that I'm going all formal on you dude, but you need to dress a little nicer around these folks."

"Okay, if you insist. I didn't really plan on staying. I would have dressed better but I figured you were cool going causal."

"I am. It's the visitors."

"Who are they exactly?"

"Just some folks I do business with." That sly smile flashed over his face again, and he turned away to hide it. "Oh shit, I can't keep it in. You're in for a cool surprise. A blast from the past, is all I'll say."

35

"You say that my brother's taken a hostage? And the FBI thinks he's collaborating with a foreign government? Please."

Kat hadn't expected an easy go of it, trying to convince X's sister Sofia that he was a dangerous lunatic bent on bringing down the government. She feared that she had only made matters worse as she tried to explain the insanity that was now her life.

Kat said, "I know this sounds crazy. God knows, I don't trust the FBI a lick. But they sent Jason Black in to spy on your brother, and he hasn't been heard from since."

"Listen, Brandon may be a lot of things but he'd never hurt a fly. He's got all sorts of wacko ideas, but they just fly around in his head for a while and then vanish."

"I hope you're right. All I'm asking is that you get us into his compound so we can see for ourselves. If this is all a pipe dream and Jason is hanging out smoking weed with your brother, reminiscing about the good old days, I'll go away and never bother you again.

"My brother and I don't speak to each other. We haven't for five years. Brandon hates his family, except for my mom and she died ten years ago. Especially hates my dad. I can't say he doesn't have valid reasons for that, but he resents me for making him support our father. So I can't help you. I'm sorry."

"You said that you remember Jason Black from years ago and he was very nice to you. He's a good man. You wouldn't do this one little thing to save his life?"

There was a pause on the other end before Sofia answered. "Like I told you, Brandon is a paper tiger. He really liked Jason. So did I. I can't imagine there's any way that he'd hurt him."

"Okay, I believe that. But are you aware that at least two of your brother's security guards are neo-Nazis? White supremacists?"

"Now you really sound off the wall, girl. Brandon would never be a party to that. He's always been a friend to minorities. That's one area where we *do* see eye to eye. One of the few. Now look, I have to go."

"Sofia, please. You know your brother and I don't, so I'll accept what you say. But the whole idea is that he's being used by people that mean to do this country harm. He's probably not even aware of their true intentions."

"You admit that you don't know him at all and you're telling me he's stupid?"

"I'm telling you that these people are ruthless. God, I sound like dialogue from a bad spy movie, but it's true. They make you think they have common goals with you and then at the end, they twist things in their favor."

"Like the jerk who won our last election?"

"Exactly. I'm glad to hear you're part of the resistance. Please, just call your brother. Tell him you need to see him in person."

"How does that help you? What does that accomplish? If Brandon's broken bad, couldn't he just hide Jason away somewhere in that monstrosity he lives in? It sounds like you're asking me to do what you say the FBI wanted your man to do. Spy on my brother. Why would I be any better at that than Jason Black?"

Kat was running out of ideas. If it was she on the other end of the conversation, she'd feel the same way. If some unknown called and asked her to betray one of her sisters, she would put up an argument as strong as Sofia Murphy was waging.

She said, "Please, just get me in somehow. Say that I work in the nursing home where your father is staying and that I need to talk to him about his care."

"Now you're really crossing the line. Using my dad's condition to take advantage of my brother? Shame on you."

"I know how that sounds and I'm sorry. But the alternative is a full blown raid by the feds. Do I have to remind you what happened at Waco and Ruby Ridge? I told you, I don't trust the FBI. They blackmailed Jason into doing this. Threatened him with deporting one of his crew. If they think he's in trouble, they'll go in full force and there will be blood."

"So I go along or the feds might kill my brother? If that's the case, why aren't *they* calling me instead of you?"

This was a smart woman. Under different circumstances, Kat could see them marching on the same picket lines. She was frustrated that every plea she made was being batted aside with ease by someone she had hoped would be an ally.

"I'll try to explain one last time. These bastards from the government blackmailed Jason into this. He didn't want to do it, but they threatened him. They had the power to ruin his life. They'll use him as a pretext to raid your brother. Tear gas, flash bangs, automatic weapons. Humvees. Jason is a pawn who gets sacrificed. Your brother might be a rook or a bishop, but he's expendable, too. If you ever cared about Brandon, help me. I need to stop this from spinning out of control and I need your help. Please."

She had finally softened Sofia's resistance. "Tell me about this blackmail. Who would they be deporting?"

"A young man from El Salvador that Jason took under his wing and is training him to be an electrician. If this damn government could ever get off its ass and give kids like this a chance to become citizens, Paco would be a great American. Works hard, sends money home. You won't meet a finer kid."

Sofia was into the cause. "It's a sin what we're doing to these people. It's one of the things that make me ashamed of my country. The man in the White House makes it sound like they're all drug dealers and rapists when they're actually less likely to break the law than whites who were born here."

"You and I have a lot in common, Sofia. I'm surprised I didn't see you last month at our rally to take down those Confederate statues, sister."

"I was there. Look, Brandon is my brother and as much as I've tried to write him off, I love him. It hurts that we don't talk anymore. He used to call me every morning, no matter where he was or what he was doing, just to see if his baby sister was okay. I miss that."

"Maybe this gives you an excuse to make things right again."

"Neither of us is getting any younger. Okay, I'll call him. Things between us can't get any worse than they are. Who knows, it might start a dialogue."

"Oh my God, I can't thank you enough. You might be saving his life."

36

X had a huge smile on his face, an inauthentic smile that Jason didn't trust. He'd seen that same smarmy look on the faces of promotion men who told him that his new album was awesome, after it became obvious that they hadn't listened to one note of it. Or that they had and didn't get it.

Why was Brandon so insistent on him meeting the newly arrived visitors? Were they business partners? Financiers for a new project? Or as Gilmore had feared, Russians in bed with him?

X said, "Head up to your room and clean up. Fifteen minutes enough time? Meet us in the dining room then."

"Yeah, works for me. Who are these people anyway? Just don't want to say the wrong thing, you know, if they're straights. Like, uptight."

"Don't worry about that, my friend. I want this to be a surprise and I think you'll find it a really nice one. Now, scoot."

Jason felt like a kid, not knowing what the 'so called' surprise was. A reunion with some of his old band mates, maybe. Or some independent label producer, willing to take a shot with an old singer. Is that why X was asking him so much about his old music and how he got into it?

He mounted the stairs and walked down the wide hallway to his guest room, which was located on the opposite side of the mansion from Brandon's quarters. The door was ajar. Since he'd brought no personal possessions, he didn't worry about theft or anything that might give him away. The maid who brought the clothes had probably left it unlatched.

Upon entering the room, he caught a whiff of something he hadn't smelled in years. It was Shalimar, the perfume that Wendy favored. The scent carried him back to those days. Heading out to the next rally or concert, coming home and making love. His conversation with Brandon had stirred memories of Wendy. How they met when she auditioned for the band. She couldn't sing a lick, but one look at her and it didn't matter. Could those memories stimulate his olfactory sense?

He shook his head to banish the thoughts. As he walked deeper into the room, he noticed that the bed had been made, a dozen fluffy pillows on top. Pillows he'd cast to the floor to make room. At the foot of the bed, there was an oaken chest, on top of which was the outfit someone had selected for him. Black slacks, long sleeved crimson polo shirt and a dark woolen blazer with brass buttons. Were they going on a cruise?

He sensed another presence. Upon reaching the bed, he saw a woman. He couldn't see her face. Her back was to him as she looked out over the grounds from the dormered window seat.

Was this the surprise? One of Brandon's Russian supermodels? A quickie before lunch? It would be just like X to think that Jason would welcome the diversion.

He said, “Excuse me ma’am, do I have the right room? This place is so huge, I may have walked in the wrong door. My apologies.”

“No, you are in the right place, Jason.”

The voice was familiar. But it couldn’t be.

When she turned to face him, she was holding a gun. “Surely you haven’t forgotten your first love.”

Jason had never fainted in his life. But now, he felt dizzy, his heart pounding. She was older, but looked remarkably the same as she had all those years ago. It was Wendy Walton.

37

Aaron was certain that Sofia Murphy was a lesbian and told Kat so. Between her appearance and the fact that she hadn't married by age 52, he trumpeted his findings as if it had taken skilled detective work to reach that conclusion.

Kat shut him down. They had a reluctant ally in Sofia and her sexual orientation was irrelevant. Aaron could be annoying with his calcified beliefs but she needed him now.

He backed off. He derived great pleasure tweaking her about her liberal views, even those he agreed with. He relished a good argument, if for no other reason than to test the mettle of his opponent. There was no reason to challenge Kat on those grounds now. He had long ago accepted that she was tougher than the rest.

They sat in Sofia's condo overlooking the May River, sipping tea. Sofia was a small woman, barely over five feet, her dull grey hair clipped short. Her face was pleasant enough but pocked by the ravages of adolescent acne. She had dark brown eyes that had seen their share of misery, Aaron thought.

Her place was neat. Furnished by Ikea or the like. The building was not top-end luxurious but its size and location along the river made it desirable. She had purchased it before Bluffton had gentrified and it was worth multiples of what she had paid. Perhaps with her brother's money.

Kat explained the plan to Sofia and the tiny woman went along with few objections, mostly due to her fear that things could get out of hand. Her last contact with her brother had not been pleasant. He was subsidizing her and their father with his millions, and used it as a cudgel whenever they disagreed about their childhood. It was safer just not to talk, rather than risk those still raw emotions from overspilling.

"I'm nervous about this," Sofia said, when they had finalized their strategy. "I don't like lying, especially about my father's condition. But if you think it could save lives, I'll do it."

She rang Brandon's cell and he picked up right away. Strange, since he'd shown no interest in speaking with her over the last few years.

"Yeah, what's up?"

"It's Sofia, Brando. Your sister."

"Duh. How many sisters named Sofia do you think I have? I'm kinda busy now."

"That's all you have to say after all this time? I need to talk to you. It's about dad."

"What? Did the old fuck finally kick the bucket?"

Sofia glanced up at Kat with an 'I told you so' look.

She said, "No, and don't call our father that."

"What should I call a man who beat the shit out of both of us and sent me off to military school when I was twelve? To make a man out of me, he said. If he knew how many queers there were at that school, he'd have thought twice about it. Or maybe not."

"Brandon, we both had our problems with him, some of mine you don't even know about. Thing is, he's our dad and he's in a bad way."

"Hey Sofe, I'm shelling out six grand a month to keep that old shit going. I'm doing my part. You wanna torture yourself by looking in on him, that's up to you. The way he's fucked up now he wouldn't know me anyway."

"Brandon, he's dying. We need to do the right thing."

"You calling to borrow a gun?"

"Shut up. I want to send over a couple of people from the home. They'll have papers to sign. I've made my decision but I need them to explain the legal ramifications to you. You and I can talk some other time but this can't wait. We need your input today."

"Here's my input. Give him a hot load. Put him out of his misery, like a dog."

Sofia shook her head. She expected X to be difficult, but he was taking this to another level. She knew that once she got past his tough guy act, he was a decent hearted guy. She suspected that old man who came with Kat, Aaron, was the same type. All bluster, but a softie when it came down to it.

She said, "Whatever you're doing can wait. Just give them a half hour. You have power of attorney. I've already signed off on it but the people from the home have to outline it for you. Then it's whatever you decide."

"I have important visitors. Heavies. I can't put them off."

"This is life and death, Brandon. I'm sure whoever you're dealing with can spare a few minutes for you to deal with an important personal matter. If they can't, then you shouldn't be doing business with them."

"Why me? Can't you make the call?"

"He's your father and you're technically his legal guardian, being the oldest. Think about how you're going to feel someday when you're in his position, God forbid. Would you want your only relatives to blow you off?"

"I got no kids and neither do you. Okay, I can give them a half hour. But that's it. If I have to sign something, make sure they bring the papers. Okay?"

"They can be there by three."

"Done. You really need two people from the home?"

"Yes. Three o'clock. Tell the goon at the gate."

~~~~~

Brandon mopped his brow. He was more tense talking to his baby sister than any of the VIP types that were at his compound now. And actually, there were only three visitors, besides Jason Black. Nadia and two of her cohorts.

Nadia's visit had been scheduled for a while but he was afraid that Jason's presence might be an issue. But even though the partnership with Nadia was coming
~~~~~

to an end, he felt he should tell her that a stranger was on the premises. He volunteered that he'd ask Black to leave if it posed a problem.

He was surprised when she recognized the name. She had known him very well years ago and would be thrilled to see him again. Make sure he's still there when I arrive, she insisted.

X was happy about that. It would be a great surprise for his newly reacquainted buddy, a boost for his damaged ego. Nadia had told him that she wanted to surprise Black. X had fantasies that she'd be naked in the bed, wearing just a ribbon, like Daniela Bianchi in *From Russia with Love*, his favorite Bond movie. The old woman was too creaky for him to be interested in --- he'd never slept with anyone over thirty. But if his old touring partner was more open minded and it caused him to be late for lunch, well, so much the better. The veggies could wait.

38

Of all the reactions he could have had --- should have had --- the first thing that Jason thought was how great Wendy looked. She must be at least in her early seventies and her fashionably styled hair was silver gray. Her porcelain skin was still smooth and the cobalt blue eyes were as captivating as they had been decades ago.

She was dressed in a tailored pantsuit, the open jacket revealing her still tight abdomen. Wendy looked as tall and athletic as the last time he had seen her, frog marched away naked, in cuffs.

The gun she pointed at him put a damper on things.

Jason didn't know how to start. He said, "I can't believe you're really here. God, I'm so happy you're alive. I've thought about you every day."

"Thought about how you sold me out? Betrayed me. You made love to me then turned me over to your government."

"And I've hated myself ever since."

"Good. I'm glad. You deserved to suffer for what you did. And you'll suffer more. I can promise you that."

Jason couldn't think straight. Wendy somehow knew he'd be here. She was prepared for this moment.

After her arrest, he often rehearsed what he'd say if their paths ever crossed. But in time, he had come to accept that Wendy Walton was likely dead and that he'd never see her in this world again. If there was an afterlife, would they be sent to the same place?

He said, "Wendy, please put the gun down. I need you to understand why things happened the way they did."

"My name is Nadia. Wendy Walton died many years ago. She never existed really. She was a KGB invention. Although, modesty aside, she was hot stuff in her day."

He had always marveled at how she had mastered the American idiom. She had never shown a trace of foreign accent, no awkwardness with slang. She could have been born and raised in upstate New York, so complete was the façade.

He said, "You'll always be Wendy to me. Please, can we talk without the gun?"

She kept the gun pointed at him, but was amused by the reference to her old name. "The name Wendy came from Peter Pan, a fairy tale. The surname? Well, there was nothing more American at the time than the Waltons. As for the gun, we can talk with it aimed at your heart. If you have one, that is."

"How can you say that? I loved you with everything I had. You ruined me for every woman I've known since. No one ever measured up to Wendy Walton, whether she was real or not."

"Is that supposed to make me feel better?"

"No, it's just that my feelings for you were most real thing I ever felt. I need you to understand that I'm sorry. It wasn't supposed to happen the way it did."

"You expect absolution? Is that what you're asking for?"

"Your mission was to infiltrate the antiwar movement. Fan the flames. I was your way in. But it was more than that with us. It had to be. You couldn't have lied about all of it."

She scoffed. "So *I* was the one who lied? Our goals were the same, you said. Your country was interfering with another's right to determine its own course. Your corrupt presidents, Johnson and Nixon, sent thousands to their death. And not just Americans, who had no business being there in the first place. You said you believed in the cause. Was that the truth or were you playing the game you accuse me of?"

"I never set out to betray you. I wanted to protect you. The feds told me you were a spy. I wanted to show them that they were wrong so we could be together. Wendy, I know you loved me. That was real."

"Loved you? You were a naïve little boy. Peace and Love. Flower Power. You had no idea how the world works. How could I love someone that simple?"

Jason still couldn't accept that his whole adult life had been based on a deception, the dream of the beautiful Russian girl who had loved him. Yes, she had started out with a mission. But then she had fallen in love with him. No matter what she said now, years later, he'd never believe otherwise.

He said, "The night they arrested you, I asked you to run away with me. Go to Canada, Mexico, even

Russia for Christ's sake. Somewhere they couldn't find us."

"You wanted me to defect, to turn on the Motherland. Your handlers would have loved that. But you never could have lived in Russia with me. You'd swallowed the whole myth of the American dream. You're a fucking carpenter now, exploiting your workers and taking advantage of down and out people."

He said, "That's not the way I work."

"You want me to think you're still a believer in our cause? What have you learned? I suppose you believe that Iraq was a just war. American exceptionalism. Please."

"And what about your workers' paradise? Your country is run by an ex-KGB dictator, with pretend elections. Is the average worker better off now? Go ahead and shoot me, Wendy. Take your revenge on that naïve kid from fifty years ago. See if you can live with it, like I have."

"Oh, poor you. Do you have any idea what your government did to me? I was naked when they kidnapped me. They didn't give me anything to cover up until they threw me into a rat infested cell. Just enough putrid food to survive. Sleep deprivation. Extreme cold, followed by extreme heat. Total darkness, then blinding light. Hundred decibel music, then silence. I don't think you would have recognized your Wendy Walton after a month of *de-briefing*, as you Americans so delicately put it."

"They promised me you'd be treated humanely. They said you were traded for a captured American."

"Your shelter animals have it better. They did trade me, but not before telling my people that I had given up all their secrets, betrayed others in the movement. I never did."

"They lied to me. At least you got back with your own people."

"My interrogation in Moscow was no walk in the park either. I was lucky to find a sleazy colonel who wanted my body and took me in. I had to live with that old man for ten years. Endure his nicotine breath and the vodka stench from his pores when he was on top of me. Ten years of hell, but by the time he died, I had friends in the politburo. During Glasnost, I was rehabilitated."

"I had no idea. Had I known you'd be subjected to all of that, I never would have agreed to do what I did."

"Like I said, you were a naive little boy. I gave up body and soul to stay alive. There were times I wanted to end it, but I carried on."

She pulled up her blouse, exposing her midriff. He looked away, embarrassed.

She said, "Look at me, Jason. Look what they did to me."

An angry red line slashed its way from just below her breasts to her navel.

"This is what the prison doctors did to me. Exploratory surgery for a chronic stomach ache. It couldn't have been the hideous food, crawling with maggots. This was their solution."

Jason couldn't imagine the torture this woman had endured, a woman he once loved. He said, "I don't blame you for hating me. So get it over with. Kill me."

He closed his eyes, awaiting the bullet.

She shook her head and said, "Do you think you're here by coincidence? You artists are so gullible. Peace and love, la di da. I planned it so carefully. And it almost worked perfectly except Richard Gilmore isn't here to share the moment."

"Gilmore's a part of this? What are you talking about?"

"I wanted to pay you both back for what you did, but he had to go and die of 'natural causes' before he could join in."

"Gilmore's dead? That's not possible. I spoke to him yesterday."

She smiled, an ugly, mean smile. Something he couldn't have imagined from the time they were together. "That's right. No doubt X cut you off from the outside world, paranoid amateur that he is. Gilmore had a fatal heart attack last night. So don't expect him to come galloping to your rescue."

"Wendy, Nadia, whatever the hell you call yourself. Please, just get it over with."

"In time. I want you to know what a fool you've been. I set this in motion months ago. Let me savor the moment. How did Gilmore tell you about what is going on here?"

"He said he got a report that some junkie had crashed this place and seen Russians swarming around with suitcases full of cash."

"You think some drugged out homeless man could get past those Nazi bastards who guard this compound?"

"So Brandon was in on this?"

"Not this. Your buddy Brandon was already doing what he could to chip away at your country. All we did was make his amateur dabbling more effective. Disrupt your currency with counterfeiting. Hacking into your social media to inflame your citizens against the government. Promoting crazy men for high office."

"So both of us fell under the 'useful idiot' category, a few decades apart?"

"Oh, but it's so much more than that. *I* fed the junkie story to Gilmore. Made it seem like it came from an anonymous agent within the bureau. The agent said that he knew how Gilmore had used a musician to break up a spy ring in the seventies, so this would be a perfect way to cap his career. He took the bait and ran with it. It planted the seed that this would be a perfect opportunity to re-unite with his old tool, Jason Black."

The longer she talked the more time it gave him to figure a way out. Although not given to violence, his years working construction had made him strong. Fit as she may be, she was years older.

"Weren't you taking an awful chance that he'd convince his superiors to bump it up to a full fledged raid and wreck your little game?"

"Gilmore? He was a relic of another generation that no one took seriously. And X has already served his purpose. When we started with him, we needed a base in this country. Now with friends like Guccifer, we can operate hack into your systems from anywhere. We have easier ways of money laundering that you don't need to know about. We're shutting down this operation permanently, as of today. You and Gilmore would have put a nice bow on it."

She didn't need to explain it further. X was toast. By the end of the day, the two old touring mates would be dead.

He said, "After all he's done for you, you wouldn't give X a chance for asylum?"

"The fool wouldn't take it. It was a little tricky to convince him to sell all his Apple stock and buy gold bars over the years, but he did. Our toughest job today will be loading them up and trucking them out of here. Hey, maybe you can help us with that. The good news for you is that it will buy you a few more hours of life. Then my new mission will be complete."

"A new mission? Sounds like the same old one. They sure picked the right girl to do it, didn't they?"

"I'll admit, I've been typecast by my people. I relate to American musicians."

"So Brandon was your mark, same as me. You seduced him to recruit him, just like me."

"Your friend likes them young so I never had to make that sacrifice. You must have noticed the so called maids he keeps. That was one of the fringe benefits for him. We provide him with a steady stream of young lovelies. He'd get bored with one harem, we'd ship another in."

"So you kept him plied with weed and sex. Just like you did with me. Except I never believed in Lenin and Marx. Are you sure X does?"

"He thinks if the system comes crashing down, altruistic people like himself can take charge and rebuild your country into a modern Utopia. Marxism 101. We tried that a hundred years ago. It was just a dream some of us had."

"So what now, my love? Are you going to pull the trigger yourself?"

"A gun is so crude. So quick. I think your demise should be more creative, more lingering and painful."

Maybe bull-rushing her would be the easier way out. Force her to shoot him now, instead of torturing him. But he couldn't do it just yet, holding out hope that someone would come to his rescue. At this point, he'd settle for one of the Nazis, if they weren't in on the game.

He said, "What I don't understand is why you waited until now. I have a business. My address is online. How hard would it have been to find me and kill me years ago?"

"Personal revenge is subordinate to my work. I couldn't do anything to compromise that. I'm a patient woman. This is my last dance too. As they say, revenge is a dish best served cold."

"And I suppose you've heard the one about digging two graves."

He started towards her. She looked past him, into a corner of the room. "Yuri."

From the shadows, a massive Russian emerged, holding a liquid soaked rag. Before Jason could turn to face him, the man forced the cloth over his face. It took five seconds for the folksinger to melt into unconsciousness.

The big Russian lifted Jason over his shoulder like a sack of grain, and followed Nadia out of the room.

39

The first part was easy. The twin at the guard station, the one answering to the name of Karl, had been told that two officials from the nursing home were to be waved through with no hassle. Karl had objections, but X insisted.

"No hassle," he emphasized.

So when the SUV pulled up to the gate, a nod from Aaron and Kat was all it took. Twin #2, Walter, didn't even venture down from the mansion to escort them up the long driveway. Karl radioed his brother that the car was on its way, and told them to 'have a pleasant stay' in the most earnest tone he could muster. Then he went back to watching the WWE extravaganza he had recorded the previous evening.

When the Tahoe they had rented reached the tree canopy, they pulled over and Julius extracted himself from the rear compartment.

"Man," he said. "That was tight and hot in there. Kat woulda fit in much better."

"No argument there, but X wasn't expecting a large black man," Kat said.

"You coulda given me a little cap and suit and I could have posed as a chauffeur. Yes, sir. Yes, ma'am."

Julius was joking, trying to mask his trepidation about the mission.

Aaron had brought a Walther .22 with a chamois holster. Kat had a .38. The assortment of small arms was hidden in the SUV, in case one of the guards body searched them.

The plan was for Julius to leave the vehicle while hidden by the tree canopy, out of sight from the house and the front guard station. Dressed as a day laborer, he would cover the front of the building and position himself to intercept any reinforcements X might summon.

Kat said, "Julius, all you are is insurance in case there's something really dirty going on. Hopefully, this is just our paranoid government worrying about an eccentric billionaire."

Aaron said, "There's no reason to think this can't be resolved peacefully. Just remember, our goal isn't to prove X is working with the enemy. It's just to get Jason out safely."

As they approached the house, they saw a large man dressed in black loading something into the back of a Range Rover. He was being aided by three women, all young and blonde and shapely. Aaron whistled and Kat slapped him on the wrist.

They were greeted at the front door by X's space cadet secretary. It seems he'd been called into an important meeting at the last minute and she couldn't say when he'd be available. He was expecting them and she had been told to make them comfortable. To that end, she ushered them into the dining room, where the buffet lunch was getting cold.

~~~~~

The wine cellar was Jason's personal dungeon. Yuri carried him there and tied him to a chair, while the singer was still unconscious. The room was underground and maintained a constant 57 degrees, year round. The wine thrived on the cool temperature; humans --- not so much.

Nadia had been in the game long enough to suppress her emotions for the sake of her mission. She needed to focus on the task at hand. Punishment for past grievances could wait.

She summoned Brandon. To this point, X's contribution had been an instinct for throwing sand into the right gears of government to achieve the most cost effective damage. He provided the SVR a safe haven from which to operate. He became skilled at seeding disruptive campaigns from unfit fringe candidates. He schooled the Russians on which falsehoods on the internet would seem most plausible to low information American citizens. He helped them launder money.

As she saw it, he took a joker's delight in creating chaos and watching helpless bureaucrats attempt to repair the damage he had caused. It was all a game to him, a game he believed in his heart of hearts, might not be won. But he enjoyed playing it.

To the Russians, he had proven to be a *polezni dvrak*. His money and desire to topple the system had worked for Nadia, but she had always known that someday, he might need to be sacrificed. This was the
~~~~~

day. She'd received orders to shut things down, the exact timing was at her discretion.

The oasis that Brandon Murphy provided was no longer necessary and its exposure could compromise more important operations. Once she was satisfied that the job was completed satisfactorily, it was up to her to tie up loose ends. That would include Brandon.

X thought it strange that she wanted him to meet in the wine cellar and almost sent for one of the twins. But he decided against it. Nadia probably just wanted his approval on what wine to serve at lunch as she celebrated her reunion with an old lover. Given Jason's anti-government views, he and Nadia might already be allies.

~~~~~

Walter Hoffmeier patted the .22. He'd never shot anyone with it or any other weapon for that matter. He'd threatened to do so many times, mostly when his twin was around. They fed off each other that way. They were big strong guys who were able to intimidate others by their mere size. But they had never put it to the test against really dangerous opponents. They'd roughed up a few lefty protesters here and there, but had never been arrested.

Walter sensed this situation might be different. He called his brother, currently enthralled by Ronda Rousey, as she took down a masked adversary.
~~~~~

Walter said, “Karl, better get up to the house. We got trouble.”

“Shit, can’t you handle a dyke and an old man by yourself?”

“Ain’t that, bro. That old bitch Nadia made him come down to the wine room by himself. Wouldn’t let me come along. I don’t like it.”

“No sweat, Wally. Probably just a business meet they don’t want us to know about. And to be true, I think we’re better off not knowing some of the shit he’s into.”

“Still, it’d help if you were here too, ‘case things go FUBAR.”

“No one’d be watching the gate if I did that. You know what they say about leaving your post. I’m thinking I better stay put here. You call me if there’s any trouble and I’ll be there in a flash.”

“Whatever you say. I just got a bad feeling about this.”

40

There are few true basements in the Lowcountry, because of the high water table. The mansion was built over a tall crawl space, and the wine cellar was a few steps below the first floor. Like the rest of the house, it was well appointed. Paneled in aromatic cedar, there were stone counters and wooden storage racks for several hundred bottles. Slate floors, old oak whiskey barrels --- empty, just for show.

Brandon X Murphy came alone, as requested. Yuri answered the door and gestured for him to enter. When he saw Jason tied to the chair, his head recoiled in disbelief. “What the hell? Jase is my guest. What’s this all about?”

Nadia said, “Mr. Black is a mole, sent by a government agency to spy on you. Most likely FBI. That’s why I wanted him to be here when I arrived. So I could find out what he knows.”

“That’s outrageous. I’ve known Jason since the seventies. He’s a righteous dude. He’d never work for the man.”

She shook her head at his susceptible nature, the very facet of his character she had used to exploit their relationship. “Jason Black worked for the FBI, infiltrating the peace movement in the seventies. He betrayed me to them and I suffered for it in ways you can't imagine. This man is not what he seems to be. He's the worst kind of treacherous slime."

X started pacing. Black was conscious now, barely. Brandon couldn't believe that his tour buddy was everything she said he was, but Nadia was not given to paranoia.

X said, "So what do you do? Interrogate him? Torture? I didn't sign up for that."

It would have been easier to kill them separately, she supposed. But her newly improvised plan was to make it look like Black was in on X's subterfuge all along. Gilmore was the only one who could have exposed that for a lie and he was dead.

She said, "We'll take care of everything. Jason Black will disappear. He had dinner, stayed over and left the next day. You're an American citizen; you have rights under your feeble justice system. If anyone questions you, they'll have nothing to tie you to his disappearance. They'll go away."

"Let me get this straight. You mean to torture him and kill him? Hey, that's not happening, lady. He doesn't know a thing. He never left his room last night. He was with me all morning. He made one phone call to his business. I heard it. It had nothing to do with us."

This is the price we pay for getting into bed with amateurs, Nadia thought. If she had any doubts that X had to be killed as well, they were eliminated by his reaction.

She simply said to X, "We have no alternative."

"Yes, we do. We hold him here. I think I can persuade him that we were doing the right thing. Either way, you're in the clear. You had me wipe all the servers clean. You said the operation was done. We can let him go. He *didn't* see anything, not really. He's a harmless old guitar player, that's all. Worst case, I'll buy him off with some of the gold."

"Oh, Brandon, you can be such a fool sometimes. He saw *me*. He knows who I am and what I did. Jason and I were lovers when he was a stupid college troubadour. He turned me in when he found out who I really was. He'll do it again in a heartbeat."

Brandon was stalling for time, mindful that Nadia was dangerous and willing to carry out her threats. "But you can be long gone by then. If they have any line on you, I'll say I hooked up with you as a chick I was boffing from the old days. I'll play dumb. Black doesn't know I know who you really are."

"Brandon, you're talking nonsense. Jason Black cannot be allowed to leave here alive.

"I don't know who dumped who when you two were exchanging fluids, but ain't this a little extreme?"

Nadia was getting tired of explaining herself to this fool, but she tried again. "You think you can trust this man? Yes, we were lovers years ago. Back when he was a mole for the FBI."

"Not Jason, man. He hates the feds."

"He worked undercover for them and no doubt still does. Trust me. He turned me in. Claimed I was a Russian spy using him to infiltrate the peace movement."

"Excuse me, ma'am, but isn't that true? That's what you are. Hey, you and me have no illusions about this shit. We're after the same thing. *Anarchy in the U.S.A.*. Stole that from the Sex Pistols or the Clash, I forget who. But point is, we're both trying to bring down this corrupt government here in the States."

Nadia rolled her eyes. "You were spending your money and wasting your time in a piddling effort to make waves. We offered our expertise and more sophisticated methods."

"What does this have to do with torturing my friend?"

"You've always been a naïf when it comes to the end game. And certainly when it comes to security. You hire a couple of steroid freaks to head your detail and think that's enough."

"You're talking about Walter and Karl? I'll put my men up against Boris here or whatever the fuck his name is any day and we'll see who comes out on top."

Yuri, the silent Russian muscleman observing the exchange glowered at X. He understood English well enough to know when he was being insulted.

Nadia said, "Two neo-Nazis and their beer swilling Kraut friends do not a security team make."

"If you're so worried about security, why haven't you said something before?"

"We act when we see problems. *Talk is for losers and fools*. You see, I know your rock and roll, too."

X said, "Mighty bright of you, lady. But this is my place and my ballgame. I took your help as a *junior* partner but I'm the one calling the shots. Just because Jason fucked you up years ago don't give you the right to tie him to a chair and kill him. Bottom line is, you were shutting this thing down anyway. You guys are ready to split. You made me destroy any evidence you'd ever been here. I did that."

"Exactly my point. Jason Black is the last bit of evidence that we were here. He has to go. Why can't you see that?"

"I get why you're pissed at him. I saw the old pictures. You were a real looker back then. Easy to see how you could lead him around by his dick. He was young."

She was tired of arguing with this simpleton. "You're a bigger fool than we ever thought you were, and that is saying something. He's out to destroy you. And us in the process. There's no way out of this for him. He dies. If you're so lily-livered, we'll do it when you're not in the room."

"I'm not going to let that happen."

"We're going to make him talk. Then, we're going to make him die."

"*Goldfinger*, eh. I liked *From Russia With Love* better. That's one reason I hired the twins, they look so much like Robert Shaw in that flick. What the fuck am I saying? Hey, this is my house Nadia. I'm telling you to leave. Now. I'll keep him tied up until you're out of the country or wherever you're headed. I'll take the heat if he talks. I'll tell them it was all me. No outside help. He doesn't know anything and you're in the clear. But there's no way I let you do what you're talking about."

It had already dawned on Brandon. If Jason was a loose end, what did that make him? If Jason had to be eliminated, how could *he* be allowed to live? Her henchman had a gun. She did, too. She might somehow rig it to look like Jason and he had killed each other. There was no way out.

Nadia didn't want to waste any more time with Brandon. The sooner she got out, the better.

She said, "You want to spare him the torture for old time's sake? Okay, I'll compromise with you on that and make it quick and painless. Yuri, shoot him now."

41

They had been in the dining room for less than a minute when they heard the shots. They all ran to the lobby, the direction from which the sound came. When they got there, they almost collided with Walter, who came running in from the opposite direction.

Aaron said, "Those were gunshots. Came from directly below us."

Walter was cool. "And how would you know what gunshots sound like, old man?"

"I served two tours in 'Nam, punk. I heard more guns in one hour than you have your whole life, I'm betting. If you're too chickenshit to do your job and check it out, I will."

"Careful who you call chickenshit, old man." He pulled his sidearm and held it at his waist. "Ain't no big deal. You stay here. I'll go down and see what's what."

With that, he rushed to the edge of the lobby, opened a concealed door and disappeared down a narrow staircase.

Kat said, "Aaron, we need our guns. And tell Julius to get his ass in here."

Aaron wasn't used to taking orders from a woman, but he was thinking along the same lines. He said, "Call the FBI. Tell Sanford in Savannah that we're here and shots have been fired. Tell him to send in the troops and hurry up about it."

Kat said, "How do we keep them from storming the place and everybody getting killed? You said that could happen."

"By the time they get here, I'm hoping we'll have things under control. We need their help. They won't go crazy shooting knowing we're here. Just do it."

She made the call. The signal was weak, but it got through. She couldn't get Sanford, settling for Sarah Bernstein, who told her to back off and find a safe place to hide. She promised to get there with reinforcements as soon as possible. The call was finished by the time Aaron ran back into the lobby with the guns. He handed Kat a .38 Sig Sauer, keeping a .45 Colt and the .22 for himself. Whatever was happening involving gunplay couldn't be good, and it was best to be prepared to fight fire with superior firepower.

He said, "I couldn't locate Julius but let's roll. He'll hear the commotion and be with us soon."

They moved toward the door where Walter had descended. As they neared the staircase, they heard more shots, the sound muffled from the enclosed basement.

"More bad. Let me go down alone," Aaron said.

"No way. If Jason's in there, I'm going with you."

"Be a real waste if a hot lady like you gets all shot up, but I ain't got time to argue with you. Just do what I say and don't ask questions. This Walter fella might be on our side now, so don't just blow him away on sight. X might not be pulling the trigger down there."

"If he's nuts like Jason said, why not? Don't apply logic to crazy."

Aaron said, "Just be ready for anything and let me lead. There's a difference between winning best in show with paper targets and live ammo against someone shooting back."

The door to the wine cellar was ajar and they heard moaning from inside. Aaron edged toward it, sideways, Colt raised. He eased the door open further.

He had told Kat to be ready for anything, but what he saw was more gruesome than he had imagined. Three large men were lying near each other, one dead, the other two moaning and bleeding out.

A blonde with a crew cut and neck tats. It was Walter, one of the survivors. On top of the dead man, there was a man matching X's description. He'd taken a round to the stomach, but was still alive.

Aaron had no idea who his late opponent was. He sensed there were others in the room, but couldn't see them from behind the door.

"We don't need any more bloodshed. I'm coming in. Let's talk."

A woman's voice answered. "Who are you? Don't open that door any more unless you want to join your friend."

With that, she fired. Walter's head exploded like a water balloon, the debris a sickening mass of skull and atomized cortex.

Aaron backed off and whispered to Kat. "You don't want to see what's in there. Two dead guys, grisly shit."

"I heard a woman's voice. Who is she?" Kat said.

"Damned if I know. Could be one of X's harem, freaking out on acid. You'd best go back up and try to see if you can locate Jason. I don't see him here."

"What are you going to do?"

"See if I can get in and talk to psycho chick. Get upstairs, find Julius and make damn sure that anybody else who wants to come down here is a friendly. This crazy women may not be acting alone. Now scram."

"Yes, sir." She gave him a mock salute. "Just be careful. Maybe our best bet is to wait until the coppers get here."

"Get your pretty ass up those stairs. Stat."

She winced at his crassness but complied. When she was safely out of sight, he moved back toward the wine cellar door.

"Listen, lady. I'm not a cop. I just want to talk to you. Let's try to find a way out of this. I'm a friend. Drook."

There was silence for a beat. She said, "Nice try with the language. You come in slowly, hands up. If I even see the hint of a weapon, I'll blow you away."

Aaron had a way of charming the ladies, but this was no spinster asking for new kitchen cabinets. He hoped she'd listen to reason. Self survival was a powerful instinct and he'd do all he could to convince her that he could pave her way out of this mess.

"Yes, ma'am. Here I come."

He laid the Colt on the floor and tucked the smaller gun into his waistband, behind his back. Although he'd abandoned the church decades earlier, he crossed himself. If he was about to die, he'd be covered either way.

He pushed the creaky door fully open and slowly walked into the room. More carnage. The man he assumed was Brandon was now lying face up, bleeding from the stomach and breathing heavily. Blood and brains from Walter had spattered all over his body. He had seen worse in Southeast Asia, but that was a long time ago. You never get used to it.

A tall woman stood behind a chair where Jason was tied up. She held a gun to his head. He was awake, but looked woozy.

Aaron, doing his best to keep his voice calm, said, "Tell me what happened. There's no need to have a gun on Jason. He's on queer street and he's hog tied up good."

"What are you, some kind of half-assed buckaroo? Who's with you, old man? Who's in the house?"

"You're hurtin' my feelings lady, calling me old man. Looks like I don't have a lot of years on you, tell the truth."

"Answer my question. Who else is here?"

"No one. Far as I know, there gate guard's still at his post, 'lessen somebody called for him. I came alone. Tell me what happened."

Aaron sized her up. She *was* old but had followed the recommended maintenance intervals and still was awfully hot. But the thing that struck him most about her was her eyes, the cold blue eyes of a killer. That was something he would have picked up on even had he not seen her end Walter's time on earth so casually. She looked as if nothing out of the ordinary had occurred and there weren't three bloody bodies in the room.

She said, "You don't need to know what happened here. What you need to know is that I have to get out now. I don't care if you think you're a friend or not. You and I and this man are going to walk up the stairs. When I get to a vehicle, I'll let you go but he's coming with me."

"Look, lady, I expect this dead Nazi called the cops when he heard the shots. You're not just walking out of here. They'll have the exits blocked. Hostages ain't gonna help."

"Just shut up and do what I tell you."

"Just sayin'. All I saw is you killed that Nazi bastard, which I applaud you for. Don't get yourself killed for nothing."

"How chivalrous of you. I'll take my chances. Walk over here slowly. Untie your friend and march him up the stairs. I'll be right behind you."

This woman was a pro and knew her way around deals like this. He wondered if she had a cyanide pill or preferred death by cop, because that's where this was headed.

Limit the damage. His goal was to make sure that Jason and Kat weren't caught in the crossfire. X was still alive; barely breathing.

This lady was built like an athlete. Strong in a wiry sort of way. She backed off from Jason's chair and motioned for Aaron to untie him from behind.

Damn, she's good, he thought. She moved away far enough so that he couldn't reach her, yet she was in can't-miss firing range if he tried anything. He struggled with the rope. They were good knots and it took a while.

Jason tried to get up as the rope fell away but was still feeling the effects of the drug.

"Help your friend up, then back off," Nadia said.

Aaron did as he was told. He barely noticed the movement behind him and even if he had, it wouldn't have made a difference. With panther-like speed, the woman smashed him across the back of the head with the butt of her gun. He fell to the floor.

42

Nadia had an escape route. She anticipated a BOLO from the authorities. She'd head to a secluded landing field in the woods near Savannah. She was an excellent pilot, with access to a small plane that could get her to Cuba. The owner of the airstrip had it fueled and ready at a moment's notice. The generous monthly stipend they paid him ensured his cooperation. She had hoped to have a large quantity of X's gold bars with her, but that was secondary now.

Yuri was dead. Her other accomplice had been loading the shiny bullion into the SUV they'd rented. She hoped that he'd heard the commotion and would come to her aid, the gold be damned.

The hard part now involved something she hadn't planned on --- getting out of the compound. She couldn't burn any more time. Any delay would give the police more opportunity to close off the exits. She had to move quickly.

The most practical solution was the one she had first conceived. Use Jason as a hostage to force her way past whatever might obstruct her. Once out of the complex, she'd put a bullet in Jason's head. Then steal another vehicle and race to the airfield.

She would have liked for Jason to die slowly, given what he had done to her. She *could* try to take him back to Russia, but that would cause complications. Besides, she could travel faster alone. Slow torture for the sake of vengeance wasn't in the cards. She would have to settle for being the instrument of his demise.

Once his bonds were shaken loose, she said, "We're leaving now, Jason. Up the stairs. We'll stop right near the top. If someone's up there, you say I have a gun on you and I'll pull the trigger if anyone tries anything."

"God, Wendy, didn't you learn anything when we worked on lyrics together? That sounds like a B movie cliché."

"I'm sorry I didn't have time to compose anything more elegant. Now get up the stairs and say what I told you to. None of your fucking hippie embellishments. Move."

"Why should I do anything you tell me?"

"So I don't just shoot you now and be done with it."

"Why don't you do that, Wendy? You think I don't know you're going to kill me anyway, first chance you get? Why should I help you get away? I'm dead no matter what."

"Maybe, maybe not." She had to make him do what she wanted now. The clock was ticking. "The thing is, if I have you for a shield and you have other friends here who're smart, they'll let us pass. No more blood. But if I have to shoot my way out, that old man won't be the only casualty. He'll need a doctor, sooner than later, especially since he might have a cerebral hemorrhage."

"Aaron? He's got a hard head. He'll be fine. But I have to warn you, if I know him, he brought some pros along. They'll pick you off the second you show your face up top."

"Nice try. If there really were *pros,* they wouldn't have sent an old man down to beg for your life. You're wasting my time. You move now, or your friend's death will be on you. Although you won't be around to agonize over it."

She was ready to die, probably had faced that possibility many times. Either that, or her acting skills had gotten even better.

He'd go along. He had no idea who, if anyone, had come with Aaron. Maybe Julius and/or Paco. He couldn't endanger them. He'd been groggy but conscious when she'd finished off the twin. Wendy would shoot all of his friends without flinching. His old lover was a cold blooded killer. Maybe she always had been.

He looked over at Brandon X Murphy, still alive but ebbing fast. His old touring partner had saved his life, temporarily. He had tried to stop Yuri from shooting him as Nadia had commanded. In the struggle for the gun, despite the Russian's size advantage, Yuri took a bullet to the neck, dying instantly.

Nadia had a clear shot at Brandon and didn't miss. Would she finish the job now to make sure he wouldn't talk, or let him die in agony, his blood pooling on the flagstone floor?

Jason raised his hands and headed toward the stairs.

43

Jed Sanford and Sarah Bernstein were on their way to Hardeeville, but even with the bubble on, it was a half hour ride from Savannah. Jed was at the wheel, Sarah clinging tightly to the grip above her door with every high speed turn.

Jed said, "I told that woman not to do this. I should have known. Checked her record. A bunch of arrests for civil disobedience. DISOBEDIENCE. She just does what she wants to, consequences be damned."

"What else could you do, sir? You warned her."

"If we weren't so short of manpower, I could have assigned an agent to follow her and the old man. At least we'd have had a head start. Now, on top of that, we'll have a problem with the locals. I *had* to call them in. They're much closer than we are and it's technically their jurisdiction. I'm going to have to wrestle it away from them. Once those rubes from county are there, there'll be no stopping the leaks. If it gets out that McCann came to us first, it'll look like we blew it. Just what the bureau needs. More shit soiling our rep."

Sarah had never known Sanford to think politically in these situations. He had always focused on doing the right thing. But as his prospects rose in the Bureau, she imagined that spin was part of the game.

This was unschooled territory for her, thankfully so at this point.

She said, “So what’s our plan once we get there?”

“No idea what we’re walking into. A hostage situation? Casualties already? This McCann woman said that shots had been fired. Said she came with the geezer. She doesn’t know who fired the shots or if anyone was hit.”

“At least it gives us probable cause to go in.”

“There’s that. If the locals don’t completely fuck it up before we get there, pardon my French. All our Bluffton agents are up in Columbia for some goddamn sensitivity training. I don’t want to call Atlanta for help until we know what we’re dealing with and they’d be too late anyway.”

Another indication that Sanford was thinking politics, rather than the interests of all involved. How bad it would look for him if this was a false alarm, rather than a potential bloodbath. Had he always been this way, or had he changed, frustrated by his slow progress up the ladder?

Or maybe he was just being wise. The more agents present, the more chances things could escalate. And more questions at the inevitable review. Sanford was keeping it tight. She deferred to his experience and prayed that it was the best course.

44

"Whoever is there. My name is Jason Black. A woman has a gun to my head and she'll use it if anyone tries to take her down. Please. Just let us pass."

His little speech was met with silence. Jason felt like he was in a pitch black room, taking his next stride on faith, hoping there was a solid floor underneath but fearing that he could be stepping into a bottomless pit. A chill shuddered through him. He felt his death close at hand.

There were four bodies in the cellar they'd just vacated. Two were dead for sure. Aaron should recover, but it looked like X would be history if help didn't arrive soon.

Light came streaming through the half open door at the top of the stairs. *Who and what awaited them?* The question tugged at him the whole way up. Aaron wouldn't have come alone. What about Brandon's security team? The FBI or local cops? He could only hope that it didn't include some trigger happy yahoo who had never been in this kind of standoff and was itching to play hero.

He prepared for the worst while hoping for the best. At least he had made his provisions. Julius would get his tuition. There was enough money for a lawyer who could help keep Paco in the country. Aaron could run the business as long as he wanted. If there were lean times at the restaurant, Kat could weather it. He took comfort in that.

Nadia/Wendy nudged him up the final stair and into the lobby. It felt only slightly warmer than the wine cellar. A delayed reaction to whatever they drugged him with? Or his fear of what was to come next?

He was stunned by what he saw when he reached the top. Kat stood there, alone, and in firing position, a gun pointed directly at his belly. Was this a double betrayal by the two most meaningful women in his life?

His tormentor cleared the final step and seemed equally surprised that a striking middle aged woman was her only obstacle.

Nadia said, “Put the gun down. Go outside and get the Range Rover parked by the side door. The keys will be the ignition. Pull it up to the door. If you don’t do as I say, I’ll kill you both.”

Kat didn’t blink at the threat. Her voice bore no trace of fear. “I don’t know who you are or what you think you’re doing, but all the exits to this place are blocked,” she lied. “You try to drive through the gates and they’ll shoot you. You won’t get far.”

“If they shoot, this man is dead. Put the gun down and he has a chance. Don’t do it this second and you both die. Now.”

Kat thought she was playing it smart. Keep talking. The longer she could stall, the better the chances that cops would arrive and take over. If this woman was surrounded by a team of well armed pros, she’d have no choice but to surrender to the superior force. And no reason to kill Jason Black.

Unfortunately, Nadia had navigated similar waters before. She gave Jason a shove forward and opened fire on Kat.

Was it Pilates? Hot Yoga? Superior genes? 20/15 eyesight?

A combination of them all served Kat well. The second she saw Nadia push Jason aside, she dove for cover. She slid along the marble floor toward the round table in the middle of the lobby. In desperation, she flipped it over so that the top faced Nadia. She scrambled behind it, giving the Russian no clean angle. The first volley made a hash of the cherry wood, but found no human target.

Jason's reflexes were still compromised by the drug and he reacted slowly to the chaos surrounding him. With Nadia's focus on Kat, he spun and pushed at his former lover. She jerked her weapon toward him and fired at the movement, no time to aim. The round tore through his left hand.

Before she could fire the kill shot, another ear-splitting percussion rocked the room and Nadia was thrust backwards. Jason's move had given Kat enough time to rise and shoot, and her bullet found its mark. Nadia grabbed her thigh where the round entered, her gun tilted toward the floor.

Jason shoved her to the ground in an awkward tackle, his damaged hand grasping for the gun. She resisted with all her strength, as he pinned her down with his elbows, using both hands to pry the pistol away.

As he felt her left hand weaken and pull away, he was sure he was on the verge of disarming her.

She was a highly trained operative and he was a musician and carpenter. He never gave a thought that the gun wasn't her only weapon. With her left hand free, she pulled a knife from an ankle sheath and stabbed him.

He yowled in pain and spun off her. She turned the gun on him to finish the job. But Kat didn't hesitate now that she had a clear shot.

Her bullet found center mass. In shock, Nadia dropped her weapon and sank to the floor.

She was dead within seconds.

45

After the shock wore off, the pain came. Jason's hand was mangled and bleeding. The stab wound didn't hurt as much, but it was a bloody mess. He lay on his back as Kat rushed over to him.

Before she reached him, she kicked at Nadia to make sure she was dead. No doubt. She screamed, "Aaron. Julius. Anybody. Help."

She ripped off Jason's shirt and tightened the fabric over the knife wound. She'd heard stories of super human strength in crisis situations, now she was living it.

"Hold on, baby. I'll get help."

She was elated to see Aaron lumbering up the stairs from the wine cellar, looking like he'd just awoken from a three day bender. He said, "Holy shit. What happened? She dead?"

"Yes. I shot her. Who is she?"

"Damned if I know. Bitch clocked me upside the head." He saw Jason on the floor behind Kat. "Did she shoot our boy? Where?"

"I'm applying pressure to this wound. She stabbed him. Don't know how deep or if it hit anything vital. Shot him in the hand too. I called for help."

"You done good, sister. Where's Julius?"

"He never got here. Look Aaron, I don't know who this woman is or if she was acting alone. She may have friends here. Go out front and see if anyone's coming. Damn, we don't know if there'll be friend or foe. Better to keep a gun on 'em until you know for sure."

"You sure you weren't in a tunnel with me in 'Nam, lady? Stay with Jase, I'll be back soon as I can."

Aaron went outside. As he opened the heavy iron door, he was relieved to see Julius trussing a bulky man to a lamppost with a heavy orange extension cord.

"Jules, what the fuck is going on? Had me worried when I didn't see ya inside. Damn good to see you still standing, hoss."

"Likewise. Kept this dude from rushing in. Told him to stop, but he kept coming and said something sounded Russian so I clocked him with a haymaker. Figured I'd best keep him out. I figured you could handle things inside. Looks like I was right."

"Truth is, it was all Kat. But we ain't out of the woods yet. There might be Commies in the trees, lad."

He walked over to Julius's prisoner. "Hey, comrade. Name, rank and serial number."

The big Russian spat on the ground and cursed. Something that sounded like *Poshel Ty*.

"Like I thought," Aaron said and shot the man in the foot.

46

Sarah Bernstein and Jed Sanford arrived ten minutes after the county sheriff and his deputy. There was an EMS truck parked in the cobblestone courtyard and the sheriff's vehicle, flashers on, blocking the entry door.

Sheriff "Patch" Davis was a stern looking fellow, old and wizened, skin a jaundiced shade of yellow. Squinty brown eyes, heavy earlobes. His hair was thin and an unnatural shade of orange as it sprung from under his official tan fedora.

Jed found Davis in the lobby. He flashed his badge and introduced himself, full title.

"What brings the feds in on a routine shooting case?" Davis wanted to know.

"I don't consider any shooting routine, sir. I'm not sure what you already know, but we were called in first. We alerted your office since we had no way of getting here as quickly as you could. We hoped that if there were active shooters, you might be able to keep the casualties to a minimum. The owner of this house is a person of interest in an ongoing investigation."

"All well and good, agent, what was your name again?"

"Sanford. Like in *Sanford and Son*. Easy to remember that way."

Sarah was surprised that Jed would resort to the obvious racial reference this quickly. Would Davis pick up the implication that Jed had sized him up as a backwoods cracker who didn't like the idea of a 'nigra' outranking him?

Davis chuckled softly at the mention of the old TV comedy. "Always liked that show. That old Redd Foxx was a hoot."

Jed was finished 'funning' with him. "Down to business. What's the situation?"

"Well in hand, your highness, well in hand. You see that dead woman over there. Two bullet wounds, thigh and chest. Lotta blood. Be a bitch to get it off them marble floors. Stuff ain't like granite, stains easy. Anyway, shooter admitted doing it, she's with my man and a bunch of other ladies in a room upstairs. Couldn't tell you which one, place is so goddam huge."

Sanford didn't really want to discuss the permeability of marble versus some other stone. He walked over to the body, careful not to make contact until the forensics team got there. It wasn't Katrina McCann.

He said, "Agent Bernstein, would you go upstairs and relieve Sheriff Davis's man from minding the shooter and separate her from these other ladies?"

She shot him a look which said, *I'm a highly trained federal agent, not a babysitter.* He got the message but continued, "I'm sure that the deputy has read this woman her rights and has more important things to do."

Sarah understood. If *McCann* was the shooter, she'd need to convince her not to say anything to the locals until Sanford could come up with a plan.

Jed said, "We were interested in a man named Jason Black. Is he here?"

"Out in the EMS truck. Shot through the hand. No big deal. Stab wound in his side but they said it didn't look so bad. Didn't hit nothing vital. I'm saving the worst for last. Got a real slaughterhouse down in the basement. Three bodies. All male. All gunshot wounds."

"One of your men down there?"

The sheriff gave him a condescending smile. "Nope. Dead men ain't going nowhere. Just brought one deputy. Figured that was enough till we sussed things out. Like I told you, he's with the female shooter and the rest of the folks we found in the house. A couple of real honeys. Oh yeah, and we found some guy all trussed up outside. Shot in the foot. He's with EMS guys. They got here pronto. Give 'em credit."

Sanford was amazed that after an urgent call from the FBI about multiple shots being fired, this idiot had seen fit to come with only one man and an ambulance. "I'm going down below. Please let your people know they're not to touch anything to contaminate the scene. We have no idea if the people your man rounded up are good or bad."

Davis didn't miss the implication this time around. "Excuse me, Mr. Federal Agent, sir," he said. "Who you think you're dealing with here? I was busting bootleggers in this county when you was still shittin' your diapers. I know the drill. And if it's allowed by your frigging federal regs, I'll go down in the basement with you."

"Sir," he finished, sarcasm noted.

"No offense intended. Just making sure. Of course you can come down there with me. Extra set of skilled eyes is always appreciated."

Sanford decided to back off the passive-aggressive insults. No need to create an enemy who could poison his relations with the locals. He needed their cooperation now and in the future. A call to the Atlanta office was imminent, but he wanted a complete assessment of the damage first.

They walked down the short staircase to the wine cellar. Sanford immediately recognized the first body. It was Brandon X Murphy and he was dead.

~~~~~

The rest of the day was consumed with procedure. An FBI forensics crew helicoptered in from Atlanta. The Bluffton agents were recalled from Columbia and arrived an hour after that.

Sarah talked with Kat. She held nothing back, even the parts that might land her in trouble.

When she finished, Sarah said, "You're going to have to repeat all of this in a written statement and I'm sure there'll be more questions. Jed, I mean, Agent Sanford will be pissed when he sees you, but he's a fair man and if what you've told me is true, I can't imagine there'll be any charges, at least at our level."
~~~~~

"I'm willing to deal with whatever you guys cook up. Wouldn't be the first time."

"Where's the old man who was with you?"

"Aaron? He went outside after the shooting. He was going to see if there were any more Russians around who could hurt us. He isn't back?"

"Maybe he's with the other group. So do you have any idea who you shot?"

"None. All I know is that she was going to kill Jason. She was holding him hostage to make her getaway. I told you, she shot at me first."

"You think she was Russian?"

"She didn't sound or look like it. Seemed like a well kept older lady who lunches. See them all the time in my restaurant. But looks don't mean anything. She sure didn't hesitate to try to kill me and Jason."

Sarah thought for a beat and said, "Here's what's going to happen. You'll probably be kept in custody for up to forty eight hours. As a material witness or person of interest. I'll lobby to keep you out of lockup. Try to sequester you in a motel room somewhere."

"When can I see Jason?"

"That's part of the point of putting you in custody. You may have already done it, but we can't have you syncing up your stories. I believe you, but you *did* admit to killing another human being. We can't let that slide and we can't allow you two to collaborate on a story."

"Can I just see him to make sure he's all right? Please."

Normally, Sarah would veto that idea. But this woman had put her life on the line for Black. She deserved to know if he had survived.

"I'll see what I can do. You won't be left alone with him, but a quick visit shouldn't be a problem. Jed'll be okay with that."

There was a tapping on the door.

"Yes?"

"Agent Bernstein? Sheriff sent me up to take care of the suspect. Your boss wants to talk to you."

Sarah opened the door and a fully decked out deputy stood on the other side. He almost saluted her.

Sarah squeezed Kat's arm and whispered, "Don't say anything to this guy. I'll smooth things over with my boss. Stay cool."

47

The two men sat on a park bench in Savannah, overlooking the river. Behind them, the soft rumble and twinkling lights meant that Huey's was doing a brisk dinner business. One of the men had vetted the area for surveillance cameras prior to the meeting. The other just showed up at the appointed time.

The streetlights shimmered with a rugged glow, but the bench was dark. The first man was attired in sweats, as if he had just returned from an evening jog. The other wore a black fleece jacket and workman's dungarees. Neither looked suspicious or out of place in any way.

The jogger said, "So far, the damage has been contained, in no small part due to your efforts."

"Yeah, well like I told you, this is it. No more. You put me in a tough spot and I don't need this aggravation."

"And you no longer are in need of our rather generous compensation?"

"This was never about money."

"To quote a wealthy American business leader, *when they say it's not about the money, it always is.*"

"That was a sportswriter. Okay, the money did help at one point. But that was a bad scene yesterday.

Some innocent folks were almost killed. As it is, five people are dead."

"Nadia was an amazing woman. She was a patriot, but she was aware of the risks. Brand X? Well, he had to know this day might come, unless he was a bigger fool than we thought. The others were expendable. Collateral damage, as they say."

"So what happens to me now? Am I expendable? You know, this ain't the old mafia, where no one gets out alive. I can hang it up and not look back. You promised right from the start that I was free to quit anytime I wanted."

"That promise was made many years ago by men long dead. Things change. But rest assured, there's no purpose in eliminating you. That's not how we treat our friends."

"Why don't I believe you?"

The jogger looked out at the slowly moving gray river and sighed. "You've been swallowing the Hollywood propaganda about us. We reward those who help us, not punish them."

"I'd like to believe that. Just know that if you're set on trying something, I'm gonna be locked and loaded. And I wrote a letter telling everything. It'll get released if anything happens to me, other than natural causes."

"Oldest ruse in the book and not what you would call credible. Still, I prefer to part as friends. Trust my words. Your usefulness to us was appreciated. We bear no malice."

"What about others? Revenge for Nadia?"

"I think both sides understand there's no need for further bloodshed. Detente. Stalemate. However you want to put it."

"I'll take you at your word, but I'm not buying it 100%. I'll still be taking my precautions."

"I'm sorry you're so cynical. We've always kept our promises to you."

The noise level from Huey's was rising, making it harder for them to speak as softly as they would have liked. "So where's this all headed?"

"You'd like me to say world domination, or some such paranoid flight of the imagination? No, it's simpler than that."

"And what's that mean, exactly?"

"Respect. Call it fear, if that suits your vocabulary better. The way it's viewed in Moscow is to take back what is ours. Unite all the Russian speakers. We're content to leave the imperialism to you. Get back to where we were before we had toothless leaders like Gorbachev. You know the American side, or you should by now."

"Yeah. Leave us alone. We ain't policing the globe any more. Treat us right and we'll do the same."

The jogger pulled a small flask from the track suit pocket. "To common goals."

He offered it to the other man, who shook his head. He didn't trust that it wasn't laced with some slow acting poison.

His counterpart shrugged and took a sip of top shelf vodka. "Da svidania, my friend."

48

"Hammer, yes. Guitar, no."

The female doc gave Jason a wistful smile. She had been born in Mumbai, and was tall, slender and darkly attractive. She said, "I didn't really know who you were when you got here, but I looked you up and listened to some of your stuff on You Tube. I liked it."

There had been times over the past day that he could swear she was flirting with him. "Back up a second," Jason said. "You mean I can't ever play the guitar again?"

After the EMS docs patched him up as best they could, they ferried him to Savannah General. The knife wound was shallow, it required little more than stitches, but it took five hours to piece his left hand together from the through and through. The surgery was pronounced a success, but Jason wouldn't call it that if it meant he couldn't play guitar.

The doctor said, "I shouldn't have said that. There are twenty seven bones in the hand, and that bullet affected seven of them. You have enough stainless steel in there so that you'll never fly again without being stopped at security. I'm not a musician, but I would think rehabbing to a level of competence would be difficult for a man of your age."

Literally adding insult to injury, Jason thought. Solo shows might be out, but maybe he could find a young guitarist, a protégé. Hopefully, he could play basic chords well enough so that he didn't have to fake it --- pretending to play like Elvis did sometimes, without being plugged in.

He said, "Well, thanks for the encouragement, doc. Although I think your bedside manner could use a little work."

She stuck out her tongue, something he'd never seen on Doctor Kildare or Ben Casey, the big hospital dramas he'd grown up watching. *Not a good idea to piss off your doctor*, but she'd get over it.

Someday, he'd show her what a determined fogey could do when he set his mind to it. He never had been Eric Clapton, but in his heyday, he could give Paul Simon a run for his money on a dreadnaught.

She turned back to him on her way out the door. "You have a visitor. Flashed some sort of credential. I didn't really pay attention to it but it looked official. Okay to let him in?"

He nodded. He'd welcome the company, regardless of who it was. He'd been in the hospital for over a day now. No Kat, Aaron or Julius. Had they been arrested? Injured? On the lam? Maybe Mr. Credential could provide some answers.

A well dressed man of color entered the room, no badge or other official signage displayed. In a deep baritone, he said, "Jed Sanford. Agent in charge, Savannah FBI."

"Didn't you stop by while I was in the EMS truck?"

"Wasn't sure you'd remember that. They had you doped up on painkillers. Be careful about those things. They can be highly addictive."

"This public service message brought to you by.... So what brings you here, as if I didn't know? Do I need a lawyer?"

Jason had already considered that option. Lawyers were expensive. He hadn't done anything remotely indictable as he saw it. If anything the government owed *him* compensation.

He knew the drill from the legal advice he'd been given in some minor court appearances. *Don't volunteer information. Answer the questions as succinctly as possible. Don't get too comfortable with the "good cop" and incriminate yourself.*

Sanford said, "That's up to you. I just came to ask you a few questions. When you're up to it, we'd like to have you in for a formal debriefing."

The very term made him quake, remembering how Wendy had described her 'debriefing' at the hands of the U. S. government. He didn't anticipate any such harsh treatment, especially since he was the victim. But he also knew how things get twisted and how scapegoats can be fashioned from innocent parties.

"Am I a person of interest? A suspect?" Jason asked.

Sanford displayed his full wattage smile, brimming with confident authority. "Oh, no. It's just that you might have some details that could aid the investigation going forward. We have a couple of anomalies that maybe you can sort out."

"Fire away."

"Let's begin with your encounter with the decedent and how you became her hostage. Ms. McCann told us that the lady held a gun to your head and threatened to kill you if you didn't cooperate. Is that correct?

"Yes. She forced me up the stairs at gunpoint and when Kat didn't immediately drop her weapon, she shot at her. I rushed her then, we fought, that's when she shot me and stabbed me. She was about to finish me off when Kat did what she did."

"Why was Ms. McCann armed?"

Jason recalled another instruction he'd gotten from his attorney. *Don't speculate. If you don't know the answer, just say so.*

"I don't know. I haven't spoken to her since she saw me in the ambulance and all she wanted to know then was if I was all right. I think she wanted to say more but one of your people rushed her out. Is she okay?"

"Her knees were a little scuffed but otherwise, she's in perfect health. Now, you wrote a letter to her, saying that you were visiting Mr. Murphy and there might be some danger involved? Is that correct?"

"Yes." He wanted to add that she wasn't supposed to open it unless she believed he was in imminent danger, but Sanford hadn't asked.

"Were you aware that she came by our office and demanded we rescue you? And rescue you from what?"

"I didn't know that. As to rescuing me, no one could have known that this woman would be there and that she'd try to kill me."

"Did you know this woman?"

He couldn't lie. Sanford probably knew his history with Wendy. But he suspected something that Sanford might confirm. "Let me ask you something? Why isn't Richard Gilmore here asking these questions. Isn't he leading the investigation?"

Sanford scratched the side of his head. He took a breath, contemplating how to answer. Black seemed like a decent sort. But he had to be careful with what he said, perhaps more careful than Jason. Legally, the bureau could bear full responsibility for the actions of a rogue agent. A messy court case would result in more embarrassment for the agency, the last thing they needed now.

"Agent Gilmore died three days ago. In the line of duty."

Nadia had told him as much, but she was an accomplished liar. Gilmore was supposed to have had his back. He now knew he had been flying without a net at Brandon's.

"I'm sorry to hear that. How did it happen?"

"Mr. Black, my time is limited and I need to focus on the incidents at the house that day. Now please, answer my question. Did you know the woman who attacked you?"

Jason was on painkillers, maybe enough to trip him up at the hands of a skilled interrogator. He needed to talk to someone who could give him advice on how to play this. Even though she had tried to kill him, if he didn't denounce her in the strongest terms, might they infer that he was colluding with her?

"Agent Sanford, I'm very tired now. They tell me I should be out of here soon. Can we arrange a meeting right after I'm released?"

Jed Sanford wasn't happy with the prospect of dealing with a lawyer if that's what Black had up his sleeve. Up until the last question, he had been cooperative. Why was he shutting down now? Was there something he'd missed that could turn this case upside down? As it turned out, he didn't know the half of it.

49

Sarah Bernstein had been schooled. Sanford would have preferred to employ a more experienced agent to babysit Kat, but manpower being what it was, she was the best he had. In her favor, there were gender issues that might even make her preferable to a more seasoned male. He instructed her to probe gently, try to gain Kat's trust. Ask questions, don't answer them. Don't lie, but don't reveal what you know about Gilmore.

Be careful about saying *anything* about the late Richard Gilmore. Although he was operating on his own without the bureau's sanction, any admission that he may have skirted the law could come back to haunt them.

Even though Sarah did this for a living, Kat was nearly twenty years older and wise in the ways of the world. Her knowledge of the whole affair was incomplete --- Katrina only knew what Jason had deigned to tell her before going in. They were due for a serious conversation when they were allowed to speak to each other.

Kat was tough enough to survive on a cot at boot camp. At times after her divorce she had lived in relative squalor, but these days, she denied herself few luxuries. She had worked hard to afford them, and felt no guilt at indulging herself in spa weekends or pampered retreats with her girlfriends. Sarah had volunteered to sleep on the room's cramped loveseat, but Kat had nixed the idea and insisted they share the lumpy queen bed.

But sharing a tiny cheap motel room with an FBI agent was beginning to chafe, especially since there were things she needed to do. As much as she valued her staff, the restaurant needed her. This was especially true in an industry where one unsatisfying experience can not only sour a patron from ever returning but inspire them to spread scathing reviews on social media.

Upon waking the third morning, Kat figured that the forty eight hour clock had expired, something Sarah neglected to mention. She got up a few minutes before her keeper, quietly freshened up and got dressed.

When she was finished, she announced, in a loud voice, "Time's up. Since you haven't filed any charges, I assume I'm free to go."

Sarah was in bed, groggy from her fitful night's sleep. She sat up and said, "Hold on. Let me clear it with Agent Sanford."

"No. I gave you people a written statement. Told you all I know. If Jason says something different, it's up to you to figure out who's telling the truth. That's what you do, isn't it?"

"Ms. McCann ..."

"Oh, it's Ms. McCann, now? Going formal, are we? Look, *Agent* Bernstein, I'm out of here. I've been a good girl, very cooperative. I've got an UBER waiting."

"I was going to say, let me stay with you. For your own protection. You killed a woman who might have been an agent of a foreign government we don't consider friendly. They may want revenge."

"I'll take my chances."

The dingy room smelled of rotting take-out. The maid service was spotty under the best of circumstances, and Bernstein had refused to let anyone into the room. Even though she didn't live at the level Kat was accustomed to, her own digs were far nicer than this dive. She would be thrilled to leave for better accommodations.

"Where are you going?" Sarah asked.

"Not really your business, is it? But I suppose there's no harm in telling you. I'm going to see Jason."

"You don't even know where he is, do you?"

"I'll find out."

Sarah got out of bed. She was wearing a yellow tee that she'd picked up at the motel's gift shop, proudly proclaiming, *Hilton Head, SC. Island Paradise*. It was the nicest sleepwear she could find on short notice. Hers was yellow, Kat had the same shirt in pale blue. Neither would be caught dead in the cheap polyester weave under other circumstances.

"I'll make you a deal, Kat," she said. "I'll come with you to see Jason. I know where he is. I won't come into the room with you. You can speak in private. How's that?"

Kat considered it. She had come to like young Sarah Bernstein. She didn't like the FBI. If things were different, she could see recruiting Sarah to help manage the restaurant and maybe become a junior partner if she ever decided to expand. She was competent, conscientious --- devoted to her work in a no nonsense manner. She thought well on her feet, this offer being the latest example.

She didn't want to get Sarah in trouble with her boss. She imagined that Sanford would ream her out if she allowed Kat to run off unsupervised.

She trusted Sarah enough to believe that she would be true to her word and not try to trick her into some sort of trap. But she couldn't rely on just instinct. Too much was at stake.

She said, "All right. But I don't want you calling Sanford until I'm alone with Jason. You have my statement. I'm assuming that one of your colleagues has debriefed Jason. He and I have to talk about what happened. And we can't do it in front of you or anybody from the government. Them's my terms, lady."

"Let me get dressed. Not that I don't trust you, but you need to stay in the room. Don't look if it makes you uncomfortable."

Kat winked seductively, as if she relished the thought of seeing her naked. It made Sarah uncomfortable. That was the point.

~~~~~

They sat in the Starbucks shop in the hospital, the aroma of burnt coffee beans permeating the air, a relief from the antiseptic smell of the rest of the building. Sarah Bernstein was stationed an appropriate distance away --- too far to overhear the conversation, but close enough to react if one or both of them bolted.
~~~~~

She had upheld her end of the bargain. She drove Kat to the hospital and had refrained from calling Sanford until they were situated at the Starbucks. Black had moved gingerly from his room to the cafe on a lower floor, so she doubted that he'd be able to run away, if he was so inclined. *And why would he?* She thought.

She dialed Sanford.

"Yes, Sarah, where are you?"

She explained the situation and he took the news calmly, as he did with just about everything. That didn't mean he endorsed what she had done, only that he was processing the decision in that analytical mind of his and would weigh in later with approval or criticism.

"Let them talk," he said. "I'm sending a car to pick him up. He agreed to talk with us after his release which I'm told will be within the hour."

"What do I do if he refuses to go?"

"Follow him. We can't force him or detain him. You might try to tell him that if he refuses to cooperate, it makes us believe he's hiding something. That'll make our job more difficult and subsequently things more difficult for him. But we have no grounds to hold him."

"Can't we keep him as a material witness? He technically wasn't in custody while he was here."

"Sarah, some things have happened in the last few hours I can't get into now. Just do as I say and I'll fill you in later. Bye, now."

Terse, even for him. Sarah couldn't imagine what the politics were in this. She only knew that the whole incident had been squelched as far as the media was concerned. There were sensational stories online about a domestic disturbance resulting in multiple deaths at the X compound. The implication was that somehow the recluse rock star had gone bonkers and shot up the place. No mention of foreign agents and espionage rings. Somehow, the bureau had kept a lid on Sheriff Davis and his man. How long could that last?

She ordered a latte and tried to relax, keeping Kat and Jason in her direct line of vision. So far, neither of them had picked up a phone, so it was unlikely anyone other than Sanford's car would be coming to pick them up. She watched and waited. It was all she could do.

50

Jason wasn't in a lot of pain and was ratcheting down to just Advil, eschewing anything stronger. His hand throbbed and the stitches in his side itched, but he could manage it.

Kat said, "So, what happened? Who was that woman? Start wherever you want. I'll just listen, Jase."

"I thought I was a dead duck. Gives me a lot to write about, if anybody cares."

"Jason, I love your music but can't you see that this is a wee bit more urgent?"

"One thing I realized lying in that hospital bed is that you deserve to know everything there is about me. Even if it makes you hate me."

"Come on, how could I hate you, Jason? I can't imagine how that could ever happen."

"The women who tried to kill us both was the first woman I ever loved."

"Oh." She was taken aback by that answer. So much so that the flood of questions in her mind never made it to her mouth. She looked at him, a blank look. Waiting for elaboration.

He said, "I was a feckless kid. Middle class. Into girls, music and cars, probably in that order. Knew more about the last two than I did the first. My dad and I never had the 'talk', so I grew up learning about the birds and bees from scuttlebutt at school and whatever I could pick up from the Playboys in my dad's sock drawer. Love was something I saw in the movies."

He sipped his tea and shivered.

"So when I went away to college, I was a virgin. Had a few make out sessions in high school, but I really didn't know what came next. It didn't take long till I found that out. Also figured out that my guitar was the best tool of seduction I had. Studied more on that than any class I took, freshman year."

Kat was an elegant lady, no matter how she was dressed or made up. Today, she looked unrefined. Older. Cheap tee shirt and jeans. Dark circles ringing her green eyes. He'd done that to her.

He went on. "I wasn't political at all. My dad was a cop. I was raised to be respectful to elders, don't question authority. That's before I met Wendy Walton."

Kat was trying not to let her face betray anything other than empathy. She wasn't sure what that looked like.

"Wendy was my first love. She taught me so much about life. Gave me stuff to read that I'd never been exposed to. Watched foreign films I'd never heard of. Helped me write songs. My harshest critic and my muse at the same time. We spent every waking moment together or that's what it felt like."

His tea was lukewarm by now but his throat was dry and his voice was starting to crack. The tea didn't help much.

He said, "During my time with Wendy, Richard Gilmore found me. Said the FBI had reason to believe that Wendy was a Soviet agent. They wanted me to let them bug our house and trick her in admitting it."

No amount of tea could ease the fullness he felt in his throat. "I couldn't believe that Wendy was a spy. But finally, she admitted to me that she'd infiltrated the peace movement and was manipulating it in service to her country. The feds now had proof and hauled her away."

He stared ahead, eyes glassy.

Kat gave him a moment to compose himself, then said, "So what happened after that? With you?"

"I drank a lot. Was clinically depressed, they'd say today. Finally turned to writing about it and I suddenly became a sensitive singer-songwriter dealing in broken hearts. Went from being a Dylan wannabe to a commercial success. All because of what happened with Wendy."

"That's the romantic in you, Jason. It's there, no matter how you deny it."

"Now maybe you can see why that even though you were everything a woman could be, you couldn't match the myth I'd built around Wendy Walton."

Sarah couldn't lip read, but from the body language, it was obvious that Jason was confessing something serious to Kat. An infidelity? That would be a crushing revelation to a woman who had risked her life to save his.

The other possibility, however vague, was treason. Could it be that Jason had been working with the enemy all along? Was the hostage situation a ruse to allow the woman to escape?

She realized she was just making things up using the loose construct of facts she had at her disposal. Jed Sanford had intimated that there was much more to this beneath the surface. She tried to imagine what it could be and wondered if he'd ever be in a position to tell her the whole truth.

That is, if they even let *him* know.

~~~~~

Jason had hit the bottom of the teacup, but he kept working it, which gave him nothing other than drippings from the exhausted bag.

He continued his story. "You know how it went down with Gilmore if you read my letter. He tried every trick in the book to get me to do what he wanted."

"Couldn't you go to his superiors and let them know what he was doing?"

"And exactly who would I go to? They must have been in on it. Paco *is* here illegally. He showed me a green card when I hired him, but later he admitted he'd paid for it and it was a forgery. If I piss the wrong person off, he'll be gone in a flash. But now that Gilmore's dead, it hardly matters."

"Wrong. You've got a lawsuit against the government. I know some big time progressive lawyers who would love to claw back at the feds. We could be talking millions here."

"Ever hear *I fought the law and the law won*? I start that up and Paco's gone, and that's just for starters."

"We'll talk about it later. So how did this Wendy happen to be at X's compound?"
~~~~~

"She was there to shut the operation down, she said. She was back to doing what she did so well: seducing musicians and using them. Makes sense in a karmic sort of way. I was back to doing what I did: infiltrating and betraying someone who thought I was a friend. Were we really that different?"

"Tactics were the same, but you were working for the good guys. Or should I say, the better guys. Our side isn't spotless."

"I know. The sad thing is, Brandon was really great with me. Like old friends. Poor guy didn't realize what he was dealing with until it was too late. Kat, I helped the feds so long ago. Who'd ever suspect that's what I was doing again? I've been a builder for years now."

"Well, somebody knew. Who else was Gilmore dealing with? Is there a mole in the bureau? Otherwise, how did they get word to shut the operation down?"

"That's why Wendy was at the mansion. No one was more shocked than I was when she turned up and held a gun on me. She was ready to kill me on the spot."

"So what stopped her?"

"Brandon. Brandon wasn't into bloody revolution. More like anarchy, chaos. The guy was like a merry prankster. He had millions to play with and he thought that the country was really messed up and needed to start over again."

"I might agree with him there."

"Yeah, me too."

"What you need to understand is that instead of blaming yourself all these years, you should have blamed Wendy. I hope you see that now."

"Yeah, I guess I do. Wendy never really cared about me. She was Nadia --- a stone cold killer. The other day, she needed to get out of the country and I was her ticket."

"Did you have any idea I'd be at the compound?"

"No. I assumed Aaron didn't come alone but I figured it would be Julius and Paco or maybe some old army buddy. Seeing you holding a gun was my second biggest surprise of the day and thank God for that. I owe you my life."

Kat lowered her eyes, embarrassed. It was true, but it set up an imbalance in their ledger that he'd never be able to repay. She knew he'd try, it was in his DNA. Might even ask to marry her to square things.

That was the last thing she wanted. If they were to be together, it couldn't be because he felt guilty. She knew that Wendy had poisoned every relationship he'd had for almost half a century. He needed to heal a lot more before he could make a go of it with anyone. Including her.

Sarah was watching them from across the room when two men approached her. Medium height, medium build, medium faces. A completely useless description that she'd heard from countless eyewitnesses.

Even their dark suits were medium. One of them spoke in a hushed voice.

"Sarah Bernstein?"

"Yes?"

"We're here to pick up Jason Black. We were told you were monitoring him."

"Jed Sanford sent you?"

The man nodded.

"That's him in the corner with the lady."

"Our instructions are to bring them both in. You stay put, but be prepared if we need backup, unlikely though that is."

"But..."

"Just do what I say, Agent Bernstein. You're wandering way above your pay grade."

51

Sarah Bernstein called her boss as she watched the agents approach Jason. She was just being careful, in case there was something afoul and these men weren't really the ones Jed had sent.

Sanford answered right away. "Yeah, Sarah, what's up?"

She explained the situation.

He said, "I didn't send them but they *are* FBI. I was going to tell you in person, but we've been big-footed on this. They sent a man down from D.C. to handle this. We're off the case."

"Why?"

"This has the capacity to backfire big time and they don't trust us lowly Savannah-ites to handle it. If it makes you feel better, they bypassed Atlanta, too."

"Well, if it makes *you* feel better, McCann and Black are going along without objecting, as far as I can tell. Do you want me to follow them in?"

"Why not? Don't announce it to the world, but if someone's lying to me and running these folks to some secret safe house for enhanced interrogation, I want to know. I'm not trying to feed your paranoia here, just making sure."

"Gotcha, chief."

"And don't call me chief."

"Okay. See you soon, I hope."

Sanford rang off. He realized Sarah had no idea why he'd thundered the line about chief. She was too young to have watched the old *Superman* series on TV, when editor Perry White would scream that expression at cub reporter Jimmy Olsen. Even at his age, he'd only seen the re-runs on ME-TV.

He wasn't permitted to use his own office now. The arrival of the Washington brass shunted him off to a small room with a makeshift desk. An object lesson on who held real power.

When they arrived at the Savannah bureau, Jason and Kat were sequestered into separate quarters. Neither room was originally purposed as interrogation areas, but one of them had been re-tasked with audio and video recording devices that fed directly into Sanford's office, now occupied by a higher up from headquarters, a man named Dan Logan.

Logan made sure the recorders were off as he entered the room where Jason was being kept. He was dressed casually --- sport jacket, open collar shirt and khakis. Comfortable, rubber soled Eddie Bauer shoes. He had deliberately chosen the weekend garb. His dark intimidation suit would come later if his 'regular guy' tactic didn't work.

He introduced himself and showed Black his credentials, allowing him to peruse them for as long as he liked. When Jason was satisfied, he began.

"Mr. Black, may I call you Jason?"

Jason nodded. Another ploy toward making this seem like a relaxed conversation rather than a grilling session.

Logan said, "Great, it's Jason then. I want to begin by assuring you that this conversation is not being recorded. You are not being charged with anything, nor are you a person of interest in this case. You may be considered a material witness down the road. You do have a right to representation if you so choose, but I hope we can keep this as just an informal sharing of information. I do have an excellent memory however, so I must warn you that if you change your story at some point, I will have made contemporaneous notes."

Jason's head was swimming at the lengthy preamble. It seemed like Logan was telling him that he wanted to have a free and open conversation without consequences, but he'd be held liable if anything he said proved to be false. He wasn't sure he should go ahead without an attorney.

Logan didn't look like a tough guy. Late fifty-ish, balding, with a closely cropped fringe of red hair peppered with gray. He looked like the suburban dad he was. A shade under six feet with a waistline that was expanding but hadn't totally given up the fight.

Jason decided to trust his instincts. He said, "I'm fine with that. But I do reserve the right to bring someone in if I think we're going in the wrong direction and you haven't been completely honest. I have to tell you in my dealings with your agency, I've been lied to more than once."

"For that, I apologize. There may be some sensitive areas I can't discuss with you, but take my word --- I won't lie to you. That's not how I operate."

"Okay."

"Let me begin by telling you what we know. The dead woman was Russian. As far as we can trace, she's been in this country on and off for the last twenty years. Came over during glasnost. The name she used was Nadia Bailey. Any of this news to you?"

"All of it. I knew her as Wendy Walton. I'm sure your files back that up. She was a Russian agent back in the seventies and I helped you guys get the goods on her. I was told she was part of a prisoner exchange and I lost track of her. Over forty years ago."

"You see Jason, you're our only link as to whether this Nadia and the woman you knew are the same person."

"There's no doubt in my mind."

"But thing is, we have no evidence that she was working for the SVR. Did she say anything about that?"

"She was up to her old tricks, working for her old masters. She told Brandon that I had to be eliminated since I saw her and knew who she was."

"Let me play devil's advocate. You turned her in, betrayed her. Might she have just wanted revenge for that, regardless of what she was doing now?"

"She could have just killed me in the guest room, but she wanted to make me suffer for what I did. They were using X to launder money, that much is clear. And I'm sure you saw they were stealing his gold, or at the very least, moving it somewhere out of the compound when all the shit came down."

"When she forced you up from the cellar, was Brandon was still alive?"

Jason hesitated. "I can't be sure. I was pretty out of it."

Logan switched gears quickly, which made Jason think something else was at play. The agent said, "Can I get you anything? Coffee. Water?"

"No, I'm good. Are you saying you aren't convinced she was a Russian spy?"

Logan rubbed the top of his head, fluffing up the stubble. "We have nothing to tie her to anything now. Our digital forensics team has been pouring over the servers at the compound and so far, we've found no linkage to the Reds. I still call them that. I have no idea how to describe their government now."

"So you're saying that none of Brandon's computers show he was into anything illegal that would help the Russians?"

"Nothing that specifically ties him to the Russians. Spreading lies and wacky theories on the internet is reprehensible but not against the law. Donations to fringe candidates is allowed in a democracy. Today's fringe might be tomorrow's majority."

He shook his head and raised an eyebrow as if to say he thought that this had already taken place. "We were hoping to find money laundering but they've covered their tracks well if that's what they were up to. We'll stay on that thread but so far, nada."

Jason was gobsmacked. He'd risked his life to compile evidence against X and the Russians, and in spite of all the danger, his foray had yielded nothing. Nothing but a busted up guitar hand and a knife wound that had missed a vital organ by inches.

He had never wanted to do this in the first place. Now Wendy and X were dead.

Jason said, "What about the guy they found outside who was shot in the foot? Can't you get him to talk?"

"He's dead. Died in the EMS cart."

"Shot in the foot and died? Really?"

"That's raised our suspicion as well."

Jason figured that all this international intrigue was complicated, but he was having trouble tying the pieces together. It seemed the feds were in the same boat. He said, "One other thing. You know that Richard Gilmore and I weren't exactly buddies, but the poor guy was just a few months away from retirement. How does he come out in all of this?"

Logan grimaced as if the next revelation gave him stomach cramps. "There *is* something I need to clear up with you now. You see, Richard Gilmore was no longer FBI. He retired last fall."

"He told me he was scheduled to retire in June. This was supposed to be his last hurrah. Another one of his lies. Son of a bitch. Right to the end."

"He didn't leave voluntarily. He was forced into early retirement."

Jason said, "Since he was onto them, you ever think that the Russians forced his retirement, then killed him when he wouldn't let go? Made it look like a heart attack. They would have gotten me too if Kat hadn't been there."

Logan extended his palms upward. "Jason, Jason, Jason. You're an artist. A creative guy. If I was writing a spy novel, I might go with your scenario. That'd be a better plot than what really happened. But

Richard was cashiered for a reason that had nothing to do with the Russians."

"I'm listening."

"This goes no further. Our intention is to honor him as a fallen hero."

Any thought he had of pursuing damages against the bureau would be futile now. Even though Gilmore might still have had a pipeline to FBI files, it would be hard to prove that he was working with their knowledge and consent. Logan might be lying about that, but uncovering the truth would be nearly impossible, not to mention expensive. Strike three.

Jason said, "So how can you be so sure that the bad guys weren't behind his forced retirement, as you put it?"

"I'll deny ever telling you this if it ever comes out. Several women came forward. Since his wife died, Richard had become a bit of a problem when it came to female coworkers. We tried to handle it quietly, but it was getting out of hand and we had to act before it went any further. It doesn't say so in his dossier, but he was terminated for sexual harassment."

52

Kat and Jason sat indoors at Huey's. It was too cold to sit outside, but the sun was bright. From their window seat, they could see the river reflecting the cloudless Carolina blue skies, even though they were actually in Georgia.

They were waiting for Jason's truck to arrive. The feds had taken it from the compound and inspected it until they were satisfied that it yielded no evidence. They had hired an outside party to drive back it to its owner and he was late.

Jason was nursing a craft beer. Kat had ordered a vodka and tonic, "*in honor of our Russian friends*", she toasted, heavy on the sarcasm. She said, "I don't speak the language, but I looked up the name Bailey, Nadia's surname. After I waded through a bunch of Cyrillic hieroglyphics, it translates to White."

"The opposite of Black. Another hint how much she hated me. I guess I would too if I went through the torture she did."

"You're still giving her the benefit of the doubt, aren't you?"

The place was virtually empty an hour before the supper crowd drifted in, but it still smelled great, a result of whatever they were pre-assembling for the early diners. Unobtrusive New Age music played in the background.

Jason said, "Was she brainwashed as a child? I guess that's giving her the benefit of the doubt. But you saw her. She would've killed us both without a second thought. That's who she was."

"Brainwashed. I'm sure they'd say the same about how we educate our kids. They lost over twenty five million in World War Two, yet our history books only talk about how we saved the world from Hitler in 1945."

Jason said, "Yeah. So they just locked you in that little room and no one from Washington came to talk to you?"

Kat signaled the waiter for another round. "Just my old pal Sarah. I think she snuck in without them knowing. Told me that she was officially out of it but that she was still going to be monitoring things as best she could. They haven't found Aaron yet. I haven't heard from him either. I hope he's all right. He went out after the shooting to see if Nadia came with accomplices."

"He's the last guy you need to worry about. He's a tough old goat." He put his beer down. "Ah shit, I'm worried about him too. It's not like him to keep us on edge. I hope nothing happened to him."

"Hope so. I know you miss him and so do I, smelly tobacco juice and all. Anyway, I got the sense that Sarah'd be willing to leak stuff to me. I feel kind of bad for her. She's getting her first taste of what those assholes in D.C. are really like. She's all about truth and justice, and they're all spin and politics. This Logan guy seem like a straight shooter to you?"

"I think so but I've been burned by those bastards before. He told me a lot of stuff that most suits wouldn't, I guess. But he did convince me that we can't tell the story about what really happened to anyone. If the Russians *were* involved, they might see us as a threat and send someone to silence us. He wants us to keep quiet and it sounds like we should go along. I told him I'd talk to you about it."

The second round of drinks came and Kat took a long sip. "And if I refuse to play ball?"

"Do we really want to test them? Logan said they'll keep digging to see if they can prove there were Russian ties. They don't have a provable case now. If we blow the whistle, what does that accomplish? Puts us in danger and compromises their investigation."

"I just hate being a pawn in their game but I guess we don't have much of an alternative. I hate those motherfuckers, except for Sarah. She's a good kid. She told me that they think X didn't bleed out from the bullet. The first coroner on site thought he might have suffocated."

"I think this was all a fun video game to him and he got in over his head. You never met him. Brandon was so frigging rich, he decided to use his money to do what he thought was right instead of pissing it away on toys. But he got into bed with the wrong people. He thought he could control them."

"The arrogance of a fool."

"A fool like me. Wendy played me the same way. I didn't believe the professionals when they told me about her back in the day. None of us are so smart we can't get fooled by a slick con."

"Yeah, look who's president."

"You never stop. You know, Logan told me that most of the rooms in that mansion weren't even furnished. Like a Potemkin village. Lots of servers feeding bullshit on social media, but other than a couple of finished guest rooms, nothing. The master was just a king mattress and a big TV."

Kat *had* never met X, but had formed a mental image. "Sounds like Brandon was a teenage kid. Bottom line, the Russians found a rich dupe. Wanted a revolution."

"Like John Lennon said, *we all doing what we can.*"

"And I for one, will keep doing it. We may not know all the ins and outs, but I do know using blackmail to force you into this is downright wrong."

"Gilmore got booted from the bureau for sexual harassment. Then he threatens deporting my worker and ruining my business. Maybe he still had enough contacts in the government to make that happen. Or maybe it was an elaborate bluff. And here we are at Huey's, where it all began. Full circle."

"While you're doing your final balance sheet, don't forget Aaron and Julius. Julius had to hide himself under the cargo lid when we smuggled him in. That wasn't fun for a guy his size. The feds grilled him, but he didn't really know anything. And how about Sofia Murphy? Without her help, we may never have gotten in. It still got her brother killed."

"But you left somebody out. A lady named Katrina McCann. Fastest gun in the East and a hell of a looker." He took her hand. "It took me too long to finally say it, but she's someone I really love."

"You're damn right it took you too long."

He couldn't disagree. "Yeah, that's on me. I'm sorry it took something like this to make me realize that. X might have been a fool, but in a lot of ways, I've been a bigger fool. Wanna get married?"

"No."

This was not the answer Jason expected. He was braced for a *well, let's see how things go* or *let's wait till the dust settles on all of this*, but a terse 'no' without an explanation was out of the realm of his expectations.

After a long moment, she said, "You like to quote songs you wish you had written. How about your idol, Joni Mitchell? That song *My Old Man*, where she said, *We don't need no piece of paper from the city hall, keeping us tied and true*."

"I just thought I'd make an honest woman out of you," he said. He knew it was a lame cliché, but he couldn't think of a better line.

"I *am* an honest woman, Jason. Maybe too honest. You're the one who's been keeping secrets. But now, you've finally told me the truth. I was always in second place to a memory. A fraudulent one at that. And now I'm supposed to believe that you're finally free of Wendy Walton/Nadia Bailey or whoever she really was. Sorry, but I say, prove it."

"You tell me how can I do that and I will. Anything."

"Everyday. With everything you do. Best I can do is move in with you. I'm willing to do that. But I'll be keeping my own place. We'll take it a day at a time and see how it goes. That work for you?"

He nodded. This wasn't going to be a negotiation. She was dictating terms, take it or leave it.

She said, "One more thing. Much as you and I like Aaron, when he finally surfaces, that rocking chair goes and he just comes over when invited. No morning surprises when I come out to make coffee. If I'm going to live with you, it's just you."

"Yes, ma'am," was all he could say in surrender.

53

Dan Logan knew all the tricks. He was a lifer, with a keen instinct for bureau politics and external optics. When the crisis in South Carolina arose, the director himself tabbed Logan to handle the fallout. So far, he'd done a masterful job containing the media and the principals. Now, he had to massage matters internally.

To that end, he invited Jed Sanford to join him for an update. He'd delegated some menial tasks to Sanford and Bernstein to keep them busy, stressing that any information on the X case, regardless of how minor, must be cleared with him first.

To Sanford, it was emasculating. Now he sat in his own office, in front of his own desk while Logan leaned back in *his* chair, acting like he owned the place. He didn't know much about Logan --- his interaction with him had been minimal. But he knew that his career would be affected by Logan's impression of him. He tried using his DC contacts to research the man, but he'd learned precious little. He had no option but to play this meeting by ear and hope for the best.

Logan welcomed him with a friendly smile and a Cohiba Esplendido. When Sanford hesitated to take the cigar, Logan said, "Don't worry, these are clean. We confiscated quite a few of these before the embargo was lifted. Rather than let them rot in a warehouse somewhere, the ones that aren't needed as evidence are auctioned off. We get first dibs, so they rarely make it to the public. Can't say that I paid market rate, but they weren't free." He winked. "I've heard you're a cigar man. So enjoy, Agent Sanford."

Sanford accepted the forty dollar smoke. He wasn't sure if Logan was testing him to see if he'd be susceptible to a petty bribe. It could also mean that the man accepted him as a member of the club. All he said was, "Thank you, sir."

"Let's take care of business before we fire 'em up," Logan said. "I read your report on this Julius Truman character. Sounds like he didn't know much. Just went along to help his boss. Seems like a good fellow. Agree?"

"Yes. Honor student at UGA. Almost made the NFL. Attending law school. Taking the bar exam in a few months. He admits to cold cocking that Russian and tying him up. His role in this was minimal, and he wasn't privy to all the details."

Logan frowned. "He said that this Aaron Hendricks shot the Russian in the foot. Claimed Hendricks was provoked. Is it possible he blamed Hendricks, knowing he was AWOL?"

"We tested everyone for GSR. Truman was clean."

"Have we located Hendricks yet? Any leads?"

"No. I have agents staking out his house and Jason Black's place, where he hangs out a lot. No one's seen him since the incident. Truman's worried that he might be lying in a ditch somewhere. He took off looking for more Russians and that's the last anyone's seen of him. No credit card usage. The X estate is pretty big and mostly wooded. We've combed the area but there're lots of places to hide a body."

"Hmmn. Very possible he might be dead. Well, keep searching the grounds but call off your men at his place and Black's. I'd like to see if he can fill in some blanks, but I need to allocate our manpower elsewhere."

"Yes, sir."

"Don't need the sir, Sanford. Director Logan will do." He shrugged. "What the hell, call me Dan. We're brothers-in-arms, after all. Now, let me read you into where we are. Unless you have anything more to add."

"Not at this time."

"Okay. This is going to be an ongoing investigation for quite some time. As of now, we can't make a case that Brandon X Murphy was doing anything illegal. Even if we could, the man's dead so all we can do is go after his accomplices. Where we're stuck is that we can't even say for sure that he was working with the Russians. I believe he was, but they seem to have covered their tracks pretty damned effectively."

Sanford was surprised. "Nadia Bailey was a Russian agent. The two men with her were Russian. The stuff that X was doing helped their cause. Plus he had those four Russian girls running his household. Walks like a duck, et cetera, et cetera."

"Ever try taking that to a judge? Problem is, this Bailey woman, who seems to have been his main contact, *was* a spy, fifty years ago but we can't be sure she still is. Or was."

"What was she doing at the X compound? How do you explain that?"

"We traced her credit card records. She comes down here three or four times a year. Apparently loves Hilton Head and rents a place there on the beach. The two dead guys with her worked as bouncers for a club in Savannah. Here legally, again for years. We're still in the process of tracing their background but so far, we got ungotz. Sorry, that's New Yorkese for nothing."

"Again, what was she doing at Brandon Murphy's place?"

"A couple of the women at the house thought she was sleeping with the boss. Apparently, she was a big music fan. Her time with Black must have got her interested in American music. But far as we can see, her main objective was to torture and kill Jason Black. She suffered some unspeakable things because of his betrayal, as she saw it."

Sanford rolled his eyes. "And we're buying that?"

"What I'm saying is, that's all we can prove. Look, I can't keep a lid on this much longer with the press. We need to keep the Russian angle out of it. We make it out that Nadia had bitter feelings against Black for dumping her back in his pop star days. She was shacking up with Brandon, which Black didn't know about until he got there. Apparently she never forgave him and things got out of hand. A big coincidence that led to a tragedy. A woman scorned is the way we'll play it."

"And the media will swallow that?"

"We'll make it out that she was deranged. She's old enough to have a touch of dementia. We found emails on Gilmore's computer from an anonymous source tipping him off to something fishy going on with X. We suspect she sent them, trying to lure Gilmore into the compound so she could kill two birds with one stone, punish them both for what they did to her. That's for your ears only. For the media, she had a torrid affair with Black years ago. Never got over it and the sight of him with his new woman sent her over the edge."

"And tried to kill him out of jealousy? Really?"

"We play up the sex and drugs and rock and roll aspect. Playboy mansion East is how we position it. Hot supermodel types in the grotto. Hedonistic lifestyle. It'll be tabloid material for a few days and then they'll move on to the next scandal. People will remember X and Black from their youth. They'll buy into it."

"What about the Russians who came with her? And Murphy's security guard?"

"Caught in the crossfire. Tried to help out but this woman was enraged and shot everybody who got in the way. The twin brother stayed at the gate, otherwise he might've bought it, too."

"Seems to me you have three major problems. Black, McCann and Sofia Murphy. Add Hendricks if he's alive. They know what really went down. You trust them to play along? Especially this McCann woman. She's got a mind of her own and she has no use for the FBI, that's for sure."

"I'm aware of that. But she loves Black. Wouldn't have risked her own skin if she didn't. If he tells her to go along, I'm betting she'll play ball. And I have a plan for Sofia Murphy."

"One you can share?"

"Sure. Brand X was worth a lot. The compound alone is worth tens of millions. We *could* find a way to confiscate it, or at least tie it up in court for years. Or we could expedite things so it could go to his only living relative, his sister. She signs a non-disclosure and we make it happen."

"Local sheriff and his man?"

"Already done. You did a fine job compartmentalizing them until I got here. They know *what* happened but not why. I sold them on a scenario where McCann had to shoot Nadia Bailey in self defense. We'll turn it around and make him look like a hero. They'll go along and keep it tight."

"But they saw the gold bars."

"Nothing to do with Nadia. X was just moving his assets to a safer place."

Sanford couldn't believe what he was being told. He suspected there was a lot more going on, but saw no gain in pushing Logan much further, other than to satisfy his own curiosity. "If I may be so bold, may I ask why you're covering this up?"

"I'm not covering it up, just protecting our case. I told you, this'll be under investigation for a long time. Money trails, cyber activity.

"What about if the Russians retaliate against Black for killing Nadia?"

"It's not their style. She may not have been active for them for quite some time. We let them know if they go after Black, we start expelling some of their rezidentura guys. Not worth it for them."

"What about witness protection? For Black and McCann?"

"Black is a semi-famous face. Without massive plastic surgery, he'd be recognized. McCann has a thriving restaurant. That'd be a big disruption in their lives that I doubt they'd agree to it."

"Don't we have enough circumstantial evidence to make a case against the Russians?"

"We can't flat out accuse a foreign power without concrete proof. An airtight case is going to take time. We don't need the media speculating on our every move. We don't need the Russkies aware that we're aware. Maybe they breathe a sigh of relief that we think it was just a domestic dispute and they get let it ride."

Logan gave Sanford a stern look, like a high school principal might to a talented but unruly student. He said, "Listen, I don't like using misdirection with the public and media any more than you do. I'm not telling you anything you don't already know, but transparency can ruin an investigation. This way the whole mess gets chalked up as a sex thing and goes away. Until we're ready to break the case."

Sanford gave up trying to decode what was really going on and decided to flatter his superior. This man was impenetrable. "Wow. I can see why you are where you are. You're playing chess, and us underlings are playing checkers."

"Bullshit. Just doing the job I've been trained to do for thirty years. You're on the same path, I'm just a little further along."

Sanford accepted the flattery for what it was --- an attempt to make him part of the conspiracy. "My fear is that this all could backfire. One small piece falls out of place and boom! I have to give you credit. You do seem to have all the bases covered."

"Not really. There are a couple of unresolved actors in this. They're named Sanford and Bernstein. Sounds like a law firm. Or a sixties group. I haven't told you what's in store for them, have I?"

Sanford had already contemplated his next move but he'd let Logan show his hand first. He figured he was severely out-gunned, but he did have the truth on his side.

He said, "Should I ask Agent Bernstein to join us?"

"No, I'll talk to her separately, Jedediah. Yours is not a common first name these days, is it?"

"My parents were big *Citizen Kane* fans."

"As am I. So much so that I've been waiting for the chance to use your whole first name. So Jedediah, good news, bad news. The bad news is --- we're closing the Savannah office. They've been dredging the river for years now and that inland port is almost ready. We're going to expand the Bluffton office and they'll cover the port and your city as well. The good news is that the head of the Atlanta station is leaving and I'd like you to replace him. And I certainly will be monitoring your progress should further opportunities arise."

It was a bribe. *Keep your mouth shut and you get the promotion*. Who knows, he might have gotten it anyway. Jed rubbed his forehead with his right hand and drew it down across his face.

What were his choices? Tell the world he thought the Russians were involved? What purpose would that serve, if in fact Logan was being truthful about developing more leads? Any report he filed would flow through Logan. Trying to go over the man's head could end his career if it reached the wrong hands.

Sanford bowed his head and said, "I'd be honored. Effective when?"

"Soon. But not immediately. That *would* look suspicious. Now, if I may ask a favor of you. When I talk to Agent Bernstein, I have a big assignment for her. Is she ready?"

He really liked Sarah and believed that in time, she'd be a great asset. But he had to be honest, especially if Dan Logan was to become his shepherd in the bureau.

"She's a little green but she does take direction well. I'm bringing her along and I'd like to take her to Atlanta with me. My protégé, if you will."

"I have something else in mind for the immediate future. But after that, I'd be happy to send her to Atlanta with you so you can continue her development. Now since we're in agreement, let's see if this batch of Espendidos is as good as advertised."

54

After the meeting and cigar rituals with Sanford, Logan excused himself and went outside for some fresh air. The sun was setting and the warmth of the winter day was fading into a seasonal chill. He found a park bench in the square and took in the essence of the old city for a moment. Sherman had spared it, unlike Atlanta, and there was a lot of history here. Even though Logan was within shouting distance of sixty, he hadn't thought much about retirement. But when he was ready, there would be worse places to settle.

He pulled his secure phone and punched in a number that less than a dozen people knew about. The director of the FBI picked up within seconds.

"Speak to me, Daniel."

"Taken care of, sir."

"Everything tied up?"

"Pretty much. Black wants to forget the whole matter and move on with his life. The publicity actually might give him a boost. Sex sells. It could help fill a few concert dates or move some digital product. If his music ambitions are over, we could contract his firm to expand and renovate the Bluffton office."

"And the woman?"

"We need to keep an eye on her. It seems she's formed a bond with Sarah Bernstein. She hinted to young Sarah that she might be someone she'd groom at her restaurant. We could encourage her to take the restaurant job and work undercover. Tell McCann she's disgruntled with the FBI. After a year or so, she could say that the food business isn't for her either and come back to us. At least, that'd be what she tells McCann."

"And you're convinced Black won't follow up on his own? For his old buddy X?"

"As far as X goes, Black won't want to go there. He hasn't been a very involved citizen in recent years. Not like his radical past. He just goes about his building business, does some small concerts. He's gone to a few rallies with his girlfriend, mostly over inequality issues. I think he's content to let sleeping dogs lie when it comes to geopolitical things like this."

"Excellent. And if Agent Bernstein stays close to McCann, she can keep her ears open with Black too, no?"

Logan sighed. "Shame about Gilmore. He was a good man. It's not an excuse, but when his wife died, he went off the deep end. They were together for forty some years. Probably the only woman he was ever with."

"I know. He was a creature from another era. You helped us keep the harassment thing under wraps, but he had to be cashiered. If that hadn't happened, we might have given him something else to do before his retirement and he never would have chased Brand X. When are you coming back?"

"A couple of bits of business to clean up here first. Maybe by the weekend. You need me back up there?"

"No urgency. Just keep doing what you do so well. Enjoy the city. The food down there is pretty fine and the historic part of the city is worth exploring. It's snowing up here now. If I were you, I might fly the wife down for a little romantic weekend. You deserve it."

~~~~~

Despite being in his own bed for the first time in nearly a week, Jason was having trouble sleeping. His hand was really hurting now, not just a dull ache but twinges of real anguish as the drugs administered in the hospital wore off and Advil alone was his sole defense.

He hadn't filled his Oxycontin prescription and was regretting that decision. But it wasn't just the physical discomfort that was keeping him up.

In his mind, he kept replaying the scene with Nadia, imagining different outcomes. Could Kat's second shot have been debilitating but not fatal? Could he or Aaron have subdued her in the wine cellar?

Under all these scenarios, Nadia/Wendy might have survived. But for what? Life in an American prison or Gitmo? Another exchange with the Reds? He wasn't a believer in *better off dead* under most circumstances, but in her case, she would have chosen the actual outcome.
~~~~~

The house was silent. Paco had taken Jasper while Jason was away and he wasn't due to return the dog until the next morning. Jasper always made some kind of noise at night --- scratching, licking his paws, or whining over a doggie nightmare.

And then there was Aaron. He'd gone AWOL before for a few days, but never under such conditions. The old man could take care of himself, former military and all, but might he have been ambushed and killed? Or shot by an over eager cop, who then covered up the shooting by ditching the body somewhere in the swamps? That was a theory Kat had tossed out. Jason chalked it up to her scorn for the local authorities and dismissed it.

He finally fell off at around three, alternating between an Alpha state and short bursts of REM. When a soft scraping sound woke him, he had no idea of the time or where he was. It was dark outside. The alarm next to his bed was blinking. The power must have gone out at some point.

He heard another noise that sounded like a drawer opening. He got out of bed, unsteady on his feet. He picked up the aluminum baseball bat that lay next to his nightstand. He kept nothing of real value in the house, and most robbers would have a hard time transporting and selling his huge flat screen. If the intruder was armed, he was welcome to take whatever he wanted.

If the Russians had sent an assassin, he could only hope to get the jump on him in the dark. A gun would have come in handy. In his bare feet, he moved toward the kitchen. It would be difficult to swing the bat with his damaged hand, but it was all he had.

He breathed a loud sigh when he realized that the intruder was Aaron Hendricks, a large duffel bag slung over his shoulder.

Jason said, "Jeez, you could have called. Where were you? Kat and I were worried sick about you."

Aaron didn't reply.

"Okay Hendricks, what are you doing? What's in the bag?" Jason said. "You're not ransacking the place, are you? Now that I can't fight back very well with one hand?"

Jason had to pause for a minute. Was it a dream? Delayed reaction to the drugs? No, this was real. The house smelled like it always did, faintly of wet dog. His eyes were open, his senses keen.

He said, "Aaron, come on, man. I covered for you with the feds. I'm not sure why, but I did. I wanted to hear it from you first. They're pinning it all on Wendy's jealousy."

Aaron was silent. Jason went on.

"They asked me if X was alive when she pushed me up the stairs. I said I didn't know for sure. But I do remember. He was breathing. Awful sounds, gasping. The feds said he suffocated. Wendy didn't do it. I guess she figured he'd bleed out on his own."

Aaron had nothing to say.

"The only one alive down there was you. You killed Brandon. Maybe he would have died anyway. But I need to know why you did it."

"How about this: he wanted me to. Poor guy was in such agony, he begged me to put an end to it."

"Nice try. But knowing Brandon, if he had any chance of surviving, he would have held on and begged you to save him. Wendy was ready to die. He wasn't."

"That's my story and I'm sticking to it, bubba."

"Cut the shit. I think I deserve more than a glib answer. Because the only thing I can come up with is that you wanted him dead so he couldn't talk. I don't have to tell you where that takes me, do I?"

"Lookee, pal. I'm sorry you got shot. I'm sorry your old flame got dead. But in the end, you survived and the folks you consider the bad guys lost. Let's leave it at that."

"That *I* consider the bad guys? You mean the Russians. You don't consider them the bad guys?"

Jason had begun to have his doubts about his friend when he learned that X hadn't died from the gunshot wound. He hadn't said anything at the time, hoping there was an innocent explanation. There was only one motive he could come up with on his own, and he didn't like it.

Jason said, "How long have you been working for the Russians?"

"I don't work for them. I do them favors once in a while. Ever since 'Nam."

Jason was aghast. Twice in his life, he'd been suckered by the enemy. One was a lover with whom he shared everything; the other a close friend who practically lived under the same roof.

"What the hell, Aaron? You did two tours. You've always bled red, white and blue. Why?"

"You, of all people, should understand. Your history protesting the war. Your anti-establishment politics."

Jason said, "I draw the line at treason."

"Treason, eh? That's not how I look at it. I see myself as the *Equalizer*. Remember that old TV show? Those Denzel flicks? I balance things out when they lean too far one way."

"You've lost me."

"Thought I might. My second tour, I realized that we weren't any better than the folks we were fighting against. We just had the bigger battalions. They saw themselves as revolutionaries, kinda like we did in 1776. Why was that okay for us and wrong for them?"

Now Jason was the one searching for the right response.

Aaron said, "Come on man, you know the truth. We just do what's good for our economy. And that means whatever big business wants. That's it. Ain't no higher morality involved. You were smarter than me back in the seventies. You protested the war, knew it was wrong from the start. It took me two tours to find that out. Once I got wise to that, I decided that when we fuck up, we need to get called on it."

Jason scoffed. "So you see yourself as self appointed guardian of our values. Bringing the moneychangers to justice."

"Think about it. Those in power always wiggle out of it and never really get held accountable. Even old Tricky Dick. He resigned, gets pardoned, and lives large in a mansion in New Jersey. Gets the establishment's respect again for being a foreign policy genius who writes bestselling books. And there's dozens of others who done worse and are still in power."

"So you help our enemies? That's your answer."

"When they're right and we're wrong. Damn straight."

"I can't believe I'm hearing this. How did they get to you?"

"Hey, I gotta be out before sunup, so I'll just give you the Cliff Notes. I got to know a Russkie colonel in 'Nam. He was an 'adviser.' Kept running into him at a brothel we both dug. Told him that after the war, I might be able to help him out once in a while. Few years later, he was KGB and took me up on it."

"Did they pay you?"

"I don't work for free. But you could say I did it out of patriotism. When we drift off course, I correct it, that's all."

"But bottom line, it's treason. You were colluding with a foreign power. If you felt so strongly about America making mistakes, why not be like Kat? Protest. Work the system from within."

"Takes too long and it don't work. You hold all the little pep rallies you want, nothing changes. Million women march on DC and a dude who grabs ladies' crotches is the one holding all the cards. My way gets results. Deflects things in the right direction. Not that I haven't been wrong once in a blue moon, but I'd put *my* record up against any of our frigging leaders."

If X had to be silenced, would he be next? Was that why Aaron was here before dawn?

"Are you here to kill me? Like whatever you used against that Russian you shot in the foot. He died in the EMS truck. What did you do to him?"

"Smart, Jason. You picked up on that. Yeah, we couldn't leave anyone around to talk. Just a little pinprick."

"Even Wendy?"

"Your Wendy wasn't going to say nothing. I wouldn't have done her. 'Sides, she croaked while I was still out from her conking me upside the head. Kat hadn't shot her, she would have either gotten away or taken one for the team. A cyanide pill."

"She pretended not to know you. Was that for my benefit? To keep your role secret?"

"Nope. She didn't know. We never met. They do a good job at keeping things compartmentalized, they call it. I didn't even know about you and her till it was too late. Jase, I wasn't part of some big ole spy network. Nothing like that. I just did some odd jobs for them. When it suited my purposes and theirs at the same time. Trust me, I turned down more work than I took. They were cool, they accepted whatever help I could give and left me alone if I said no. Got the most for their rubles that way."

He said, "So did they tell you to cozy up to me?"

"No. They never said nothing about you. You and me getting together was just like it seemed. I was an electrician. You needed one for your work. We had mutual interests and hit it off. Football buddies. Family. That's why I risked it all to save your ass."

"Kat saved me, not you."

"Just worked out that way. I woulda stopped the crazy bitch if I could."

"Right."

"You think I trust them Russian bastards? They were sending somebody to shut Operation X down and wipe away any trace of their involvement."

"And was I one of those traces?"

"You may not wanna believe this, but I didn't find out about this whole deal until you told me about Gilmore. That's when I got in touch with my Russkie contact. You remember I tried to warn you to stay out of it."

"I couldn't risk letting them deport Paco."

"Once Gilmore was dead, Paco was safe. Look, I made them promise to leave you be. They never fucked me over before, but problem is, this Nadia went rogue on them. Her job was to clean up the X op. That meant your boy Brandon had to go. That's all she was assigned. You and Gilmore, she did on her own."

"She told me she had this in the works for months."

"That much might be true. They saw the end coming for X, but they needed to button it up clean and leave no loose ends. Took some planning and they don't usually act on impulse."

"It sounds like you're more afraid of your comrades than the FBI."

"I accept that they're more ruthless, yeah. Don't make 'em bad guys. Just protecting their interests."

"False equivalency. You know that, Aaron. Don't bullshit me."

"Think whatever you want. Truth is, even though they promised you wouldn't get hurt, I wasn't just going to take their word. So I snuck in with Julius and Kat to make sure you got out all right."

"So why didn't you just shoot Wendy in the wine cellar?"

"I would have, but she had a gun on you and then she hit me from behind. I said the Russian word for friend. Drook. I hoped she'd pick up on that. I was hoping you'd never find out what I just told you."

The cranky old curmudgeon that he'd worked with for years, shared meals and stories with, was colluding with the Russians and he'd suspected nothing. Jason felt as foolish as he ever had in his life. Blowing all his money on the movie deal and trusting Wendy's charade were the life changing mistakes he made when he was younger. He was older now and should have been wiser, but he had been exploited by someone he thought he could trust.

Aaron said, "I'm leaving now. I love you man, but I'm not gonna tell you where I'm headed. Maybe I'll send you a postcard once I'm settled. The Reds said they were okay with me ending our deal, but it ain't like them to leave things be. You wanna call the fuzz after I leave, go right ahead. I'm betting you won't. Even if you do, I'll be long gone before they can do anything to stop me."

"So you're not going to kill me, Aaron? You let me live and I might tell that FBI man, Dan Logan. They'll piece it together and hunt you down."

"You say you draw the line at treason. I draw the line at killing my partner."

"Wow. So there is a limit to how low you'll go."

Aaron stayed calm despite Jason's affront. He said, "Whatever. I been laying low the past few days 'cause I knew they had eyes here and at my place. I left some stuff here I figured I'd need."

For the last minutes, the confrontation had taken Jason's mind off his pain, but a sudden spasm in his left hand reminded him. He'd fill the Oxy prescription and use it when he couldn't tolerate the hurting.

He said, "You killed two people. That doesn't bother you, Aaron?"

"I put one out of his misery. The other was a spy who knew what he was getting into. I thought I might have to kill the other Nazi security guard on my way out but I skated. Truth is, killing that bitch Nadia to save you wouldn't have troubled me. I killed a bunch of gooks in 'Nam before I came to my senses and realized they was just like us. Doing like their leaders told 'em. Buying into the bullshit."

Jason didn't know how to react. Maybe this was a vivid dream, brought on by the meds. "Well, adios, old friend. You were right about me, Mr. Hendricks, if that's your real name. I'm not going to call the feds."

"Didn't think so. No offense, but you're soft, Jason. Big guy with a heart of gold. You always amused me. You march and protest, sing your little songs, do your little dance, but in the end, you won't do what needs to be done."

"I suppose that's the difference between us. But don't lie. You wanted me to hear your story. You wanted me to know the truth."

"Like I said, I figured I could sneak in here and gather some of my things. I'd be out before you got up. Figured they'd drugged you up good."

"Like whatever shit you left here was so important. You wanted me to know you were alive and well."

"Okay, you got me. I figured you should hear the truth. Straight out of the horse's mouth."

"I had you pegged as a harmless old rebel, big talker, no action. My mistake was thinking you were a true friend, someone who had my back. It was all a lie, wasn't it? I bet you don't really even have prostate cancer, do you?"

"I wish. Early stage, slow progression, they tell me." He squinted at his friend in the predawn light. "I *am* your friend Jason, more than you'll ever know. I could've just taken their word that they'd leave you be and not gone with Kat into that compound. If I hadn't, you and me wouldn't be standing here bullshitting right now. I'd be getting ready for your funeral, *if* they found your body, that is. And I'd be shedding real tears, amigo."

"You should cry for the man you killed. Brandon X. Murphy."

"I do pity the fool. We were doing kinda the same thing, weren't we? Difference is, I'm a pro and he was an amateur bumbler. Well meaning, but an idiot."

Jason's temper broke through. He was mad, at himself, at Aaron, at the world. At the fact that he was powerless to do anything to make this right. People were dead and the bad guys were going to get away with it.

And the man he thought was his best friend was one of them.

He said, "No, the difference is, he wasn't a cold blooded killer. Even in the wine cellar, when he knew I came to expose him, he pleaded for my life. Then he took a bullet for me. And rather than help him, you killed him to cover up for your pals. That's something I can never forgive you for. *Amigo.* Now get out of my house. I'll let the feds think you're dead, Aaron. Because that's what you are to me."

55

They sat on the front porch of the cabin, watching the sun as it was sinking over the western skyline. The purple Rockies in the distance were still capped with snow, despite the August weather on the high plains. The nights were already getting colder as summer yielded to early autumn at this elevation.

Aaron Hendricks sipped his bourbon. His guest settled for club soda, mindful of the drive ahead of him. They spoke sporadically at first. This was an unexpected visit but the man who had lived in the cabin for the past half year welcomed it. He didn't get many visitors.

He said, "You could have emailed or texted."

The other replied, "That would leave a digital trail. I had business on the coast and I thought I'd make a side trip to see how you were getting along. Besides, you deserve to have your questions answered. I know how hard it was for you."

"Hardest thing I ever done. I killed people before, you know that. Didn't take that lightly, but truth be told, this bothers me more. Shit, I practically lived with the man for years. He thinks I'm a low down traitorous skunk."

"That was the price we had to pay. To keep your friends safe." The visitor shuffled his feet over the rough hewn floorboards. "You think we *like* to do things like this? The reports are he's pretty depressed, even though he's got a damn fine woman living with him."

"Kat. We turned her into a killer and she has to live with that. She's a tough broad, but that'd be hard for a man. A lot rougher on a woman. This is what you spy dudes call collateral damage."

"Yes, but it could have been so much worse. Those two have each other and if they're as strong as you say, they'll come out all right. The FBI has already hired Black to do the Bluffton office project and the publicity from the love triangle bumped up his catalogue sales."

"The extra loot couldn't hurt but I don't see him doing many music gigs with that bum hand."

"Everyone took a hit here." The man took a moment to savor the peacefulness of this wild country. "But you made out okay. You get to spend your twilight years in a safe place. No worries about money. Your health issues are under control, much anybody's can ever can be. I know it hurts, but Aaron, it *would* have been a lot worse if it weren't for you. I know having your best friend thinking you're a rat has to be devastating, but think about the alternatives."

"Jason would have been killed, wouldn't he? By us."

"I have to be honest; this would be decided over my head. If the big boys thought he couldn't be trusted, I can't promise that they wouldn't take extreme measures. No point in the other side going after him. They know we'd retaliate."

"Back to your bosses, you really trust them to leave Jason and Kat alone?"

"You know Black. He'd never let Truman and Compaña know you were a mole. He'd rather they think you're a dead hero than a live traitor. He's going along with the jealous woman story. It makes X a victim too, and I don't think he wanted his old friend exposed as a Russian dupe."

"Jason's loyal to his friends. I told him that was weakness, but truth is, I admire the hell out of it."

"You guys were a family. Gotta hand it to you, it takes a strong man to lie to his best friend's face. Even to save his life."

"Yeah, but are *your* people buying into it?"

"They seem convinced that this will hold. They'll keep Bernstein in place to make sure. She's become a confidant of McCann. She's saying that Kat and Black are focusing on putting their lives back together. Outwardly, they're acting like it never happened. And taking a page from Gilmore, we do have the Latin kid as leverage. We're keeping ICE away from him. He's the insurance policy --- the boy's safe here unless Black starts to talk."

"Jason never had a real family of his own. Me and Julie and Paco were his family. Paco's a great kid. Deserves to be a citizen someday. What about Julius? He take the bar exam yet?"

"He did. Results won't be known for a while. Bernstein's keeping tabs on him. He believes you're dead, buried somewhere in the swamps. Misses you a great deal."

"He'll make a good lawyer. That boy's got what it takes. Plus he'll scare the shit out of people on the witness stand, with his size and all."

"He might make a good U.S. attorney. We'll keep an eye on him."

"Why're you guys being so bighearted now? I half expected you came out here to kill me."

"Aaron, you *do* understand the difference between us and them, don't you? We don't like loose ends either, but we do everything we can to avoid bloodshed. Witness protection. Incentives. Yeah, even blackmail. The other side skips all that and takes the shortest route. Just pull the trigger. Or use poison or radiation if that makes it harder to trace back to them. Whatever it takes."

"I know both sides have done wet work, so let's not lie and say we never have. So what about Sofie? X's sister. You sure she won't snitch?"

"She's getting the compound and all his money, tax free. She's planning to turn it into a shelter for battered women. That won't be finalized for a while but she's happy that Brandon's millions will be put to good use. She'll keep quiet. Even though their relationship was strained, she's going to name the place after him. A memorial to her crazy brother."

"The man I killed."

"She thinks Nadia did it. As do the locals. Aaron, you made a judgment call and it was the right one. Brandon Murphy was a crazy man. An anarchist. There's no way he could be trusted to keep this all on the QT. You did the right thing. The Russian goon, well so what?"

"The Russkies don't bother me so much. Jason thinks X wasn't a bad guy, but he was pretty stupid trusting that the Reds wouldn't turn on him the minute it suited them."

"That's another difference between us."

Aaron wasn't going to let him get away with that one. "One thing I'm not clear on --- did you guys sanction Richard Gilmore and make it look like a heart attack?"

"No. We thought the Russians might have, but we don't think so now based on the forensics, unless they have something invisible we don't know about. Desk job, no exercise, rich foods and he smoked. The pressure, the excitement that his big moment had finally come. Docs wanted him on meds but the prescription was never filled. No, it was a heart attack. Natural causes."

The Western sky was electric now and they stopped talking for a moment to take in the scene. The crickets were warming up for their evening symphony and the wolves and others wildlife were chiming in. The visitor said, "It sure is nice out here. Lonely though, I'd imagine. You okay with that?"

"Suits me fine. I have satellite TV, football package. All the books I can ever read on Kindle. And there's an escort service in the nearest town that delivers when the need arises."

"Our deal covers all your expenses and we're not keeping a close ledger so enjoy, my friend. You've served your country well for a lot of years. A shame no one will ever know."

"You don't see any way I can square things with Jason before I go?"

"If that time ever comes, we'll let you know. Never say never, but I doubt it'll happen. It's likely he'll go to his grave thinking you were a spook for the bad guys. I'm sorry. I wish there was another way. Ease your mind, old friend. If he thought the Russians might have killed you but wasn't sure, he'd never stop digging. And that woman of his would think it was the local cops or us that did you in. They wouldn't sit by quietly for long. You did it to protect him and your country. You did what you had to do. Take solace in that."

"Someday, maybe. But now, it eats me up alive."

"Well, I need to go before it gets too dark. You take care, and let us know if there's anything more you need. Anything at all."

They shook hands and parted. Aaron Hendricks went back into his cabin and turned the heat up a notch. Too early for a wood fire.

Aaron wanted to believe that he was safe, but he'd taken precautions. Video cameras, alarms, and a small arsenal. His main comfort was that if anyone wanted him dead, they probably would have done it already.

He was glad that the lies, dead drops and coded messages --- all his acquired tradecraft --- were finally in the past.

He'd managed to deceive them all. He didn't lie to Jason about one thing --- he did consider himself the Equalizer. He had finessed both sides since returning from 'Nam. Sometimes he aided the Russians, sometimes the Americans, depending on his judgment as to who held the higher ground. He was a double agent many times over.

It had been dangerous work. If either suspected he was dealing with the other, he'd be eliminated --- slowly and painfully, after extracting whatever information they could.

He'd tipped off the Russians when Jason had told him about his impending penetration of the X compound. Aaron reasoned that the exposure of a conspiracy of that magnitude would exacerbate tensions between the two powers. With all the other trouble spots in the world, heightened paranoia in a freshly stoked cold war would be counterproductive. That was why he'd told them to wipe away all evidence of their involvement and why he had killed X and the Russian.

It almost backfired when Nadia disabled him, but he recovered in time to limit the damage. He found it fascinating that the media were continuing to present the whole business as a sex, drugs and rock and roll scandal. No enterprising investigative reporter had uncovered the truth. They'd rather do a feature on the Kardashians.

Regardless, he was giving up the game, hoping that nature would find its own balance. He'd kept the equilibrium for a long time, averting all kinds of international mischief. At least, that's how he saw it.

Ironically, the whole debacle added to the legend of Jason Black, making him into an outlaw hero and an aging sex symbol. The ruggedly handsome photos of him created legions of would-be female rivals for Kat. She wasn't concerned nor was he interested. The two of them 'no-commented' whenever asked about that day, and the inquisitors' curiosity faded in the wake of juicier scandals.

Content that his friends were protected, Aaron had taken the Americans' witness protection package rather than explore what the other side might offer. He trusted his homeland's principles more, but not completely. The combination of his age and the slow progress of his disease made it unlikely he would be a threat to them. The only caveat was if they decided to target Kat and Jason, he'd be in their sights as well. He didn't discount the possibility, but had done all he could to prevent it.

It would take a great deal of effort for the Russians to find him and he was betting that they wouldn't bother. To his knowledge, they believed that his assassination of X and Nadia's bodyguard had been done to serve their interests. If they had been captured alive, they may have talked. The idea that Wendy/Nadia had chosen suicide by cop was credible.

He was well stocked with provisions for the harsh winter months ahead. He poured another bourbon and turned on his satellite system, featuring an even larger screen than the one at Jason's. There was a preseason football game coming on soon.

He opened up the word program on his computer and added some notes. His memoir was almost finished. He wasn't sure if he should take some liberties --- change some names and places and turn it into a novel, or tell it exactly as it went down. In any case, he figured it'd be released it posthumously, if at all.

He'd wait until morning to work on the next chapter. He hadn't come up with a proper ending yet.

EPILOGUE

Dan Logan was on a dark, lonely highway heading toward Jackson Hole, where he had a breakfast meeting scheduled with a former vice president. Then it was on to San Francisco for a much needed vacation with his wife, who had already checked into the Hotel Union Square. It seemed like a million miles away.

While he drove, he was on the secure phone with the director. After he gave his boss a quick summary of his visit with Aaron Hendricks, he added, "So, Hendricks doesn't suspect that we knew all along he was feeding information to the Russians. He has no idea the stuff he gave them was leaked intentionally. All misdirection. He thought he was balancing the scales when in reality, he was tipping them our way."

"That may be, but he never should have told the Russians off that Black was coming in to spy. It would have been better to close out the op on our terms when we were ready. Hendricks telling the Commies accelerated the process and it cost lives."

"He did it to protect his friend Black."

"Understood, but we should have been able to get out cleaner. But you think rather than expose him as a double agent, it's better to let him live out his days in anonymity?"

"I do. He's in no position to be of any use to the bad guys now. And if we try to punish him through channels, things will come out about what really happened that day. We don't want that."

"There are other ways to ensure he'll never talk."

"I don't think we need to go there. His active days are over. He just wants to be left alone."

"I hope you're right. You know, Daniel, you're one of the few who're privy to the long game. We're deep into the Russian computer networks in ways we believe their government knows nothing about. When we penetrated the X compound digitally, that was our first portal into their infrastructure. They still don't know and we need to keep it that way. It's better they think we're idiots who have no idea what they were up to."

"A shame that Gilmore didn't know that. Could have saved us a lot of trouble, not to mention lives."

"Who knew he'd make it a personal crusade after he was let go? The bottom line is we can't afford to have the Russians reviewing the links and discovering our penetration."

"Well, Gilmore is dead and so are the principals. But people died that day who shouldn't have."

"Three were Russian agents. One was a neo-Nazi. Brand X was the exception but he knew the risks. And that's tragic. The good news is we don't need that portal anymore."

Logan was cautious. "But if it ever comes out about South Carolina, they'll review everything they gathered from that source and we'll lose that edge."

"Or maybe they retaliate and start a full scale cyber war, although some would say they already are. Our geeks versus their geeks. It's better we handle this diplomatically. Back channels in small rooms."

Logan had one more item to settle before he could begin his working vacation. He said, "Meanwhile, I'm convinced that no one involved in this knew that Murphy was working with us from the start. Black thought X was a true believer. Hendricks didn't know he was on our side either. He thought making sure Brandon X was dead helped the other guys."

His boss said, "Who knows, if push came to shove, maybe Murphy would have let the other side know he was our guy. Like you said, all that disinformation we fed them would be useless. We would have offered X protection if he'd been found out, but Hendricks rendered that academic. X's use to us had run its course, just like with them. With the technology now, they're much better off operating from overseas."

"I do feel bad about X, though. He was a patriot, even though he bought into a lot of anarchy nonsense. People thought he was just lucky backing Apple early on. The guy was eccentric, but also a genius who foresaw the computer age."

"Casualty of war."

"Yeah. In the scheme of things, the only thing that hasn't fallen into place is Sarah Bernstein. She says she really does see her future as a restaurateur. She agreed to keep us posted if McCann and Black waver, but she may not come back to us. Sanford was crushed to hear that."

"He'll get over it. He's off to a good start in Atlanta."

Since everything had been sorted out, there was no point in sanctioning Black and McCann. They had sworn not to reveal what had really gone down at the compound that day. They would be monitored to make sure they didn't renege, but Logan was confident they would honor their commitment. As for Aaron, the old man could live out his days in peace. Overall, he had been an asset to his country, although unintentionally on occasion.

That's the difference between us and them, he told himself. We only take human life when there is no alternative. They are ruthless; we are merciful when we can be.

He told the director, "All of this is way above my head, sir."

"Mine as well. The reason we're discussing it now is that someday you might be sitting in my chair and you should be aware of these things."

"I'm honored that you say that but there's no way I could fill shoes as big as yours."

"I've never known you to be a suck up, Logan. Don't start now."

Too late, Logan thought. It was already an essential part of his job and he was good at it.

ACKNOWLEDGEMENTS

As with any work of fiction, we've taken liberties with many facts. There is no Savannah FBI office, and no plans to expand the Bluffton bureau. Huey's is a cool bistro with great beignets. The Skull Creek Boathouse on Hilton Head Island is a wonderful place to eat, as is Hall's Chophouse in Charleston.

Jason Black is not based on any one musician, but his experiences track closely with many of the singer/songwriters of the era. His love of Joni Mitchell parallels my own, but she never criticized his work or hit the road with our protagonist. The pairing of Jason and Brand X was typical of the asymmetrical tours back in the day --- witness Bruce Springsteen opening for Anne Murray. Label mates often toured together, regardless of their compatibility.

As usual, Camine Pappas and my wife Vicky did a stellar job with the design. Reed Farrel Coleman has been a great coach throughout the journey.

Duncan the Wonder Dog is dismayed by the minor role played by Jasper in this book, but he understands that all dogs are not modeled after him.

ABOUT THE AUTHOR

"Three Chords and the Truth" is Richard Neer's ninth novel, and the first featuring Jason Black.

His successful series of Riley King novels include "Something of the Night", "The Master Builders", "Indian Summer", "The Last Resort", "The Punch List", "An American Storm" and "Wrecking Ball." The next installment, "Heart of the Matter", is complete and will be released this year.

His work of non-fiction entitled "FM, the Rise and Fall of Rock Radio", (Villard 2001), is the true story of how corporate interests destroyed a format that millions grew up with.

Neer has worked in important roles at two of the most prestigious and groundbreaking radio stations in history --- the legendary WNEW-FM for almost thirty years, and the nation's first full time sports talker, WFAN, since 1988. Early in his career, he and Michael Harrison started the first suburban progressive rock station, WLIR on Long Island.

Made in the USA
Columbia, SC
14 June 2021